An Escape t

T.A. Williams lives in Devon with his Italian wife. He was born in England of a Scottish mother and Welsh father. After a degree in modern languages at Nottingham University, he lived and worked in Switzerland, France and Italy, before returning to run one of the best-known language schools in the UK. He's taught Arab princes, Brazilian beauty queens and Italian billionaires. He speaks a number of languages and has travelled extensively. He has eaten snake, still-alive fish, and alligator. A Spanish dog, a Russian bug and a Korean parasite have done their best to eat him in return. His hobby is long-distance cycling, but his passion is writing.

Also by T.A. Williams

Chasing Shadows
Dreaming of Venice
Dreaming of Florence
Dreaming of St-Tropez
Dreaming of Christmas
Dreaming of Tuscany
Dreaming of Rome
Dreaming of Verona
Dreaming of Italy

Escape to Tuscany

Under a Siena Sun
Second Chances in Chianti
Secrets on the Italian Island

Love from Italy

A Little Piece of Paradise
An Escape to Remember

T.A.WILLIAMS

An Escape to Remember

CANELO

First published in the United Kingdom in 2022 by

Canelo
Unit 9, 5th Floor
Cargo Works, 1–2 Hatfields
London, SE1 9PG
United Kingdom

Copyright © T.A. Williams 2022

The moral right of T.A. Williams to be identified as the creator of this work has been asserted in accordance with the Copyright, Designs and Patents Act, 1988.

All rights reserved. No part of this publication may be reproduced or transmitted in any form or by any means, electronic or mechanical, including photocopy, recording, or any information storage and retrieval system, without permission in writing from the publisher.

A CIP catalogue record for this book is available from the British Library.

Print ISBN 978 1 80032 767 2
Ebook ISBN 978 1 80032 383 4

This book is a work of fiction. Names, characters, businesses, organizations, places and events are either the product of the author's imagination or are used fictitiously. Any resemblance to actual persons, living or dead, events or locales is entirely coincidental.

Look for more great books at www.canelo.co

Printed and bound in Great Britain by Clays Ltd, Elcograf S.p.A.

1

To Mariangela and Christina with love

Chapter 1

Louise decided to make her return to the UK a surprise for Tommy. She hadn't seen him for ten whole weeks and she was dying to get back to him. Although she had told him she would be home on Saturday, she used some of her air miles to jump on a flight leaving Antigua on Friday morning which got her into Heathrow airport at half past seven that evening. Less than two hours later she was already back at the flat they shared in south-west London feeling a bit weary but excited at the prospect of seeing him again after months apart. He normally played squash on Friday evenings and generally arrived home around ten so her plan was to take a shower, put the bottle of champagne she had bought at the duty-free shop on ice, dim the lights and surprise him. In the lift on the way up to the third floor she was even toying with the idea of maybe digging out the rather saucy underwear she had bought for Valentine's Day last year. She turned the key in the lock with a rising sense of excitement.

Dumping her heavy suitcase in the hall she saw that the light was on in the bedroom. When she had spoken to him on the phone the previous night he had sounded fit and well and she hoped he hadn't caught a bug. It was certainly unlike him to be in bed so early. Pushing the bedroom door open, she did indeed find him in bed.

However, it was immediately evident that he wasn't alone.

Alongside him, partly covered by the duvet – Louise's own favourite duvet, she noted in a daze – was an attractive dark-haired girl and neither of them was wearing a stitch of clothing.

'Tommy!' Louise's hand flew to her mouth as she croaked his name. It sounded like somebody else's voice.

He leapt out of the bed in disarray while the girl burrowed deep under the duvet and covered her head with the pillow. Louise just stood there blankly, idly noticing the clothes strewn across the floor and the ice bucket by the bed with an upturned empty champagne bottle in it. It was an indelible image that would return to haunt her time and time again for weeks to come.

'Louise, I didn't think you were coming back till tomorrow…' He was standing by the side of the bed, cupping his hands over his nakedness, his face as red as the discarded bra lying on the floor by his feet.

Afterwards, all sorts of possible retorts came to her, ranging from an explosion of invective and rage followed by a hail of missiles to more measured comments like, 'Maybe you think I should have knocked,' or 'Don't let me interrupt you.' As it was, words completely failed her and she just turned on her heels and headed back out of the bedroom door again, not even bothering to slam it behind her. Grabbing hold of her suitcase, she tugged it out onto the landing, relieved to find the lift still on this floor. She pressed the ground floor button and barely heard the door hiss shut behind her as she was still reeling at what she had just witnessed and struggling to come to terms with it.

Back outside in the damp night air she stood in the shadows and breathed deeply. Her eyes were stinging but

2

she steadfastly refused to let the tears run. In the space of a few seconds her whole life had been turned upside down. Tommy had been the man with whom she had been planning to spend the rest of her life but now those dreams were in tatters. Her head was spinning as she tried to make sense of what had happened – her thoughts a swirling mix of anger, disappointment, sadness and bewilderment. How could he...?

A grey-haired lady with a poodle on a lead came walking towards her, caught sight of the expression on her face and slowed down as she approached.

'Are you all right, dear?'

With a Herculean effort, Louise took another big breath and tried to sound normal. 'I'm fine, thanks. Just thinking...'

'Well, if you're sure.'

'It's okay, thanks.'

But of course it wasn't.

She called a cab and phoned her mum from the back seat. As the taxi headed north across the Thames she gave her mother a brief account of what had just happened, mildly surprised to manage it without bursting into tears. Her mother was understandably outraged.

'How could he do something like that? And your father and I thought that things were serious between the two of you.'

'So did I, mum, but clearly Tommy didn't.' Her voice almost cracked but she held firm.

The half hour ride passed in a blur and as she paid the driver outside her parents' house he caught her eye. 'It's no business of mine, but for my money you're better off without him.'

She even managed a glimmer of a smile in return although all she could feel was emptiness deep inside. 'I think you're right. Thanks.'

A minute later she was sitting on the sofa with a mug of hot chocolate, stroking Mog the cat with her free hand while doing her best to describe to her sympathetic parents how she felt. It wasn't easy.

Finally, at well past midnight she went to bed, but spent much of the night wide awake, eyes staring sightlessly into the dark, wondering where it had all gone wrong. Was *she* the problem? Had she not been loving enough or considerate enough or understanding enough? Of course it was likely, maybe even very likely, that her job had been part of the problem. She had been away so much he had got bored and had found himself a new plaything. Not that this could justify his infidelity, she reminded herself. She had missed him too, but she would never have dreamt of hooking up with some random man. No, whatever contributing factors there might have been from her side, the blame here lay squarely on Tommy's shoulders.

When she woke up next morning and turned her phone back on – she had deliberately switched it off last night – she found she had a dozen unanswered calls and a stream of messages from Tommy. After taking a long, cleansing shower, she sat in the kitchen with a mug of tea and read her way through them. They all ran along similar lines. He was sorry. It had been an awful thing to do. He hadn't meant to hurt her and he hoped she would let him explain and forgive him.

This was something else she had been turning over and over in her head overnight and the answer was now quite clear and irreversible: Tommy and she were history. There was no way she would ever be able to trust him again after

4

what had happened. She talked it through with her mum who backed her to the hilt. What he had done had been beyond the pale. She would be far better off without him.

She sat there and composed a text message to him. She didn't waste words.

> We're finished, Tommy, forever. We both know I'll never be able to trust you again. I'll come over with dad and Ben this afternoon to pick up my stuff. I don't want to see you. Please go somewhere, anywhere, but stay away. We'll be there at two and out by five. Don't try to contact me. I never want to see you or hear from you again.

At two o'clock she and her brother, Ben, drove over to the flat, closely followed by her father in his car, and she was relieved to find the place empty. Ben, on the other hand, looked positively disappointed. When he had heard what had happened, he had gone ballistic, and Louise was glad there wasn't going to be a confrontation. Wisely, Tommy had obeyed her instructions to vacate the flat. Although her stuff almost completely filled both cars, including the roof racks, they were able to remove everything by half past four. It was only when she stood at the door, looking back into the now half-empty rooms, that she felt the tears massing in the corners of her eyes. She had refused to let herself cry so much as a drop so far but now it finally hit her and the tears came coursing down her cheeks. It was all over. There was to be no engagement, no wedding, no happily ever after. Tommy was out of her life. She barely felt her father stretch a comforting arm around her shoulder and steer her out of the apartment. The last thing she did was to drop her keys back through the letterbox.

She knew she wouldn't need them again.

Chapter 2

She spent the weekend at home with her mum and dad. It was nice to catch up and feel their support, but deep down inside she was conscious of a cold, empty void. She had come home to London full of hope for the future and this was the way Tommy had welcomed her. Gradually she began to remember a number of times over the past six months or so when he had sounded distant, when he had stayed out for unspecified events, or nights out with 'people from work'. At the time she hadn't given it a second thought but it was now all too clear that even if he hadn't been cheating on her back then, the signs had been there and she had failed to read them.

On Sunday morning she got a phone call from her boss. Getting calls from him at odd times and on odd days was quite normal. He didn't do it to be awkward; the thing was that he worked even harder than she did and the days all just somehow melded into one as far as he was concerned.

'Hi, Louise, did you have a good flight?'

'Joseph, hi. Yes, all good, thanks.' He didn't need to hear about her private life. That was her affair, not his. She did her best to sound upbeat. 'All well with you?'

'Fine, thanks. And what about over in Antigua? From your reports it looks as though you got it all sorted.'

'I'm confident we've made the right changes. The new manager's on the case and everything's been running smoothly again. No more complaints for almost a month.' She had been sent over to the Caribbean immediately after Christmas to put the failing hotel back on its feet. It hadn't been easy, but she had managed.

'Great job, Louise. Well done. Annabelle came back most enthusiastic about everything.'

'That's good to hear.'

Louise was relieved, although not that surprised. Annabelle, the company's very bright Head of Operations and unofficial Inspector General with a lynx-like eye for the smallest detail, had visited the hotel two weeks earlier and had told Louise before leaving that she had been impressed with the changes and the results. Presumably she had handed in a positive report, since praise from Joseph was a rarity – not because he was ungrateful or unappreciative, but because he normally had other things on his mind. It rapidly emerged that today was no exception as he continued, 'Great. Now listen, you speak Italian, don't you?'

'Yes, pretty well, although it's probably a bit rusty. I spent a year over there when I was doing my degree, and that was a while back.'

'Excellent. I need you to go to Italy. I've just signed off on a deal to purchase a hotel in the hills of north-west Italy, just below the Alps. Do you know that part of the country?'

'Fairly well. I was at the university in Turin. That's close to the Alps. Is the hotel anywhere near there?'

'It's in the Monferrato, if that means anything to you.'

'I think I know where you mean. I'm pretty sure it's not far from Turin. I can remember people saying it's a lovely area, but I never got out there. Winemaking country, I believe. Tell me about the hotel. What's it like?'

'Picturesque, quirky, it's been operating for well over a hundred years. The place has a lot of potential, or so Massimo reckons.'

Louise gave a non-committal murmur. She didn't much like his use of the word 'quirky', and as for 'potential', in her experience this all too often meant needing head-to-toe renovation. Massimo Milanese was one of Joseph's contacts in the European real estate business and, although he had come up with a handful of real gems over the years, he had also produced one or two which had cost a fortune to revamp.

'And you want me to go over there and take a look?'

'More than that, Louise; I want you to go and make it hum. It's barely ticking over at present. I was only there for lunch and a quick look around, but I could see it needs a good bit of work. Do what you've been doing in Antigua. I want you to get the place back on its feet. Go through it from head to toe. Make any changes you think fit to the property itself, the facilities, the management and staff at all levels. Get rid of any dead wood and turn it into one of the best luxury hotels in Italy. If possible I'd like it to be firing on all cylinders by the beginning of July.'

That was little more than three months away so, depending on the state of the place, that sounded like a big ask. Still, she had always loved a challenge and the chance to spend some time back in Italy wasn't to be sneezed at and, of course, there was no longer the problem of abandoning Tommy to consider if she disappeared off again so soon after getting back home.

'You know I'll do my best. How big is it?'

'It has sixty guest bedrooms and grounds of twenty-five hectares. That should give you something to work with.'

'Sounds good. And what's the name of the hotel?'

'The Grand Hotel del Monferrato.'

'And is it really grand?'

'A hundred years ago it certainly was. Nowadays I think it's fair to say that it's a bit tired, a bit neglected. Your job is to get it back up there again.'

Louise felt a little surge of excitement. She loved being able to put her own stamp on a project. 'I'll try my hardest.'

'I know you will, Louise. Good luck.'

At lunchtime she and Ben went to the King's Arms for a drink and she met up with her best friend, Viv, and her husband, Rick. After telling them what had happened in the Caribbean and the fact that she would be heading off to Italy in a little over a week, she decided to tell them about the events of Friday night. She and Viv had known each other since school and Louise was able to talk freely and openly to her about the abrupt ending to her relationship with Tommy. Predictably, Viv was supportive.

'The cheating rat! I have to say I'm amazed, though. I never would have thought that of Tommy.'

This was exactly what Louise herself had been thinking. How could she have misjudged him so seriously? 'I know, right? Of course I've been away a lot...'

'So what? That's no excuse. If he was feeling left out he should have spoken up. He should not, repeat not, have leapt into bed with another woman.' There was no doubt where Viv felt the blame lay.

'You're right. There's no excuse. My job maybe didn't help but I can't blame it for him deciding to cheat.'

She loved her job as company troubleshooter for the luxury hotel chain, but it certainly had kept her almost permanently on the go – and away from Tommy. On the flight home from the Caribbean she had been thinking that the time to sit down with him and plan out the rest of their lives together had come. She had even decided to talk to Joseph to see if there might be a position in the company that would allow her to spend more time with Tommy but now, of course, there was no need for that. Tommy and his dark-haired bedfellow had seen to that.

He had been her boyfriend for over five years and they had moved in together almost exactly two years ago, although she had probably been away for at least half of that. She had loved him, of course she had, but she also loved her job. The fact that it had kept her away from him so much must have been tough on him and, while not an excuse for his behaviour, it was an explanation. But she didn't have time for further reflection as Viv did her best to look on the bright side.

'Well, you're definitely better off without him.'

'That's what the taxi driver said.'

Viv grinned. 'London cabbies know everything. And, of course, this means you're now free to find yourself a new man. Surely there must be some hunky Italian guy over where you're going. Some of those tall, dark, handsome Italian men – you know, with their shirts open to the waist exposing a suntanned chest – are just plain gorgeous…' Her voice tailed off into a dreamy sigh which even caught her husband's attention. Up till then he and Ben had been scrupulously keeping out of the conversation.

'Wishing you'd chosen a hunky Italian instead of me, are you, Viv?' Rick adopted a mock-pleading tone and an attempt at a pretend Italian accent. 'Please donna dump me. I takea Italian lessons, icea cream-making lessons, pizza…'

Viv reached out a reassuring hand and caught hold of his. 'You're fine as you are, Ricky… Mind you, a regular supply of homemade ice cream and pizza would be a bonus.'

While the two of them carried on with their banter, Louise sipped her cider and allowed herself to think of moving on, but she knew the spectre of Tommy would haunt her for a long time to come. How could she have got it so wrong? At least her upcoming trip to rural Italy sounded as though it would provide a place to escape from the memory of Tommy and his woman.

'So, are there going to be any hunky men over at the Grand Hotel? I bet there will be.' By now Viv had finished fantasising about Latin lovers and an unlimited supply of homemade Italian food and she was back on Louise's side.

'I have no idea and no interest, honestly. Tommy's put me off men – maybe not for good but for a good long while. I thought I'd found somebody I could trust but I was wrong. If I can get it so wrong once, I can make the same mistake again. No, I think I'll just concentrate on my job for now and let nature take its course. If a suitable man crawls out of the woodwork, I'll have to think long and hard before deciding what to do. For the moment I'll just keep my nose to the grindstone.' She did her best to sound upbeat. 'To be honest, one of the first things I was planning on doing this week was to talk with Tommy about the conflict between my job and our relationship and see where we could go from here. Now that he's put the kybosh on the relationship, he has at least helped me solve that conundrum.'

Viv caught hold of her hand and gave it a reassuring squeeze. 'It's been tough but you'll get over it.'

Louise gave her a grateful look in return. 'I hope you're right. Why does it have to be so hard? All I was looking for was simple, uncomplicated love. Was that too much to ask for?'

Chapter 3

The view from the aircraft as Louise flew into Turin over the Alps was spectacular with the mountains, even the not-so-high ones, still covered in snow although it was already late March and technically springtime. Evidently it had been a hard winter. Today there wasn't a cloud in the sky which made a pleasant change from the grey, over-cast London she had left. She even managed to recognise some of the places she had visited with friends when she had lived here twelve years earlier, and she was looking forward to her return to Italy although she had other things on her mind as well at the moment. All the way through the flight she should have been concentrating on reading back over the information about the Grand Hotel that Annabelle, the company's Head of Operations, had given her. Instead, she had partly been thinking about Tommy, but equally about her boss, Joseph.

Three nights ago she had been surprised, and pleased, to be invited out for dinner by Joseph. She had never mixed with him socially, and everybody in the company knew him to be so involved with the business he had little or no private life. Unlike many bosses, he was always cordial and she had never known him to lose his temper. He was probably around forty, stinking rich, always immaculately dressed and good-looking in an airbrushed front cover of *Vogue Hommes* sort of way. He was not only unmarried but he had never been seen with a woman – or a man for that matter. He was the true epitome of a workaholic, which made the dinner invitation unexpected.

What was even more unexpected was the conversation over dinner. She had brought with her a thick file containing details of all the different changes and improvements she had made in the Caribbean, anticipating being questioned by him, but such was not the case after all. His personal chauffeur had picked her up in a huge black Mercedes with discreet tinted windows, and had dropped her off at a smart restaurant in Covent Garden. Joseph must have been following their progress as she found him waiting outside the restaurant for her with an umbrella to protect her from the rain as she stepped out of the car. She felt like a movie star and was glad it was dark so he wouldn't see her blushes. She had always had an irritating habit of blushing at the slightest hint of embarrassment, and getting the personal treatment from her boss was now all it took to set her off again.

'Louise, how nice of you to come.'

'Thank *you*, Joseph. How extremely kind of you to send your car for me. I could have taken the tube.'

'Absolutely not.'

Inside the restaurant it was all subdued lighting, immaculately turned out staff and Santana playing softly in the background. The maître d' led them to a discreet table in a far corner, slid her chair in underneath her as she sat down and then opened and placed her napkin onto her lap for her. By this time Louise was wishing she had chosen something more formal from her fairly limited wardrobe. Anticipating a smart place, she had gone for her trusty forty-year-old Dior cocktail dress discovered in a charity shop three years ago and purchased for a fraction of its original price. However, in a place like this it looked positively mundane. The woman on the next table, partly veiled from them by an Ali Baba-sized earthenware urn, was sheathed in silver snakeskin that sparkled as she moved, and her décolleté was still gaping as it reached the level of the table top.

'Shall we have some champagne?' Joseph's voice interrupted her wardrobe qualms.

'That'd be lovely, Joseph. Thank you.'

This was a very different Joseph from the work-obsessed boss she was used to seeing and she wasn't sure what to make of the new him.

With a practised gesture he summoned the waiter and ordered a bottle of Bollinger before returning his attention to her, the smile reappearing on his face.

'You're looking spectacular tonight.'

'You can't mean that. I've been jet-lagged all week and if I'd known you were bringing me to somewhere like this I'd have made more of an effort.'

'You look great. Maybe a tad tired. You haven't been overdoing it, have you?' This was beginning to sound a lot more than just polite interest and Louise wondered where this was going. She shook her head to indicate she wasn't really tired although she knew deep down she probably had been burning the candle at both ends – but she also knew that that was the nature of the job and she had wanted to do it right. She decided it might be wise to turn the conversation onto work matters and launched into a detailed account of her months in the Caribbean which was only interrupted by the arrival of the champagne along with the maître d' to take their order.

After they had both ordered scallops followed by lobster, Joseph raised his glass towards her.

'Here's to you, Louise. Cheers.'

She clinked her glass against his. 'Cheers, Joseph, and thanks again.'

As she sipped her wine, the thought occurred to her that maybe this wasn't intended to be a business dinner at all. Surely he didn't think it was a date? Up to now he had only ever been her boss. Could he really be interested in a simple employee like her and, if he was, how might she feel about being in his sights? Leaving aside for the moment her resolution not to get involved with another man for a good long while, how might she feel about considering Joseph as a candidate for her affections? If it was true — and she couldn't really believe that he could be interested in her in that way when the world was full of far more beautiful women — how would she respond if he started making advances? On the one hand she would be surprised and flattered but on the other, she knew she would have to say no, and not just because she was still reeling from what Tommy had done.

Yes, Joseph was good-looking; yes, he was bright and successful and, of course, he had made enough money to buy a dozen restaurants like this without batting an eyelid, but there was no way she could imagine him as a possible life partner and she certainly had no intention of leaping into a casual affair with him that would inevitably end in tears. This world of glitz and glamour was all very well as far as it went but she knew it wasn't for her. She had been brought up fairly modestly to enjoy the simple things in life and she knew deep down that such obvious opulence wasn't for her so she spent the next two hours doing her best to keep the conversation light and, where possible, work-oriented.

The food was predictably excellent but she barely tasted it, concentrating on not drinking too much and measuring her words. Nevertheless, in spite of her best efforts, the conversation did take a more personal turn from time to time.

'So tell me, Louise, is there a special someone in your life?' Joseph followed up a chunk of lobster with a mouthful of the excellent Chablis Grand Cru he had ordered. The bottle of champagne had been finished ages ago – mostly by Joseph – and he was already making serious inroads into the white. She had never seen him drink heavily before and she wondered if this might be because he was nervous about something. Although she had a full glass in front of her, she was pacing herself, consuming it sip by sip.

She decided that this was the time for a bit of dissimulation, in the hope of returning the conversation to business matters. 'Yes, we've been together for five years and living together for a couple of years now. His name's Thomas. He's a dentist here in London.' This was all true. The only thing she omitted to tell him was the fact that it was all over.

'I see.'

She watched him register her response and waited for him to comment. It took a few moments in coming.

'And do you love him?'

'Yes, of course.' And she felt sure she had done.

'I see.' A further long pause ensued before he tried again. 'And did you know you loved him from the start?'

'You mean like love at first sight?' Seeing him nod, she paused for thought. Could she honestly say she had known Tommy was The One from day one? Probably not. 'I don't think so. It took time.' Deciding to try to find out where he was going with this line of questioning, she threw the question back at him. 'What about you? Has it happened to you?'

'Yes… At least I think so.'

His voice tailed off and he reached for his wine glass, leaving Louise still no wiser about what was going through his head. Still, she felt reassured that he appeared to have bought her little white lie about being in a solid relationship, and she set about her lobster again with a sense of relief. Although they chatted sporadically about the food, the weather and work, it wasn't until she had almost finished her wonderfully light *îles flottantes* that he returned to the subject of relationships again.

'So do you think you'll marry your boyfriend?'

If he had asked her that a week ago, her answer would have been yes. She would be thirty-three this summer and she had been asking herself the same thing for some time. She had been getting on really well with Tommy; they had a lot in common – in fact she had felt sure this was the real thing but, of course, she had got that dead wrong – but Joseph didn't need to know that. She marshalled her thoughts and decided to carry on with the fantasy simply so as to keep her boss at arms' length without offending him. 'I really think we will. I certainly hope so.'

'I see.'

And that was that. He saw her back into the Mercedes afterwards but didn't attempt to join her on the back seat. He told her his apartment was close by and said he would walk in spite of the rain. After shaking her hand formally, he wished her luck for her trip to Italy and waved the car away. The driver headed out of Central London and she finally settled back and began to relax again. It had been a stressful evening. Had she completely misread the signs or had he really been targeting her as a conquest? Hopefully if that really had been his intention, she had done enough to put him off and, if she had got him all wrong, at least she hadn't put her foot in it. But it had been hard work.

–

When she emerged from the baggage hall at Turin airport with her heavy suitcase containing enough clothes to last her three months she was pleased to find a man holding a sign with her name on it. He was squeezed into the sort of dark blue uniform trimmed with gold braid that one of Napoleon's generals might have worn. It would have looked more impressive if one of the buttons hadn't been missing, presumably having given up the effort of holding in his impressive paunch. She was glad she had got hold of a baggage trolley; if he had tried to bend down and pick up her hefty suitcase the results might have been catastrophic for any bystanders. She walked across to him and held out her hand.

'*Buongiorno, sono Louise Rhodes.*'

'*Buongiorno, signora. Mi chiamo Luigino.*'

Louise suppressed a smile. Adding the suffix *–ino* to an Italian word acted as a diminutive. No doubt this character had been a small Luigi once upon a time but such was definitely no longer the case. He reached gallantly for the handle of the baggage trolley and she left him to it but resolved to help him lift her case off when they reached his car. She didn't want her first interaction with a member of the Grand Hotel del Monferrato staff to result in a coronary.

They walked out into the crisp afternoon air and she looked around appreciatively. It was good to be back in

Italy. She took the opportunity to get in some Italian conversation practice and asked him about this year's snowfall in the mountains. The answer was unedifying.

'It's been pretty much as it should be.'

She tried the state of the roads and the traffic.

'The traffic wasn't too heavy, but it wasn't light either.'

And the weather.

'It's cold at night but the sunshine during the day warms things up.'

After equally uninspiring results to her queries about how often he made this sort of trip to pick up hotel guests, the numbers of tourists visiting this part of Italy and current affairs, she finally hit upon last autumn's grape harvest and he suddenly became more communicative.

'A remarkably good year, signora. In particular the Barbera has done well but the Dolcetto and Grignolino grapes have also produced excellent results.' He glanced across at her. 'We'll start bottling it up soon. I'm sure you'll like it. Everybody does.'

She had heard of the local Barbera wine and drunk quite a bit of it when she had been here last time, but the other grape varieties were new to her. In fairness, at uni in her early twenties she had been a penniless student and her wine consumption had mostly been from two-litre bottles of dubious quality and origin bought from the supermarket. The specifics of the grape varieties hadn't been anywhere near as important as the price: as low as possible. Since then she had been fortunate to have had the opportunity to develop a taste for fine wines and she looked forward to trying some of the good stuff this time. 'Are there vineyards in the hotel grounds?'

'Oh yes, signora, we have twelve hectares of vines.'

'So the hotel make its own wine?'

He nodded vigorously. 'Yes, indeed. The *Barbera del Grand Hotel* is well known in our area and regularly wins awards.'

'Excellent.' The idea of having home-grown wine with the hotel's name on the label sounded ideal and she filed that fact away to be slipped into her first report to Joseph.

The car to which he led her in the short-term parking block came as quite a surprise. She had been expecting something modern and functional – probably a Fiat as they were made right here in Turin – but, instead, she was confronted by an ancient behemoth of a vehicle sporting the unmistakable emblem of a silver lady with fluttering robes perched on the front of the highly polished midnight blue bonnet.

'A vintage Rolls Royce? Very stylish.' And it was. Mentally adding this to her report, she reflected that it would make an excellent vehicle for collecting VIP guests.

'Built in 1933 and it's been in the family ever since.' There was a note of pride in Luigino's voice.

'The family?'

'The Dellarosa Family. Count Vittorio Emanuele bought it and handed it down to his son, Vittorio Emanuele, who passed it on to his son, also named Vittorio Emanuele. When he died two years ago *his* son inherited the car together with the hotel, but he sold it along with everything else.'

'And is his name Vittorio Emanuele, too?'

'Yes, signora, how did you guess?' The expression on his face gave nothing away.

'And what's happened to this gentleman, Vittorio the fourth? Did he move away after selling up?'

'No, he still lives quite close to the hotel.' He opened the cavernous boot and reached for the suitcase. Without being asked, Louise helped him lift it off the trolley and was relieved not to see any more buttons come flying off his tunic. Somebody could have lost an eye.

'I look forward to meeting him.'

Luigino wiped his brow. 'He's a very private person and he keeps himself to himself but, you never know, your paths might cross. He occasionally comes up to eat at the hotel but nowadays we hardly ever see him otherwise. Not that he ever spent much time at the hotel.'

'But his father ran the hotel, didn't he?'

'Well, his grandfather mainly, until he died at the age of ninety-three.'

So this meant the hotel had been in the hands of a nonagenarian. She wondered what she was going to find when they got there. Suddenly *quirky* was looking more understandable – and daunting.

The journey to the hotel wasn't without drama; not caused by Luigino's driving which was remarkably sedate for an Italian, but by the car itself. Just after they had turned off the main Turin-to-Milan motorway where they had been rolling sedately along in the slow lane, being overtaken by huge trucks with number plates from all over Europe and beyond, smoke began to pour out from under the bonnet, partly obscuring the view through the windscreen.

'Luigino, are we on fire?' Louise glanced across at him but saw him looking remarkably unconcerned as he pulled into a lay-by at the side of the long straight country road and turned towards her, smiling encouragingly.

'It's just steam, signora. She's an old lady and sometimes she needs a bit of cooling down.'

He climbed out of the driving seat and disappeared round to the boot. A minute later he reappeared carrying a jerry can and headed for the engine compartment. The moment he opened the bonnet a white cloud billowed up and Louise decided to follow his example and get out of the car as a precautionary move. His mention of steam, rather than smoke, had reassured her but it was better to be safe than sorry. She slid off the soft old leather armchair of a seat and stepped outside.

The air was noticeably cooler now as she stood at the side of the road and she was glad of her warm coat. Off to the left of them she could see and hear the motorway with its seemingly unending convoys of trucks, while to the right the flat land gave way to a series of low hills. These were covered with a mixture of open fields, copses of trees and the unmistakable regular lines of vineyards. Unlike the Alps, there was no snow to be seen around here and Louise was relieved. Somehow she didn't think a vintage Rolls Royce and fresh snow would mix well. The trees and vines were still bare after the winter frosts but it wouldn't be long before fresh young shoots and leaves began to appear as spring got under way. The sun was just about to disappear behind the curtain of the distant Alps and she could see her breath in the air as she exhaled. The Rolls Royce, on the other hand, had by now stopped expelling steam.

'All done, signora. I just needed to top up the radiator.'

Luigino emerged from under the bonnet and returned the water container to the boot, after which they both climbed back inside and their journey continued southwards into the hills. They passed solid-looking houses, some built of stone and some of brick. Other red-roofed buildings dotted the landscape as far as the eye could see. Many of the farms were equipped with open-sided barns attached to the houses, alongside which were huge wire cages containing heaps of shiny yellow corncobs. Louise knew they would have been used to feed the livestock through the winter as well as providing the human occupants of the farms with the typical yellow flour of this area: polenta. Interspersed among the traditional older buildings were more modern houses, no doubt many of them built by people from Turin keen to get away from the cloying heat of summer down on the plains. For now, cloying heat was noticeable by its absence.

The higher they climbed, the more beautiful the views became. The old Rolls Royce took the increasingly steep slopes in her stride without overheating again and when they reached one particularly high vantage point Luigino pointed across the valley to a large building amid the trees, fields and vineyards near the top of the next hill. From here, it looked like a castle. The roof and the treetops around it had a light covering of snow and the overall impression was charming.

'That's the Grand Hotel over there.' He glanced across at Louise. 'It's in a beautiful position, isn't it?'

'It most certainly is.' Although she had already checked it out on Google Earth, Louise was impressed. The hotel looked as if it was all on its own, completely immersed in the Italian countryside with no near neighbours. She added *peace and quiet guaranteed* to her mental report and asked Luigino to stop while she took a couple of photos. Although the hotel was just a few kilometres across from them in a straight line, they then had to drop down via a series of hairpin bends to the valley floor before climbing back up again and it was beginning to get dark as they finally turned off the narrow lane they had been following. A slightly lopsided, faded wooden sign at the side of the road announced their arrival at the Grand

Hotel del Monferrato and Louise frowned at its dilapidated appearance. Still, she had to admit that the sweeping drive that led upwards in an elegant curve flanked by tall trees was delightful and the light dusting of snow on the leaves added a romantic feel to the place. The old car crunched up the gravel until at last they emerged onto a large parking area in front of the hotel itself and came to a halt alongside just half a dozen other cars. It was obvious the hotel was far from full tonight.

Louise's first impression as she climbed out into the evening shadows was *wow*, closely followed by a number of caveats. Yes, it was a fine building although not as ancient as it had first appeared – maybe nineteenth century – but it had definitely seen better days. The faded ochre plaster on the walls had come off in a few places, exposing the rough brickwork beneath, and the windows and shutters looked as though they could do with a good clean and, preferably, a fresh coat of paint. Looking upwards, she could distinctly make out a small tree growing out of one corner of the roof and one of the shutters was hanging drunkenly by just one hinge. The place could definitely do with a generous shot of tender loving care.

'If you'd like to go on up the steps, I'll see that your suitcase follows you.' Maybe anticipating Louise's concerns for his health, Luigino was quick to explain. 'Rodolfo will come and get it.'

Muttering a silent prayer that Rodolfo would not prove to be another candidate for a heart attack, Louise thanked Luigino and left him to it. Apart from the frosty chill in the air, the main thing she immediately noticed was a strong smell of drains. Presumably up here in this isolated position the hotel had to have its own sanitation system and, clearly, it wasn't working properly. She added this to the list of things to be done that she was already composing in her head, just after *painting and decorating, new hotel sign, service the Rolls Royce* and *find Luigino a tailor*.

She had barely started climbing the half dozen steps towards the front doors when she was almost bowled over as a giant of a man came running out. He was dressed in traditional hall porter garb of grey trousers, white shirt and smart green waistcoat and he towered over her, although his boyish cheeks indicated he probably wasn't even twenty. Louise had no doubt that if this was Rodolfo, then carrying her suitcase was going to present no problem – quite possibly with Luigino under his other arm at the same time. He narrowly missed bumping into her, blushed and jumped backwards, almost tipping an exquisite old terracotta pot off the terrace as he did so.

'*Mi scusi, signora… scusi, scusi.*' And he hurried on down the steps without waiting for a response from her.

'*Buona sera, signora.*'

Louise turned back in the direction of a female voice and saw a matronly lady emerge from the doors. Holding out her hand, she replied in Italian. 'Good evening, I'm Louise Rhodes. The hotel really is a lovely old building, isn't it?'

'Welcome to the Grand Hotel, Signora Rhodes.' She pronounced it Ro-ho-dess. 'We've been expecting you and I'm delighted to hear you speaking Italian. We all speak a little English but I'm afraid I'm not terribly fluent. I'm Domenica Albese, the assistant manager. You must excuse Rodolfo. He's very willing but a bit clumsy.'

Louise took an immediate liking to this friendly-looking lady. She looked as though she was roughly the same age as Luigino, no doubt in her sixties, and Louise wondered whether Rodolfo the baby-faced giant was going to turn out to be the exception to the rule as far as the average age of the staff here was concerned. She was reminded of Viv's comment about hunky Italians and from the showing so far she had a feeling that she wasn't going to find herself being tempted into the arms of any man out here in the Piedmontese countryside – which was definitely for the best, given the events of the past ten days. They shook hands and Louise couldn't miss the nervous expression on the assistant manager's face, but this didn't come as a surprise. She was all too familiar with this reaction when she appeared at hotels. After all, she was the person who could potentially put Domenica and her colleagues out of a job and she was quick to offer reassurance.

'Rodolfo looks like a useful strong man to have around. The hotel's in a charming location, isn't it? I'm most impressed.' It was on the tip of her tongue to comment on the abundance of fresh air there must be out here in the country when another rank reminder of the dodgy drains wafted past her nose. For now, however, she didn't comment. First of all she wanted to concentrate on trying to put everybody at ease. There would be time for criticism in due course. There was no point in putting anybody's nose out of joint until it was absolutely necessary. 'And what a marvellous old car I've just travelled in.'

'Ah, yes, the Rolls Royce was old Count Vittorio's pride and joy.'

'But Luigino tells me the last in the line sold it along with the hotel. Why did he sell up? I ather he didn't work in the hotel. Wasn't he interested?'

'It's not really that he wasn't interested.' The expression on Domenica's face was difficult to decipher. Louise felt she could read disappointment, but mainly it was one of compassion. 'He didn't really have the chance.' Presumably realising that further explanation was necessary, she carried on. 'His grandfather was a stubborn man – and that only got worse as he grew older. He refused to give up the reins until the end. Although his son, Vito's father, worked in the hotel with him, old Count Vittorio wouldn't hand over any of the day-to-day running and wouldn't hear of innovation or change.' She gave Louise a hint of a smile. 'I can tell you all sorts of stories but, as an example, he refused to let us put soft toilet paper in the guest bathrooms and insisted on us buying the old shiny, greaseproof stuff.'

'Wow, I didn't know they made that anymore.'

Seeing incredulity on Louise's face, Domenica explained the old man's rationale. 'He thought female guests would use the soft stuff to wipe their makeup off or steal it to use in place of tissues and it would all be wasted in no time. He was funny like that. To be honest, his inflexibility's the main reason the bookings dropped and dropped: he wasn't prepared to move with the times. Vito must have seen how unhappy his father was in the shadow of his grandfather so he decided to go off to do his own thing.'

'And what was that?'

'He's a *professore* at Turin University.'

'I see.' A life in academia was a long way away from the life of a hotelier but the man had no doubt wanted to keep well away from the frustration his father must have felt. 'And Luigino said he lives nearby.'

'That's right, when his father died, he took over his father's house by the river just down the hill from here. It's the old mill and he's been living there now for a couple of years.' Domenica gave her a nervous smile. 'But of course the hotel belongs to you now.'

Louise shook her head. 'Not to me, Domenica, to my boss. I'm just the hired hand.'

'Anyway, do come inside, signora. I expect you'd like to see your room and maybe, as you're English, you might like a cup of tea?'

Louise gave her a grateful smile. 'Thank you, I'd like nothing better, and please call me Louise.'

Chapter 4

Louise came down for dinner at half past seven as agreed and found the dining room virtually empty. Domenica had told her that they only had a handful of guests at present. The way she said it implied that they had more guests at other times but the printouts Louise had got from Annabelle said otherwise. Tonight just three of the forty tables were occupied, plus hers. There were two elderly couples – probably tourists, maybe even Brits – and an Italian family of seven.

Being charitable, Louise had to admit that mid-March, with winter still making its presence felt, probably wasn't the busiest of times for any hotel in this area. The high Alps where people were still skiing were a different matter but here, out in the country, however picturesque it might be, there was bound to be limited tourism – at least for now. For a moment she couldn't help wondering what had prompted Joseph to buy the place. Most of his hotels were city centre locations or in well-known tourist hotspots. Presumably he must have got it for a good price. The thought of Joseph brought back the conundrum that had been plaguing her for the past few days: had Friday night's dinner invitation been a date? Had all those questions about love and relationships been a prelude to declaring himself, only to bottle out when he heard that she was almost engaged? Could he really be interested in her and, if so, how might this affect her working relationship with him going forward?

The jury was still out on that one.

Before coming down for dinner she had spent half an hour prowling about the upper floors of the hotel, opening doors and poking her nose into every corner. What she discovered had been fairly heartening. Considerable expenditure on refurbishing a number of the bathrooms was going to be necessary, but the fact that every room already possessed one was unexpected and some of them were rather fine. Some other hundred-year-old hotels she had come across still only had a lone bathroom at the end of each corridor and this had meant long and messy construction work to create en-suites.

However, apart from upgrading some of the facilities, much of what she had found had been positive. The mattresses were good quality and for the most part fairly modern and – no doubt because of the drop in guest numbers – little used and, therefore, still firm. The floors were mainly bare wood but well looked-after and polished, the furniture of good quality with a few antique pieces, and the overall impression was one of extreme cleanliness. She hadn't found a single spider's web – which made a pleasant change after her discovery in the Caribbean of not only a massive web under one of the beds, but of its equally large and aggressively annoyed arachnid owner still in residence. Louise had taken one look at its multitude of black hairy legs and fled.

She was shown to her table by a tall, thin sexagenarian in a dinner jacket which was showing its age, unlike the man himself who looked fit and active. He introduced himself as Calogero. Louise had never heard the name before and wasn't sure whether this was his first name or his surname so she studiously avoided calling him anything for now. She resolved to add his name alongside Luigino's to her list of candidates for the attentions of a good tailor. He laid a leather-bound menu on the table in front of her, bowed respectfully and retired.

Instinctively, she checked her surroundings. The restaurant was an imposing room with a high ceiling and a series of French windows to the outside which were firmly closed tonight. Presumably the Grand Hotel offered the possibility of dining outside in the summer. Even up here she had no doubt it could get really hot in July and August. The cupboards and dressers along the end wall looked old and well-preserved, the floor was highly polished wood, and the overall impression was positive and welcoming. She added a provisional tick alongside *dining facilities* in her mental report for now.

The meal proved to be excellent and the bottle of Barbera del Grand Hotel lived up to Luigino's hype. It was an excellent wine. She would have preferred a half bottle but Calogero – or might that be Signor Calogero? – informed her he would cork it and keep it for her for tomorrow's meals if she didn't wish to drink it all tonight. Louise had no intention of getting plastered on her first night so she limited herself to two smallish glasses, but definitely enjoyed them.

She opted for the menu of the day and it came as no surprise to find that the first course of antipasti lasted for almost half an hour. Here in Piedmont, up in the top left-hand corner of Italy, antipasti were something of a speciality and she found herself on the receiving end of a seemingly never-ending procession of different dishes, with taster portions served by Calogero, assisted by a very tall young girl who looked as if she might even be Rodolfo's sister. Louise wondered idly whether tall Calogero might be father to both of them.

There were local hams and salami, wild mushrooms from the surrounding woods preserved in olive oil, freshly made Russian salad, vol-au-vents filled with chicken in a creamy sauce topped with aromatic flakes of truffles, and much more, including slices of boiled beef in a thick, parsley sauce. Partway through, Calogero arrived with a dish of *bagna cauda*. This local speciality consisted of red peppers roasted in the oven and served with a smooth anchovy, cream and garlic sauce. She had tasted this potentially lethal-sounding dish before when she had lived in Turin as a student and knew it to be far better than the sum of its parts. It tasted wonderful – although Louise reflected that it was just as well she wasn't going to be kissing anybody tonight.

Thoughts of kissing returned her mind to Tommy but, at least for now, she didn't have time to dwell on her defunct relationship as her phone started vibrating. It was an Italian mobile number which she didn't recognise.

'*Pronto.*'

'Louise, is that you?'

It was an Italian woman's voice and, although she hadn't heard it for years, she recognised it immediately.

'Silvana! Ciao.'

'Ciao Louise. I got your email and I was wondering if you'd arrived yet.'

'Yes, I just arrived this afternoon. So good to hear from you. How are you?' Silvana and Louise had been close friends when they had both been studying at Turin University twelve years earlier. They had seen little of each other since Louise had started working for Joseph eight years ago and had pretty much lost all contact. Of course, as Louise knew only too well, the fact was that she had lost contact with many of her friends since starting this job, as she was so often out of the country. She was delighted her email had got through.

They chatted for five minutes or so until Louise saw Calogero hovering with a steaming dish of pasta. She gave him a little smile and told Silvana she had to go.

'But let's meet up soon. I'm only an hour or so from Turin. I could try to come in and see you.'

'Have you got a car?'

'Not at the moment, but I'm thinking about renting one.'

'Well, why don't I drive over and take you out for lunch one day this week. How about tomorrow? I've got the day off.'

Silvana had been studying medicine when they had first met and she was now a surgeon at Turin's Molinette hospital. Louise agreed eagerly. 'That sounds perfect, but let me offer you lunch here. I'd like to get your opinion of the food.'

Silvana agreed to come at noon next day with her *fidanzato* if he could free himself. The word translated as fiancé – or at least long-term serious boyfriend – and Louise was looking forward to meeting him. She put her phone down and beckoned Calogero forward, noticing that it wasn't pasta on the dish in his hands but potato gnocchi, surprisingly a bright yellow colour.

'*Gnocchi allo zafferano.*'

Calogero scooped a generous portion onto her plate and stood back while she picked up one of the Parmesan-smothered gnocchi on the end of her fork. The hint of saffron added an unusual delicacy to the taste, and the consistency, with just enough background crunch from the potato, was delightful. She murmured appreciatively and saw a look of satisfaction spread across his face.

'*Buon appetito, signora.*'

This was followed by roast lamb accompanied by polenta laced with fontina cheese, and by the time her panna cotta arrived Louise had already resolved to start going for long walks and cutting back on the amount of food she ate if she was to avoid returning from her stay in Italy needing a whole new wardrobe. One thing was for sure: although the drains needed fixing, there was nothing wrong with the food. Credit where it was due, she beckoned Calogero over and asked if he could send the chef out. Seeing immediate concern on the maître d's face she was quick to reassure him that everything had been perfect. He turned away with an expression of relief and two minutes later the chef arrived. To Louise's surprise the chef, looking the part in a pristine white tunic – this time with no buttons missing – was none other than Luigino.

'Luigino, you're the chef?' He nodded. 'Well, my compliments. I've had an excellent meal and I wanted you to know it. Thank you so much.'

'I'm glad you enjoyed it, signora.'

'Please call me Louise. So, how is it you combine the roles of chef and chauffeur?'

'To be honest, sig… Louise, we've got used to sharing the jobs between us. We don't have many guests so, by each of us doing a bit of this and a bit of that, we've managed to keep the hotel afloat and save our jobs.'

Louise was pleased to hear him being so frank. From the figures she had seen, the hotel wasn't so much afloat as part-submerged and heading, Titanic-like, for the ocean floor, but it was good to hear that the staff were prepared to muck in. 'Well, that's what I'm here for. Hopefully I can try to get us more guests, bring in more business and keep everybody employed.'

He gave her a beaming smile. 'I do hope so. This place has been my life for so long now, it's a real shame to see it so quiet.'

'After a meal like I've had tonight, you don't need to worry. Once we get the word out that there's a top-quality chef here, I'm sure the numbers will pick up.' At that moment she spotted Domenica coming over to see her, accompanied by Calogero.

'I thought I'd check to see that you enjoyed your dinner, signora.'

'I've just been telling Luigino that I've had an excellent dinner – and do call me Louise, please.' A thought occurred to her. 'By the way, if you're the assistant manager, where's the manager?'

Domenica and the two men exchanged looks before she replied for all of them. 'There isn't one at the moment. You see, old Count Vittorio stubbornly refused to hand over control of the hotel and it was only when he died at the age of ninety-three that his son finally took over. He was well into his sixties by that time and had been working in the old count's shadow for decades but, tragically, he'd only been in the job for a matter of months before he was diagnosed with a most aggressive form of cancer. He died two years ago. It was all so sad.'

'And since his death there hasn't been a replacement? So who's been running the place?'

'Since he died, it's been me mostly, seeing as his son, Vito, isn't involved.' Domenica produced a weary smile. 'With help from Luigino and Calogero. It's been a collaborative effort.'

'Wow.' Louise was genuinely impressed. She had been expecting there to be several tiers of unproductive personnel to be weeded out but it sounded as though Domenica and her colleagues had been managing on a skeleton staff – albeit a pretty aged skeleton. From Louise's point of view this was good news. Hopefully, with so few staff, there should be no need to sack anybody and she always hated making people redundant – even the less productive ones. 'Well, you seem to have been making a very good job of it. Congratulations.'

The relief on the faces around her was clear to see.

She decided to go up to her room after dinner and get on with preparing her initial report for Joseph, partly because she could see that Domenica, Luigino and Calogero were looking tired and she didn't want to keep them up. There would be time to start talking shop in the morning.

When she got up to her scrupulously clean but rather antiquated bedroom, she dropped her bag on the bed without putting on the light, felt her way across to the window and looked out. It was pitch black outside but, as her eyes grew accustomed to the dark, she began to see little pinpricks of light all around. High above, the wintry sky was studded with stars, while lower down the surrounding hillsides were dotted with the lights of houses and farmsteads – but remarkably few of them.

Considering the hotel was barely an hour from a city of almost a million people, it really was in a remarkably remote location. The air was clear and she felt sure there would be a hard frost up here tonight. Thankfully the old cast-iron radiator below the window was belching out heat and she knew she wasn't going to be cold. Resting her elbows on the windowsill she felt an unexpectedly warm glow which had nothing to do with the radiator, Luigino's excellent food, or the Barbera del Grand Hotel.

Somehow, in spite of the sudden demise of her relationship with Tommy and her fear that her boss's feelings towards her might be straying away from the purely professional, she felt remarkably relaxed, unusually relaxed. Something told her the Grand Hotel del Monferrato was going to prove to be a perfect place of escape and a little oasis of calm. And she could certainly do with some of that.

Chapter 5

Louise got up early and spent the morning going through the books with Domenica, checking on all the income and expenditure. The latter seriously outweighed the former even though the wages bill was remarkably modest. Certainly nobody was being overpaid. Interestingly, income from the sale of their own wine to the public came to almost as much as the hotel revenue. It came as no surprise to see that little or nothing had been spent on the upkeep of the buildings over the past few years and together with Domenica she was soon compiling a detailed list of essential remedial work, as well as upgrades to bring the place into the twenty-first century and up to the standard of Joseph's other hotels. She asked Domenica to start getting quotes for the various jobs and sent a long and detailed email to Joseph in London, following up on the initial report she had sent to him just before going to bed last night. One thing was clear: it was just as well he had deep pockets.

At midday Silvana arrived with her *fidanzato*, Davide. Silvana at thirty-three was six months older than Louise and was looking smart and happy. Davide was a friendly, dark-haired man who looked a bit like a younger version of George Clooney. It came as no surprise to discover that he, too, was a medic. What *was* a surprise was to find that he knew the hotel and its former owners well.

Not only had he been one of the doctors who had treated the last manager, Count Vittorio, two years ago for the lung cancer that had subsequently killed him, but he had also been a close friend of the count's son, Vito, first at school and then at university. Although they hadn't seen much of each other over the past few years, he was able to tell Louise that Vito was now a lecturer in Environmental Studies and apparently gaining quite a reputation as an expert in the field of conservation.

The other thing Louise discovered was that Silvana and Davide had only just got engaged to be married and were having a party this coming Saturday in a restaurant outside Turin to celebrate. The wedding was due to take place in the middle of June and Louise was invited. She was delighted to accept the invitations to the wedding and this Saturday's party. She decided to rent herself a car as the idea of driving the Rolls Royce was far too intimidating.

Over lunch, they talked and talked and she told them about what she did for a living, but studiously avoided any mention of her personal life, not feeling up to relating the whole sad saga of Tommy's betrayal. Hopefully in a few weeks, as the hurt subsided, she would find it easier, but, for the moment, she just skated around her relationship status, telling them that she was concentrating on her job for now. In return, Silvana brought her up to date with news of the members of the old crowd with whom Louise had mingled during her year at Turin university. Among these, one name leapt out at her: Paolo.

Paolo had been Louise's first real great love. In fact, thinking back to Joseph's questions on the subject, she realised that with Paolo it really had been love at first sight. Although she had had a number of boyfriends at school in London and then at university, meeting Paolo in Turin had been a whole new experience for her. After the proverbial glance across a crowded room at a New Year's party she had been overwhelmed by a wave of infatuation, never to be repeated in her life to date, not even with Tommy. They had spent the next five and a half months together and she had convinced herself that she wanted to spend the rest of her life with him.

But it hadn't worked out. As summer and the end of her course in Turin approached, he had delivered the bombshell that he was going off to California to do his Masters. She had begged him to come to the UK to study but he told her the UCLA course was the best option for him and made it brutally clear that his career took priority over everything – including her. Their parting was bitterly tragic and she would never forget the rivers of tears she had cried for ages afterwards. Time had gradually healed her wounds and, despite regular correspondence over the next year, they had slowly drifted apart until all communication had ceased. In consequence, hearing his name risked stirring up all sorts of conflicting emotions inside her. After all, Paolo's break-up with her was in so many ways a mirror image of how she had prioritised her career and contributed to causing things to sour with Tommy.

In fact, there was little that Silvana could add to the story of Paolo. She, too, had pretty much lost contact with him over the intervening years. All she knew was that he had stayed on in the US at the end of his course and had found a job over there. Well over ten years had passed and in all probability he was married with children by now. Silvana told her she had sent him an invitation to the party and the wedding via the last email address she had for him but had received no response. Louise allowed herself a little sigh for the memory of what might have been but reminded herself that men were near the bottom of her agenda for the foreseeable future. Meanwhile, Silvana reeled off details of what the others from their group of friends had been doing and by the sound of it, Louise would have the chance to meet up with a good number of them at Saturday's party. She looked forward to hearing what they had all got up to in the intervening years and to seeing what they looked like now.

Luigino's lunch met with enthusiastic approval from Davide and Silvana and, by the time they left, Louise felt that she and Silvana were once again as close as they used to be. She waved them off down the drive and looked up. It wasn't dark yet but the sky had clouded over and it came as no surprise to feel raindrops on her cheeks. She just had time to hurry back up the steps to the front door before the rain started tipping down, almost as though somebody had turned on a tap.

It rained on and off for the rest of the day and well into the night and when she awoke next morning she found all residual traces of the snow washed away and replaced by huge puddles and a constant chorus of drips. The temperature had also risen by several degrees as a result and there was no longer frost in the air or on the ground. Hopefully spring was just around the corner.

She sat down with Domenica and Calogero after breakfast and they told her more about the hotel – and themselves. It turned out that Louise's guess had been correct and Calogero – that really was his first name – was Rodolfo and Graziella's father. Their mother had sadly died some years back and the three of them lived in the nearby hilltop town of Moncalvo. Domenica, however, had never married and she had been living in an apartment above the stable block at the rear of the hotel for over thirty years. Luigino lived with his wife in the village barely a kilometre down the hill from the hotel and he had worked at the hotel for even longer than Domenica and Calogero. It was a close-knit group, almost like a little family, and Louise determined to do all she could to ensure none of them should lose their jobs. It certainly looked as if they were all pulling their weight.

She learned that there were a couple of part-time chambermaids who could lend a hand in the kitchen if required and both Rodolfo and Graziella took turns in the kitchen washing dishes, peeling potatoes and preparing vegetables and salads for Luigino. In the grounds, there were two men who looked after the gardens and vineyard and Louise set out after lunch, wearing her battered old trainers, to find them and introduce herself. Her official – and somewhat opaque – title in the company was Support Officer, but she tended simply to refer to herself as a consultant which wasn't a whole lot clearer but was a bit more recognisable.

Finding the two men was easy. All she had to do was head for the sound of a tractor and she located the first of them in one of the fields down towards the lower part of the sizeable estate, ploughing the earth in readiness for this year's crop. She waited for him to return to the top of the field and sucked in the crisp, country air, feeling unexpectedly relaxed. She had spent most of her life in the city and there was something enchanting about these pastoral surroundings with little birds twittering in the bushes and the distant sound of sheep in a field somewhere out of sight. Looking around, the hotel was already hidden from view by the trees and the overall impression was one of bucolic tranquillity. When the tractor came back up the field towards her, she waved. The elderly man in the driving seat waved back before coming to a halt, turning off the engine and climbing out of the cab. She picked her way gingerly through the mud to meet him.

'Hello, my name's Louise. I'll be working up at the hotel for a few months while we get on with all the modernisation. I just wanted to introduce myself.'

He shook her hand. 'I'm pleased to meet you, signora. My name's Giuseppe Delmonte but everybody calls me Beppe.'

'And everybody calls me Louise.'

He was no spring chicken either and it soon emerged that he had started working here over forty years ago. One thing became clear as she spoke to him: what Beppe didn't know about the hotel and its grounds wasn't worth knowing. She spent a fascinating half hour with him learning about the crops he was growing and receiving confirmation of what Luigino had said about last year's wine promising to be exceptional. As far as winemaking was concerned, this was in the experienced hands of his colleague, Ernesto, who was even now out in the vines, checking that all was well. Following Beppe's directions, Louise set off in search of him, greatly impressed by the fact that these men had been doing the exact same jobs for so many years and must have built up irreplaceable experience. Just like the orchestra playing on the Titanic, they had carried on as normal while the hotel had slowly started to sink beneath the waves. It was now up to her to see that the future for men like Beppe and the other loyal members of staff of the Grand Hotel was secured.

After fifteen minutes or so on a muddy track that followed the contours of the hillside she finally spotted her man, but immediately discovered that her presence had already been registered not by Ernesto, but by a big brown Labrador who came bounding up to her followed by a scruffy little mongrel, both of them barking noisily. She hesitated as she saw the dogs approach but she could see their tails wagging so she assumed their intentions were friendly. It turned out they were. But it also turned out that the Labrador's idea of a greeting was to launch himself at her from several feet away and almost tip her backwards into the mud. His dirty paws turned her jeans into brown and blue striped pyjamas and she realised that he wasn't in fact a chocolate Lab. Underneath the liberal coating of fresh Piedmontese mud was a jet-black dog and Louise had a feeling Ernesto was going to have a major cleaning job on his hands when they returned home.

'Leo, come here, you pest. Leave the lady alone. And you, Attila.' Alerted by the barking, Ernesto had noticed her plight and, remarkably, the dogs obeyed instantly.

Louise wiped her muddy hands on her now predominantly brown jeans and squelched across to meet Ernesto in between bare rows of vines, the ground at her feet still littered with last year's fallen leaves, now almost indistinguishable from the mud. Glancing down, she resolved to buy herself some new trainers as by now these were the same colour as her filthy jeans.

'Hi, I'm Louise. I'm a consultant and I'll be working up at the hotel for a few months. You must be Ernesto.'

'Yes, signora. Domenica told us you were coming. I'm pleased to meet you.'

'How come your little dog's called Attila?'

He smiled. 'He's a terrier and a terror. When he was little, he destroyed everything he could find. It seemed like the right name.'

46

While they chatted, the terrier wandered off into the vines while the Labrador came over and leant against the side of Louise's right leg, tail wagging lazily. She reached down and ruffled his ears – just about the only part of him not coated in mud – as he slowly slid down until he was stretched out on his back with all four paws in the air, grunting happily to himself as his tail produced a fan shape in the viscous mud beneath him. She glanced at Ernesto and pointed towards the dog.

'I'm afraid your dogs are going to need a bath tonight.'

Ernesto grinned. 'Attila will need a good scrubbing but I'm pleased to say that this one won't be my responsibility. Leo isn't my dog.'

'Who does he belong to, then?'

'Vito... Professor Vittorio Emanuele Dellarosa. He lives in the old mill down there by the river.' Louise followed the line of his pointing finger and could just make out the weathered red roof tiles of a building among the trees. 'Leo often joins Attila and me in the fields. As for his bath, I'm sure he'll see to that himself. There's a pool down by the mill where he spends most of his life in the hot summer months and he still swims every day even at this time of year. He's been doing it all winter.'

'Wow, that fur coat must be really thick.' She glanced back down at the dog. 'Whereas my jeans are going into the washing machine.'

'Yes, sorry about that. He's just a youngster and he can be a bit over-affectionate.'

By the time Louise bade farewell to Ernesto and the dogs, she knew a lot more about the vineyards here and they had agreed to meet up the following morning at the cantina behind the hotel. He promised her a tasting of the new wine that would soon be ready for bottling and she told him she was looking forward to it, but, first things first, she needed to find a washing machine and some clean dry clothes.

Chapter 6

On Saturday, Louise drove to Silvana and Davide's party in the hotel van. Ernesto had insisted there was no need to rent a car and had given her the keys to a white van parked at the rear of the hotel. He told her he used it for wine deliveries to various local restaurants and shops and for collections of food and other necessities from suppliers, but he could happily do without it on Saturday and Sunday. It smelt vaguely of vinegar but was clean enough although the diesel engine roared like an unhappy lion most of the time. Still, it got her there.

The party was a lunchtime event in a country restaurant set on the flank of the first of the foothills of the Alps, just to the north of Turin. Access was up a tortuous and fairly narrow road and she found driving the large vehicle a bit daunting until she realised that most car drivers automatically took avoiding action when confronted with a van and she was mostly able to sail through almost without slowing down. Silvana had told her not to worry about dressing up but, to be on the safe side, Louise had dug out her old faithful Dior dress and the only pair of heels she had brought – although she only slipped these on after arriving in the restaurant car park, having quickly worked out that the pedals of the van had not been designed with high fashion in mind.

Inside she was greeted by the familiar face of Ines, one of the old group of university friends, and Louise was delighted to see her again. Together they did the rounds of the guests who had already assembled in the bar and Louise was soon renewing acquaintance with people she hadn't seen for over a decade. She was also introduced to both sets of parents and a number of aunts and uncles, knowing full well she didn't stand a chance of remembering all their names. It was only when they reached the far side of the room that the smile was wiped from her face. There, leaning against the bar was none other than the man she had once been sure she loved. The moment her eyes alighted on him, she had to make a conscious effort to stop her jaw from dropping to her feet.

'Ciao, Louise.' He didn't look as gobsmacked as she felt. Presumably somebody had broken the news to him that she was coming.

'Paolo...' She wasn't often stuck for words but seeing him had struck her dumb.

'Long time no see. You look wonderful.' She saw him study her more closely. 'How're you doing?'

Louise let her eyes range over him as she searched for something to say. Over the intervening twelve years he had, if anything, become even more good-looking. His unruly brown hair, which had been shoulder length when she had known him, was now neatly and stylishly trimmed so that it just brushed his ears. He looked great. Finally regaining the power of speech, Louise held out both hands towards him.

'I'm fine, thanks. Just a bit tired. I've recently come back from a pretty intense couple of months working overseas.' Now was definitely not the time to speak about what had happened with Tommy. 'This is quite a surprise;

I didn't expect to see you.' She almost added the words 'ever again' but stopped herself in time.

He caught hold of her hands and they exchanged chaste kisses on the cheeks. It felt really weird to touch him again after so long and after so much heartache and she could feel stinging in the corners of her eyes as long-suppressed emotions threatened to spill out. Stepping back, he explained how it was he had come to be at the party. 'It was all a last-minute thing. I've been over in Germany on business and it was just by sheer chance that I checked my old email address and found the invite from Silvana. I'd been planning to stop off in Turin for a day or two so I jumped on a plane first thing this morning and flew down.'

At that moment Silvana herself appeared and gave Louise a big welcoming hug. 'Ciao, Louise. I see you've found Paolo. I only discovered he was coming when he walked in the door ten minutes ago. Isn't it great to see him again?'

Louise nodded but she was still having a hard time coming to terms with the shock of his reappearance in her life. A host of memories came flooding back into her head and she could feel her head swimming. If she hadn't been driving, she would have asked for a large brandy but, instead, she grabbed a cold glass of sparkling mineral water from a passing waiter and took a big, calming mouthful. Unfortunately the result was anything but calming as the bubbles rushed up her nose and she erupted into a fit of coughing. At least by the time she recovered her breath, she had also managed to recover a semblance of composure.

'So where are you living these days, Paolo?' She was pleased to hear her voice sounding pretty normal. She was back in control of her emotions... sort of.

'Denver, Colorado.' Unbidden, a little shiver of disappointment ran through her. Clearly they were destined to be forever separated by the Atlantic Ocean. Paolo added a few more words of explanation. 'I've been based there for ten years now and I love being close to the mountains. It feels a bit like Turin in a way. What about you? What's this job you've been doing?'

They chatted increasingly freely and Louise felt herself relax – up to a point. She learned that he had worked himself into a senior position in a large pharmaceutical company and that he travelled all over the world just about as much as she did. He didn't mention a wife or family and she didn't ask. He also didn't query her current relationship status and she didn't offer. The only clues on display were that neither of them was wearing a wedding ring, but these days that probably didn't mean much.

The time for lunch arrived and she found she had been placed beside him on a six-seater table along with two other couples who had already been together when she had first met them twelve years ago and were now married. Ignoring the possibility of this being some kind of portent, she listened to the goings-on of the others and, in return, told them about the Grand Hotel. They all promised to start spreading the word about the top-class chef in the restaurant and then Paolo put the cat among the pigeons.

'How would it be if I were to meet you there for lunch tomorrow? My parents have organised a big family get-together in the early evening that I can't escape, but it would be nice to sit down for a few hours to catch up, just you and me.'

Sitting down together and catching up was of course exactly what they were doing right now and Louise seriously considered saying no for a moment. Her fear was that this might stir up her already whirling emotions, still seriously battered by the Tommy fiasco. After all, hadn't she told everybody – including herself – that she wasn't interested in getting into another relationship? At the same time Paolo was an old friend and, as such, maybe she owed it to him to agree. Conscious that he was waiting for a reply, she took a deep breath and said yes. She was a grown woman and she knew her own mind; it wasn't as if she was inviting him up to her bedroom after all.

The party broke up around mid-afternoon and Louise drove back to the hotel in the van. All the way there she couldn't stop thinking about Paolo and how his sudden reappearance in her life had affected her. He had looked like the old Paolo, he had sounded like the old Paolo, and being with him had felt like being with the old Paolo. Maybe it would have been wiser to invent some reason why she couldn't see him again, just in case the old attraction might be reignited, seeing as he was returning to Germany and then to the States in a few days' time but, of course, it was too late now. They hadn't even exchanged phone numbers. At least, she reminded herself, they would be meeting up in a public place where nothing could possibly happen between them even if she wanted to get involved with him again, which she didn't.

Did she?

That evening she went down for dinner quite late on, determined only to have a bowl of soup or a salad after the huge lunch. She was almost at the bottom of the stairs when she saw a familiar black shape sitting in the middle of the entrance hall, idly scratching his ear with his hind leg. No sooner did he see her than he jumped to his feet and came charging across to greet her, tail wagging. Clearly he remembered her from the other day. Tonight the Labrador was clean and dry and looking handsome, but she had to ward him off with her hands to stop him climbing all over her. As she was bending down, petting him, she heard a man's voice, but it wasn't Ernesto this time.

'Leo, leave the lady alone.'

She looked up and the funniest thing happened. In a fraction of a second all thoughts of Paolo – or Tommy – evaporated from inside her head as she set eyes on the dog's master. Presumably this was Count Vittorio Emanuele, aka Vito the *professore*. He was a tall man, maybe three or four years older than she was, and there was something about him. Okay, he was fairly good-looking – well, very good-looking really – with dark hair, unexpectedly bright blue eyes and he was wearing steel-framed glasses that underlined his *professore* status. He was tall, and had a friendly, if serious, face but it was something else. She felt an immediate and inexplicable feeling of familiarity, almost as if the two of them had already met. She blinked a few times and swallowed hard.

'I don't mind. He's a lovely dog. Are you his owner? Are you Count Vittorio Emanuele?'

'That's me, although I don't use the title. And you must be Louise Rhodes, the expert who's come to get the hotel back on its feet.'

The funny thing was that although she had addressed him in Italian he had replied in totally convincing, fluent English. She stood there stunned for a few moments before responding in English. He spoke it so well, there seemed little point in carrying on in Italian.

'I'm pleased to meet you.' She held out her hand and shook his. 'Leo and I are already old friends. We met in the fields the other day.'

'Ernesto told me what happened and I apologise.' He was sounding formal. In spite of the feeling of familiarity she had sensed, she got the impression he was more detached. She remembered that Luigino had said he was a bit of a recluse and she wondered if he was feeling uncomfortable in her presence. 'I gather he made a bit of a mess of your clothes. Sorry about that. He's still a youngster and I can't get him out of the habit of jumping up.' She saw him glance towards the door, obviously keen to get away.

'Please don't worry about it. It was only my old jeans and they've already been washed and ironed by the people here a lot better than I could have done.' Keen to keep the conversation going although it was increasingly evident that he wanted nothing better than to go off and leave her, she added. 'So, may I ask how it is you speak better English than I do? *Complimenti* as you Italians say.'

'Thank you, but if I speak good English it's because I lived there for a long time.' No detail, no explanation.

Then, just as she was about to ask what he had been doing in England, he glanced down at his watch. 'Anyway, if you'll excuse me, I need to get back. Goodbye, Ms Rhodes.'

'I'm here until the summer so we'll probably meet again. And it's Louise.'

He didn't react. He just clicked his tongue and looked down. 'Come on, Leo, we're off.'

The dog jumped to his feet and obeyed the command, even though it had been delivered in English. Together, man and dog went out into the night and she was left standing there feeling mildly shell-shocked. How could it be that a man she definitely had never met before could arouse such a feeling of familiarity in her? At the same time it was quite clear the same couldn't be said about his reaction to meeting her. He had been polite but there had been no warmth in his greeting, almost as if he regretted seeing her, and he had appeared only too keen to get away. She wondered if she would see him again or whether she had frightened him off and this would be the one and only time they met. She knew that, if that was to be the case, she would be disappointed. For whatever reason, she had enjoyed these brief moments in his company immensely.

She was still feeling puzzled as she made her way into the dining room.

Chapter 7

It took her quite a while to get to sleep that night. Her head was spinning with conflicting thoughts of four men. First, there was Tommy and the still open wound caused by his infidelity, second was the former love of her life who had moved to the other side of the globe, only to reappear like magic, third her boss whose intentions she couldn't fathom, and now, suddenly, this unknown man who had made such an inexplicable first impression on her – even though the same couldn't be said about her on him. She ended up feeling so confused she almost phoned her mum to talk things through with her. Seconds later common sense kicked in as she realised it was almost one o'clock in the morning and she lay back and did her best to relax. It wasn't easy.

When she got up on Sunday morning she just had a cappuccino and then went for a long walk to try and clear her head. Today the sky was cloudless and the morning sun had real heat in it although in the shade it was still chilly. Instead of going downhill, this time she headed uphill through the fields towards a patch of untouched woodland. The track she had been following skirted around the edge of the woods until it finally ran up against an old brick wall that appeared to mark the boundary of the estate. A convenient fallen tree trunk made a perfect spot for her to sit down, admire the view, and try to get her head straight. That same sensation of peace and tranquillity she had felt when she first arrived here gradually took over and stilled her whirling thoughts. She let her eyes roam across the patchwork of fields, vineyards and woodland and finally managed to make some sense of it all.

Tommy and she were finished and the only thing to do about him was to try to banish him from her head and her heart.

As far as Joseph was concerned, she knew nothing was ever going to happen there. She just hoped things wouldn't become awkward and come between her and this job she so enjoyed.

Similarly, Count Vito was a non-starter, in spite of the frisson his appearance had shot through her. He was from another world, doubtless a very wealthy man – she knew he must have made millions from the sale of the hotel and the estate – but, irrespective of all that, he obviously wasn't interested in her.

Paolo and she were divided by five thousand miles and an ocean so unless he appeared here today and told her he was moving back to Europe, nothing could start up again between them, even if she suddenly were to fall under his spell once more.

So the net result was that she was alone. She reminded herself that this had been her stated aim all along so she made an effort to stop thinking about men and concentrate on her job. The only obstacle, of course, was the imminent arrival of Paolo to have lunch with her.

He appeared at noon and she met him by the reception desk. He was dressed casually today in jeans and a jumper and he reminded her even more of the boy she had once loved. When he kissed her cheeks, he caught hold of her shoulders and pulled her towards him and there was real warmth in his touch. If it hadn't been for the patent impossibility of their ever getting back together she might have wrapped her arms around him and hugged him but instead she took a deep breath and stepped back, managing to produce a big smile.

'Ciao, Paolo. It's good to see you again.'

She led him into the empty lounge where two huge logs were burning in the grate. It felt really cosy in here.

'Can I get you a drink?'

'I'm driving so I'll just have a Coke, but don't let me stop you. And today's on me.'

'Of course not, you're on my territory here.' She almost went on to tell him he could pay next time, but stopped herself just in time. Of course there wasn't going to be a next time.

After asking Graziella for his Coke and a glass of Prosecco for herself, they settled down on an old leather sofa by the fire and, slowly, they started to talk. She told him more about her job and all the travelling it entailed. He told her about his life since leaving Italy, how he had finished his master's degree, found the job in Denver and worked his way up the ladder. She told him how she was trying to keep active by walking, or swimming when she had the opportunity. He told her how he had taken up golf and how every weekend in winter he went skiing in the Rockies.

Finally, he told her he had got married four years ago.

Louise managed to avoid looking too gobsmacked and did her best to respond as naturally as possible. 'Congratulations. Who is she? An American?'

'Yes, her name's Katharine and she's originally from LA. We both work in the same company.'

'And have you got kids?'

He shook his head. 'No, she decided to wait, mainly because of her career.' He glanced up and caught Louise's eye. 'To be honest, it's just as well we waited.'

'It is?' Louise didn't understand.

'Things haven't been going so great between us recently. If we had kids, it would only complicate things even more.'

'I'm sorry to hear that. Hopefully you'll be able to patch things up.' What else could she say? There was no doubt that seeing him again had reawakened feelings she had thought gone forever and if he and his wife were to split up this would mean that at least theoretically there was nothing to prevent her rekindling the relationship if she wanted. No sooner did the thought dawn upon her than she stamped on it. The man was married – all right, he and his wife were going through a difficult patch – but she was not, repeat not, the sort of woman to make a play for somebody else's husband. Besides, even if his marriage were to collapse, there was the minor matter of five thousand miles separating them.

'And what about you? Are you married?' His tone was so deliberately casual she realised he really wanted to know.

'No.' She decided there was nothing to be gained by recounting the demise of her relationship with Tommy so she just kept it vague. 'To be honest, my job makes it hard for me to sustain a relationship. It sends me off all over the world so often I'm never back home for long.'

'Does it ever send you to the States? To Colorado, even?' He was sounding hopeful.

Joseph currently had no hotels in North America so she shook her head. 'Afraid not.'

He looked disappointed. 'Well, the best of luck to you. I hope your career continues to go from strength to strength.'

'And I hope you end up running the company.' This was why he had abandoned her twelve years ago, after all. 'And that you and Katharine will manage to sort things out.'

Lunch was excellent as usual, but she barely noticed the food. It was so surreal to find herself here like this with Paolo after twelve years. So much had happened in both their lives since university and yet being here with him felt so familiar. Almost as familiar as the feeling she had experienced last night when first meeting Professor Vito. Once again she found her thoughts occupied by this man she barely knew. What on earth was going on?

After lunch she and Paolo went for a walk in the gardens of the hotel. The ground beneath their feet was a lot drier now and she could feel the dead leaves once more crunching rather than squelching as they trod on them. When they reached a rose bed he pointed out new shoots just appearing on the plants.

'Spring's on its way here now, but I'm afraid it'll take a good bit longer in the Rockies.'

'But you enjoy living there?'

'Yes… but I can't deny that coming back to Turin, to my home town, has been great. Maybe if things change…'

Presumably by this he meant if he and his wife split up, but she did her best not to think about that possibility. She had absolutely no intention of coming between husband and wife, even if it sounded as though things weren't going swimmingly for them at the moment. Tommy might have been a miserable cheat but one thing needed to be said: she wasn't cut from the same cloth. She decided to be brutally frank – just in case Paolo had any intentions of that nature.

'It's been great seeing you again. Looking back on it now, I realise that if you and I had stayed together, I'd never have got this wonderful job. And as far as I'm concerned now, that's worth more than any man.' She almost added the words 'and that includes you', but she felt pretty sure he must have got the message. Nothing was ever going to happen.

He left at three o'clock because he had to go back for the family get-together his parents had arranged. Louise had met them many times and she asked him to say hi to them if they remembered her. His reply was surprising.

'Of course they'll remember you. My mother was heartbroken when I went off to the States and you and I split up. For ages afterwards she kept on telling me how stupid I'd been to put my career before my happiness... and yours.' He gave her a little wry smile. 'The irony that this is what Katharine's now doing hasn't escaped me. My mother's convinced it's karma and I deserve it for leaving you.' His smile changed to a look of almost supplication. 'It's not that I wanted to leave you; it was a career thing. You understand that, don't you?'

Louise nodded. 'Of course I do... now. At the time it was awful, but now I get it, I really do. My career's all important to me, too, nowadays. And as far as you and your wife are concerned, I hope you manage to sort things out. You both deserve to be happy.'

'So do you, and I wish you all the best. Ciao.' To her surprise, he ducked forward and kissed her fleetingly on the lips before climbing into the car and heading off. The expression on his face was one of regret.

Louise stood and watched his car disappear down the drive, the feel of his lips still on hers, and she was genuinely moved. What if he hadn't moved to the US? The way she had felt about him back then, she was sure they would have married, just like so many of the friends she had met again yesterday. What would that have meant for her life, her career? Almost certainly she would have settled in Turin with him and in consequence – as she had told him – she would never have got her present job and all the satisfaction it had brought her. But, in return, she would have been with the love of her life. It didn't matter now; that chapter of her life was over for good.

Wasn't it?

Shaking her head angrily, she repeated her mantra that she wasn't interested in finding herself another man – and she certainly wasn't going to get involved with a married man. She went back up to her room, changed into jeans and her increasingly scruffy trainers and set out for another walk. This time she followed the drive back to the entrance and then took a track to the right running along the inside of the perimeter fence leading down into the valley. Once again, being out in the country air had a positive effect on her mood. For somebody more used to life in the city, there was something unexpectedly soothing about being here and she felt a smile forming on her face as she walked. These fields, woods and hills had been here for many centuries before her and would no doubt still be here many years after she was gone. What was it Humphrey Bogart had said about the problems of a few little people not being worth a hill of beans? Somehow this helped to put her own internal conflicts into some sort of perspective.

Towards the bottom of the hill she began to hear water and soon spotted the river, swollen after the recent rainfall, rushing down through the trees. There was a gate in the fence here which opened onto the riverbank. She went out through it and followed a good gravelled track alongside the water for a couple of hundred metres until she spotted a roof ahead of her and a gateway. Presumably this was the old mill where Professor Vito lived. Her brain was already fully occupied with thoughts of Paolo, and the last thing she wanted was to introduce this other man into the mix, so she turned off the track onto a path that led uphill into the trees, vaguely in the direction of the hotel, keen to distance herself from the mill. After all, he had made it pretty clear he wanted nothing to do with her.

She had only been walking up the narrow path through the undergrowth for less than a minute when she heard running footsteps coming towards her and she just had time to step to one side as a big black dog and his master emerged through the bushes. The Labrador took a flying leap at her but she was forewarned this time and so was able to execute a hasty avoiding manoeuvre and then bend down to greet him on his own level. She was crouching there, petting the happy dog, when she heard his master's voice.

'I'm really sorry about how he keeps assaulting you. It's all very friendly but I've got to find a way of making him stop.'

He sounded cordial and she straightened up to greet him. As she did so, she couldn't help noticing that his Spandex running shorts fitted him snugly and his damp T-shirt clung to his torso in enough places for her to realise that he was in very good shape. Doing her best not to think about his body, she held out her hand.

'Good afternoon.' She didn't use his name because she wasn't sure how he liked to be addressed. He had said he didn't use his title but she was undecided between *professore* and *signore*.

'Good afternoon.' He didn't use her name either but that might be because he had forgotten it.

To fill the ensuing awkward silence she ended up stating the obvious. 'Out for a run? I'm out for a walk.' As an opening gambit it wasn't exactly scintillating, but his obvious reticence was off-putting.

'Yes… well, good.' She saw him glance at his watch. 'Leo and I had better get off home. Come on, dog.' He turned away, but remembered his manners and looked back. 'Goodbye, Louise.'

So he did remember her name after all.

Louise carried on up the path and gradually headed back to the hotel. All the way, she found herself thinking about the uncomfortable meeting with the uncommunicative professor. In her line of work most of the people she met tended to be outgoing and talkative and she herself was usually a pretty accomplished conversationalist. Somehow, coming across such a handsome man who appeared withdrawn in her presence had resulted in her lapsing back into a tongue-tied teenager. Considering she was a thirty-something-year-old who normally routinely and comfortably conversed with strangers, this puzzled and annoyed her. When she got back to the hotel, she changed out of her mucky trainers and went down to the lounge for a cup of what the packet described as English Breakfast Tea – even though it was almost six o'clock by now. She was sitting by the fire sipping it when Domenica came looking for her.

'Hello, Louise. Your boss has just sent an email. He's coming over at the end of next week for a quick visit.'

Louise felt torn. On the one hand, there were numerous things to be discussed and decisions to be made, particularly with regard to bathroom furniture and the new colour scheme for the public areas. On the other, there was the uncertainty still lingering inside her after that dinner with him back in London. She sincerely hoped she had been mistaken about his intentions that night. Maybe after the emotional damage inflicted on her by Tommy she was just being over sensitive, so she produced a smile for Domenica's benefit. He was coming and they just had to get on with it.

'That's fine, thanks. Did he say when he's arriving and for how long?'

'Friday of next week and just the one night because he has to be in Milan on Saturday afternoon. He's coming in on the same flight you were on. Unless he has other plans, I can get Luigino to go and collect him – or maybe you'd like to drive yourself?'

Louise shuddered at the thought of driving the magnificent Rolls Royce and shook her head. 'No, thanks. If Luigino can do it, that would be great.'

'He'll be happy to do it. He loves driving the Rolls.'

'Fine, you'd better make sure there's a really nice room available for Joseph. Maybe number 124? It's big and on a corner of the building with lovely views out of two windows.'

'Or 224 on the floor above? The view's even better from up there.'

'Excellent idea.' Louise decided to take advantage of Domenica's arrival to find out more about Vito. 'Have you got time for a coffee? There's something I wanted to ask you.'

Domenica sat down opposite her and Louise recounted the exchange she had had with Vito on her walk. 'He's awfully taciturn and I was wondering if he's like it with everybody or if it's just me. Does he maybe resent the fact that I work for the company that bought his hotel?'

She saw the same expression of compassion appear on Domenica's face that she had spotted on the first day. 'It's not you, Louise, that's just Vito – at least over the past few years. I'm convinced something must have happened to him in England, but he never talks about it. He always used to be such a cheerful, friendly sort of boy but he's changed. I've known him since he was a youngster. Growing up, he played all sorts of sports – and he was good at all of them – and he had loads of friends. He's very bright and he did amazingly well at school.' She paused. 'But he's changed. He's experienced a lot of tragedy in his life, culminating in his father's cancer diagnosis three years ago. That's what brought him back from England.'

'He told me he'd been in England for a long time. What was he doing there?'

'He did his first degree in Turin and then went to Oxford University for his doctorate.' There was a note of pride in Domenica's voice. 'After qualifying, he worked over there until his father got sick. Vito lost his mother when he was quite young and he and his father were extremely close. He gave up a good job in England to come back and look after his father, and it took its toll. Those last few months when his father was dying of cancer must have been terribly tough on both of them. They lived in the old mill down by the river and Vito still lives there now, all alone. From what I hear, he hardly goes out. There's a lady from the village, Rosina, who goes in once or twice a week to keep the place tidy but, apart from her, he doesn't seem to mix with anybody around here. It's so sad to see.'

'But he teaches at the university in Turin. Surely he's got friends there.'

'I hope so, but I honestly don't know. Like I say, he's not the man he was. I've tried to talk to him a few times – he and I go way back – but I can't get anything out of him. He was here the other night but that was the first time we've seen him in quite a while and on the rare occasions he does come, he's always on his own.'

'Or with his dog.'

'Getting the dog was the best thing he's done for ages. It gets him out in the fresh air and you know what they say about dogs providing good companionship.'

Chapter 8

On Monday afternoon Louise scrounged a lift into Turin with Ernesto who was delivering consignments of wine to some of their clients, and asked him to drop her off at a car rental company to pick up a car. She planned to keep it for at least a week as there was a lot of running around to do before her boss arrived on Thursday. The first thing she did was to find a shoe store and buy a new pair of trainers to replace her old ones which were now irrevocably stained a muddy brown colour. After that, she spent the rest of the afternoon checking out a wide selection of products, from electronic door locks to luxury toiletries, and it was almost dark before she headed for home again. She was getting to know the road fairly well now and it took her only just over an hour to get back to the Grand Hotel. As the car crunched up the gravel drive in the gathering dusk she was delighted to see that Beppe had mowed the overgrown lawn in front of the hotel. Hopefully this would help make the place presentable for Joseph.

The first thing she found as she walked into the hotel was a smiling Domenica holding a huge bunch of red roses. The card along with them said simply, *I'm so sorry. There's so much I need to say to you. Tom x*. So much for telling him she never wanted to hear from him again. And as for adding that little x… She was almost snorting as she dropped her bag and took the bouquet.

'They arrived this afternoon. They must have cost a fortune at this time of year.' Domenica's smile turned to a grin. 'He must love you very much indeed.'

Louise had been getting on well with Domenica who was rapidly acquiring an almost maternal role in her life but she hadn't told her about Tommy yet. Now she didn't have any choice and she was pleased to find herself able to reply in an unexpectedly steady voice. 'I used to think he did.' She saw the smile slip from Domenica's face, so she set the flowers down on the reception desk and, as there was nobody else around, told her the whole sad story of how five years together had gone up in smoke in as many seconds. Not surprisingly, Domenica looked appalled.

'How simply awful for you. How could he…?'

Louise nodded soberly. 'Well, he could and he did. Anyway, it's all over now as far as the two of us are concerned and I'm gradually getting over the shock. Would you ask Graziella to put the roses in some water and display them somewhere? Maybe divide them up and put them on the tables in the restaurant. Seeing as they're here, we might as well put them to some good use.'

Domenica put a motherly hand on Louise's arm. 'Have you eaten today?' It was almost nine o'clock by this time. 'I thought not. Luigino's left some soup and a few bits and pieces for you in case you were hungry.' She led Louise through to the now empty dining room. 'We only have two rooms occupied tonight and both couples wanted to eat early so Luigino closed the kitchen and sent everybody home just before you got back. You don't mind, do you?'

'Of course not, and he shouldn't have bothered leaving anything for me. That's so sweet of him. I'd have been quite happy with a cup of cocoa and a couple of biscuits.'

The expression on Domenica's face showed what she thought of that as a substitute for a real meal as she guided Louise to a table and sat her down before disappearing into the kitchen, flatly refusing Louise's offer of help. When she reappeared, she was bearing a tray laden with half a dozen different antipasti, a basket of bread, a steaming bowl of vegetable soup, a carafe of red and one of Luigino's addictive desserts: *panna cotta* with white chocolate. After setting it all down in front of Louise, she added a few words of encouragement.

'Some good food always helps. At least you found out what sort of man he was before getting any more involved.'

Louise just nodded and reached for the carafe of wine.

The improvised meal was excellent, exactly what Louise needed, and by the time she had licked the spoon at the end of her *panna cotta*, she felt she had managed to get Tommy out of her head – at least for the time being – and she was feeling happier again. Of course, this might just be the effect the Grand Hotel del Monferrato appeared to be having on her.

Next morning she got up early and went for a walk shortly after dawn. The ground underfoot was dry and all around she began to see signs of the arrival of spring. It was early April now and the little pink buds Paolo had noted on the roses were already turning into shoots and tiny leaves, and there were daffodils blooming in the hedges. Above her in the trees she could hear at least three or four different bird calls, from the amorous cooing of doves to the cheerful early morning greetings of the local robin. It was a time of rebirth and renewal and she breathed deeply, mercifully a satisfactory distance away from the dodgy drains which were supposedly going to be looked at by a specialist firm this week. When she reached the end of the track above the hotel and made her now regular stop by the fallen tree alongside the perimeter wall, she looked back down over the rolling hills and hoped against hope that this new season would also bring a fresh start for her.

She spent the morning with Domenica and then drove back down to Turin in the afternoon to visit bathroom showrooms and a number of tile and carpet warehouses, searching for the exact shades to match the new colour scheme she was planning for the hotel. While she was there she texted Silvana and they arranged to meet at the end of the afternoon for coffee and a chat. After several hours sorting out all her business for the hotel, Louise drove into the centre and along the broad, tree-lined boulevard of Corso Vittorio Emanuele II, passing the statue of Piedmont's most famous king standing proud on a high pillar, cutlass in hand. She had no doubt that Vito and his male ancestors had all been named in honour of this most famous of Italian monarchs.

She eventually managed to squeeze the car into a tight parking space not far from the main station and walked up under the arches of Via Roma for a bit of retail therapy. As a student she had only been able to peer longingly into the big-name designer stores all along the main shopping street of the city. Now she had a good job and cash in the bank so she decided to treat herself.

Louise hadn't bought new clothes for quite some time and she started with a couple of new work outfits. Because of the environment in which she worked, she tended to dress smartly so she picked up two new skirts, a tailored jacket and three lovely linen blouses. One of the advantages of living and working in luxury hotels was that there was usually somebody else to do the painstaking job of ironing such things. She also bought a beautiful mohair jumper in a lovely autumnal shade of reddish-brown and a pair of light grey designer jeans that fitted like a glove. She was walking back to the car when she gave in to temptation and slipped into a top-end shoe shop and bought herself a gorgeous, if rather impractical, pair of heels to go with either her Dior dress, or with her only long evening gown currently in a cardboard box at her parents' house back in London.

She met Silvana in a chic cafe under the arches of Piazza San Carlo, looking out over the cobbled square where busy Torinesi were coming to the end of their working day and heading home or out to relax. They found a table by the window of this stylish old cafe and ordered coffee. Louise allowed herself to be persuaded – she didn't put up much of a struggle – to go for a bowl of lemon and dark chocolate ice cream at the same time. Silvana sat back, stretched her legs and let her breath out with a hiss.

'I've had a hell of a day. A gastric bypass that went wrong, followed by peritonitis. Saved one, lost the other, but that's the way it goes. Still, it's good to be able to relax. How are things with you?'

Put like that, Louise's break-up didn't sound so significant. Nobody had died, no blood had been spilled and she had emerged intact – with a bowl of ice cream and several hundred euros worth of lovely clothes as well. Taking heart from this thought, she decided that, having found the courage to tell Domenica what had happened with Tommy, it was time to relate the events of the weekend to Silvana. She managed to do this in even tones and at no point did the desire to burst into tears overcome her. This wasn't missed by her friend.

'I must say it sounds as though you're taking it really well. If something like that were to happen to Davide and me I'd be a wreck.' Silvana took a spoonful of strawberry and meringue ice cream and shot Louise a little grin. 'And I'd also probably be in custody for assault with a deadly weapon.'

'It was a major shock to the system but I *am* starting to come to terms with it. As for manslaughter, I don't think I'd have the courage. It's all right for you surgeons with your scalpels; you're used to the sight of blood.' She looked up from her ice cream. 'To be honest, now that I've had a couple of weeks to think, I suppose it was almost inevitable that he would start looking for somebody else. I *have* been away an awful lot really, and I get so caught up in my job. I probably didn't think about him as much as I should have done, even though I did miss him. Maybe it was the inevitable consequence of my selfishness.'

'That, Louise, is rubbish. There's no excuse for what he did. You love your job and it took you away from him. So what? He's the one who did wrong here, not you.'

'Thanks. I keep telling myself that.'

'Well, you keep on telling yourself that. Now of course, with him out of the equation, you know what this means, don't you…?'

There was no need for her to say more. Louise knew exactly what she meant. She told Silvana about the lunch she and Paolo had had on Sunday but she repeated her determination not to get involved in his marital affairs, ending with the words, 'That ship has sailed. It was nice to see him again one last time but nothing's ever going to start up again with him. No, I'm happy concentrating on my job for now. Apart from anything else, my boss is coming over on Friday and I need to be able to show him that I've been making progress.'

'Oh yes, your boss, didn't you say he wasn't a lot older than you?'

'I'm not sure exactly, but I would guess he's maybe late thirties, even forty – say seven or eight years older than us.'

'Is he married?' Silvana had always had an unerring ability to cut to the chase.

Louise shook her head, stalled for a few moments before finally telling her about the dinner she had had with Joseph back in London. Silvana immediately jumped on the possibilities this offered.

'So you reckon he might have meant it as a date?'

'No… yes… I don't know. It makes no sense. He must have a multitude of far more suitable women dying to go out with him, but it was the way he was talking that got me thinking.'

'Don't do yourself down, Louise. I wouldn't be surprised if he really did fancy you. He might be coming over here as much to see you as to see the hotel. Maybe more?' She took another little spoonful of ice cream and looked wistful. 'There's something about a multi-millionaire…' She sighed theatrically. 'What does he look like? Quasimodo?'

'He's actually very handsome, but he just doesn't get my motor running.'

Silvana grinned. 'Might be worth taking him for a spin all the same – you know, try out the performance, the handling, the clutch.' Her grin broadened. 'Not to mention the reliability of this particular model after the problems you've had with your previous one.'

This brought an answering smile to Louise's face. 'Not going to happen. No, men are off the agenda for now. Like I said, I'll concentrate on work, but having an affair with my boss isn't my idea of how to get on. Far too complicated, even if I did fancy him and I just don't.' She gave it a few seconds' thought. 'He's just too perfect, if you know what I mean. He's always immaculately dressed and groomed; I just can't imagine him in jeans and a T-shirt. Or naked for that matter.' She gave a pronounced shake of the head. 'Oh no, definitely not.'

'You never know, meeting up with him now that you've had some time to digest the fact that you're a free agent might make you see him in a fresh light. I wouldn't write him off just yet if I were you. Like I say, there's something about a multi-millionaire...' Seeing the expression on Louise's face she changed tack. 'What about over here? Any eligible men at the hotel?'

Louise shook her head. 'Afraid not. You've seen most of the staff and the majority of the men are my dad's age or older, while the only younger one's barely out of short trousers — so slim pickings I'm afraid.'

'Nobody else? Nobody in the surrounding area?' Silvana wasn't giving up. 'A hunky neighbour, maybe? A local farmer who could give you a ride on his tractor?'

Of course there was one hunky neighbour, but Louise had already discounted Vito because he plainly wasn't interested in her or, by the sound of it, any other woman. Besides, she reminded herself, she was not, repeat not, on the lookout for another man. No, there wasn't anybody and, she told herself firmly, that was fine with her.

'Nope, no handsome farmer, no nobody, but I really don't mind. This whole business with Tommy has shaken my confidence and trust, so I'm fine as I am for now.' She thought she could read scepticism in Silvana's eyes so she added a bit of emphasis. 'Really, I'm fine.'

Back at the hotel, she was delighted to hear that the man from the drain company had been and had already discovered the root of the problem – literally. The mechanics of the system were apparently working well but, over the years, tree roots had gradually infiltrated the old terracotta pipes, gradually breaking them open and splitting them, thus creating obstructions and leakage – hence the pong. The solution he had come up with involved digging a fifty-metre trench along the front of the hotel. The old pipes would be removed and replaced with modern ones and then the trench would be backfilled. Although it sounded like a major operation, he had told Domenica he should easily be able to do everything in a single week. Louise was relieved to hear that it wasn't going to be as complicated as she had feared.

'That's great news. Is there a week some time soon when we haven't got many bookings? That would be ideal, so we inconvenience as few guests as possible.'

Domenica had already thought of that. 'Easter's towards the end of April this year, but May's normally pretty quiet. Certainly, we have very few bookings at the moment.'

'Excellent – May it is. And is he going to send us a quotation for the work?'

'He said he'd email it tomorrow.'

Louise was impressed. 'Sounds like he's organised.'

'He's actually Luigino's cousin, so I know he'll look after us.'

Louise nodded. Family connections still meant something over here. Hopefully this meant he should be trust-

77

worthy, but she reserved judgement until she had seen his estimate.

'Good. Now, I've seen the curtain people, the carpet people and the tile people and I've got a whole heap of samples in the car which I can go through with Joseph when he gets here at the end of the week. I've also got brochures for bathroom furniture so that's moving along well. I don't suppose Luigino has any cousins who're plumbers by any chance?'

'I don't think they're related but he definitely knows one. We've used the firm before and they're good. I'll ask him to get in touch.'

They carried on discussing the various works that needed doing and Louise was ever more impressed with Domenica's obvious passion for the job and her efficiency. Although Joseph usually parachuted in a new management team when he took over a hotel, Louise resolved to push for Domenica to be promoted to manager. For now, she didn't say anything to her but she added it to her list of things to discuss with Joseph on Friday.

Chapter 9

The next days sped past as Louise did her best to make sure she had all the information she needed before Joseph appeared on Friday. As far as getting him from the airport to the hotel was concerned, early on Thursday afternoon a message arrived saying there was no need for anybody to meet him the following day as he would rent a car. Louise went in search of Luigino to tell him he wasn't going to have to drive to Turin in the Rolls and, at the same time, to discuss Friday night's dinner. The quality of the food in Joseph's hotels had always been a vitally important factor for him, and all of his chefs were constantly vying with each other to obtain recognition by the Michelin Guide or other validating bodies.

Louise was delighted to see that Luigino had already given this some thought and was evidently no stranger to slap-up dinners.

'I'll sort him out, Louise, don't you worry. Tell me, do you happen to know if he has any allergies?' He smiled. 'It probably wouldn't be a good idea to poison the new boss.'

Louise had a think. Apart from the dinner the other week, she had only ever seen Joseph eating a few times at formal events. Chief among these was the firm's annual party when everybody from Carl, the security guard at the front door, to Annabelle, the company's frighteningly organised, immaculately dressed Head of Operations, dolled themselves up in long evening gowns or rented dinner jackets and danced the night away in some posh London locale. Food there was usually canapés and nibbles so it didn't prove much as far as potential allergies were concerned.

'I don't really know. I would think he's pretty omnivorous. Last time I had dinner with him he had scallops, lobster and a sort of chocolate mousse thing. I can't remember anybody at work ever commenting about allergies but I'll send an email to somebody who knows him better and check with her, just to be sure. You're right, it's definitely best not to poison the boss.'

'Well, assuming the answer comes back negative I would suggest a typical Piedmontese selection of antipasti followed by a roast of some sort. If he wants a pasta course in between, I could make some fresh agnolotti filled with wild boar ragú, or if he prefers something lighter, some homemade tagliatelle with a pesto sauce. You tell me which you think best or I can prepare a taste of each – in fact an assortment might be the way to go. We know he likes chocolate so I'll make a hazelnut and dark chocolate tart – you'd better just check he isn't allergic to nuts – and serve it with my own zabaglione or ice cream or meringues or some such. Does that sound okay?'

'Does it sound okay? It sounds marvellous.' Although Louise had had a salad for lunch half an hour ago she was almost salivating at the mere thought of the feast Luigino would no doubt prepare for her and her boss. Somehow she had a feeling she would do well not to have a big lunch tomorrow in readiness for the evening.

After rushing off an email to Annabelle who knew Joseph better than anybody in the company, she settled down to put the finishing touches to her report for him. She had already sent him several emails with her initial impressions of the Grand Hotel, and this was a detailed list of changes to be made, works to be carried out, and proposals for the future. She was running through her plans with regard to the extra staff to be recruited in advance of the grand re-launch of the hotel under Joseph's banner in the summer when the reply came back from Annabelle and Louise wasn't surprised at the immediate response. The Oxford-educated Head of Operations was always on the ball.

The good news was that Annabelle didn't think Joseph had any serious allergies, certainly no problems with nuts, but she did mention that he wasn't too keen on rice. Louise made a note of this and hoped nobody in Milan would offer him one of their traditional risottos. Annabelle also mentioned that she would be coming over in a few weeks' time to familiarise herself with this new addition to Joseph's portfolio of hotels and Louise resolved to make sure she, too, got a good room. Although the two of them had always got on well together, Annabelle's reputation as a stickler with an eagle eye for the smallest detail preceded her.

As the shadows began to lengthen on what had been another remarkably mild sunny day, Louise put on her trainers and set off for a quick walk before dark. She went down past where Beppe was ploughing yet another field and he gave her a friendly wave as he spotted her. Once again, being out in the fresh air cheered and energised her and she spared another thought for how much she was going to miss all this once her work here was done. After another ten minutes she ended up once again on the track beside the river. Like last time, once Professor

Vito's house appeared in front of her she turned off onto the narrow path to the right and had only taken a few steps into the trees when she heard feet coming towards her at speed. Around the corner towards her came Leo the Labrador, tail wagging furiously. Forewarned, she dropped to her knees and greeted him at his own level to avoid him jumping up at her. Although the plan worked as far as keeping her safe from his dirty paws was concerned, she hadn't reckoned with his tongue and his cold wet nose, and she was still struggling to keep him from kissing her when she heard a familiar voice.

'*Leo, vieni qui.*' The dog turned away and Louise looked up to see Vito standing there in his running gear. That self-same surge of familiarity or attraction or whatever it was swept across her and she felt her cheeks flush. Presumably unaware of the thoughts flashing through her head, he continued. 'We seem to have the same exercise schedule.' There was what might have been a hint of a smile on his face. When he looked down at her there was something almost hypnotic about his blue eyes and it felt as if she was being drawn towards him. She swallowed hard and dropped her head so as to concentrate her attention on the dog until her moment of embarrassment passed. After a couple of deep breaths, she felt able to respond, sticking with the banal.

'Although my exercise regime looks a lot less energetic than yours.'

'Sorry about Leo. I really am trying to get him out of the habit of jumping up but he's just got so much energy.'

By this time Louise had gradually calmed the enthusiastic dog – and herself – and she stood up cautiously. She was delighted to see Leo remain down at ground level. Vito looked impressed.

'You seem to have got the hang of it. I must try crouching next time he jumps up at me, specially when he's got muddy paws.'

There then followed yet another silence as they stood there for a few seconds while her head completely emptied of anything to say. It was so unusual for her to find herself at a loss for words that she involuntarily started thinking of the last time this had happened, when she had found Tommy in bed with his woman. The image had a further calming effect on the upsurge of whatever it was this man's appearance stimulated inside her, and her brain suddenly started producing words again.

'I've been down in Turin picking out tiles for the older bathrooms and new curtains for all the rooms. We're trying to brighten the hotel up a bit. It's a beautiful old property but it badly needs renovation in places.'

'You don't need to tell me. My grandfather seemed intent on keeping it in the twentieth, or even the nineteenth, century.'

'I gather he ruled with a rod of iron right up until he was in his nineties. It must have been tough for your father.'

'It was terrible for him.' He caught her eye for a moment and nodded ruefully before looking away, almost as if he regretted the confidence.

Delighted to have been able to get him to exchange a few words, Louise looked for another subject and hit on science.

'I hear you're an expert on climate change. We're getting increasingly environmentally aware in the hotel business these days. Do you ever get asked to advise?'

This time there was definitely a spark of interest on his face. 'Not hotels, I'm afraid. I'm more involved with the conservation side of things – you know, the effects of climate change and human interference on plants and animals.'

'Mother nature's having a tough time of it at the moment, isn't she?'

'You can say that again. If things carry on as they are, fifty per cent of the world's animal species could be extinct before the end of the century.'

'So what can be done to stop that?' She was pleased to have got him talking, but her joy was short-lived as she saw him glance down at his watch.

'An awful lot needs to be done, but I'm afraid I need to get back home. Next time I see you I'll do my best to tell you a bit more if you're interested. Come on, Leo.' She saw him hesitate. 'Goodbye, Louise. My name's Vito, by the way.' And he and his dog set off again.

Louise bade him farewell and carried on up the path, the overriding thoughts in her head being the fact that he had not only remembered her name but had told her his and had used the words 'next time' as he mentioned meeting again. Somehow, this felt like a major victory in her dealings with this reticent man. What she couldn't get over was the fact that somehow, in spite of her resolve to avoid any romantic entanglements, she was allowing herself to be bewitched by this withdrawn, introverted man who clearly had no particular interest in her. Getting him out of her head, if not her heart, was going to be a challenge.

Chapter 10

Joseph arrived at just before six on Friday in a flashy car. Louise hurried down the hotel steps to greet him, reflecting that his idea of a hire car was a million miles away from the little Fiat she had rented. The silver sports car turned out to be a Porsche and had no doubt cost a small fortune to rent but, of course, he had an enormous fortune to draw on.

'Louise, hi. How's everything?' Joseph climbed out of the low vehicle and emerged wearing a suit that looked as if it had come straight out of the wardrobe rather than at the end of a thousand-kilometre journey.

'Hi, Joseph. I'm fine and everything here's working out well, I'm pleased to say.'

After shaking her hand he reached back into the car and retrieved his overnight bag. As he did so, Louise was pleased to see the long shadow of Rodolfo materialise and remove the bag from Joseph's unresisting hand.

'Shall I take this up to your room, sir?' The offer was delivered in impeccable English and Louise was amazed. She had been led to believe that he only spoke a smattering of the language.

'Thank you.'

'The gentleman's in room 224, Rodolfo.' Louise saw him nod and turn away. There was a smile on Joseph's face as he shot her a sideways glance.

'They breed them big up here.'

Louise grinned back. 'No bag's too big for the Grand Hotel del Monferrato hall porters.' Although until the grand re-launch in the summer, Rodolfo was the only porter they had.

She led Joseph up the steps and into the entrance lobby where Domenica was standing stiffly to attention, looking understandably nervous. Louise made the introductions and was delighted to hear Domenica respond in remarkably good English, albeit with a strong Italian accent. Clearly when she had apologised on the first day for not speaking much English, she had been overly modest. Louise caught her eye and gave her an encouraging wink before addressing Joseph.

'What would you like to do first, Joseph? Maybe check out your room?'

'I'd kill for my first real Italian coffee of the trip, to be honest. Is there somewhere the three of us could sit and chat for a few minutes?'

They escorted him through to the lounge and sat down together by the fireplace. The hotel only had half a dozen guests tonight and the room was empty. Graziella appeared bang on cue looking smart in a freshly ironed waitress uniform and they ordered their coffees.

'This is a lovely room.' Joseph craned his neck to look around. 'I was only here so briefly last time, I'd almost forgotten how attractive it was.' He glanced across at Louise. 'Any changes planned?'

'Like you say, it's rather nice as it is. It doesn't even need redecorating. I thought it could do with a couple of good-quality rugs on the floor, some new curtains and cushions, a few plants and a couple more paintings, just to add to the feel of the place. The furniture's old but it's well-made and it adds to the character of the room, don't you think?'

Joseph then went on to outline – mainly for Domenica's benefit – his plans to boost guest numbers. The company's marketing department was already gearing up to produce a high-profile advertising campaign and an all-singing, all-dancing replacement of the existing extremely basic Grand Hotel del Monferrato website. The new site would offer online reservations direct with the hotel as well as via the central booking office. There would also be links to and from the other hotels in the chain, so that hopefully a surge of new guests would fill the hotel that summer and beyond. Domenica and Louise exchanged glances and Louise could see the excitement in her eyes at the thought of the hotel returning to the glory days before its recent decline.

They sat and chatted for almost an hour until Domenica excused herself and went off to relieve Calogero on the front desk so that he could ensure that everything was readied in the dining room. Joseph looked pleased to be left alone with Louise and she gave a silent prayer that he wasn't about to become amorous. So far his attitude had been purely businesslike and she hoped he would continue to keep it that way. Maybe she had just misread the signs.

'I'm pleased to see you looking much more rested than last time, Louise. The Italian air must be doing you good.'

This was borderline personal but she didn't panic yet. 'I think it is. I'm walking every day and breathing a lot of clean country air.' Keen to keep the conversation off anything more intimate, she launched into a detailed explanation of the upcoming works to be done to rectify the hotel's sewage system. He listened carefully and nodded in approval.

'Excellent. I thought I noticed a bit of a smell in the air as I arrived.'

'Not for much longer. We've had the builder's estimate and it looks reasonable.'

She kept the conversation on business matters until he decided it was time for him to see his room. Louise asked Graziella to show him the way and as the two of them disappeared from sight she breathed a sigh of relief. So far it had been all business and she hoped it would stay that way over dinner.

She walked out into the lobby and had a quick chat with Domenica while Joseph was otherwise occupied, reassuring her that he had been impressed with everybody and everything he had seen so far. She also complimented Domenica on her command of the English language and singled out Rodolfo for special praise.

'I hadn't realised he spoke such good English. Most impressive.'

Domenica smiled. 'He studied English at school but he was never academically minded. But since he's been working here he's found a website full of useful phrases for people in the hospitality industry. He's been getting quite good at offering to carry bags or bring drinks, but don't ask him to tell you where he went for his last holiday or what he'd do if you gave him a million euros.'

Bang on the stroke of eight o'clock, Joseph reappeared and Louise led him through to the dining room. Four other tables were occupied; one by an elderly couple, one by a younger couple, one by a family of four – all blond and almost certainly from one of the Nordic countries. The fourth table had only one occupant: Tommy.

Louise's face must have revealed her shock and incredulity. She could hardly believe her eyes. What the hell was Tommy doing here?

'Are you all right, Louise? You look as if you've just seen a ghost.' Joseph followed the direction of her staring eyes. 'Is that man somebody you know?'

Louise did her best to reply in normal tones but she could hear the tension in her voice and Joseph didn't miss it. 'Yes, he is… If you'd excuse me for just a few moments, I think I'd better go over and have a word with him.'

'Do you want me to come with you – a bit of moral support?' Joseph sounded concerned and genuinely caring.

Louise managed to flash him a hint of a smile. 'Thanks, Joseph, but I'll be all right.'

Taking a deep breath, she walked over to where Tommy was sitting. He jumped to his feet as she approached but she stayed out of range and made a point of keeping the table between the two of them. Doing her best to keep her voice low so as not to cause a scene, she looked him straight in the eye.

'What the hell do you think you're doing here, Tommy? This is my workplace. I'm with my boss. You can't just come bursting in like this.' She did her best to keep her voice down so as not to be overheard by any of the guests or by Joseph.

'I had to see you, Lou. I had to tell you how sorry I…'

Trying hard to suppress the wave of anger that was building inside her, Louise cut him off. 'I specifically told you I never wanted to see you or hear from you again. What part of "never" don't you understand?'

'Lou, I just had to. I'm sorry but I have to explain. And the only way to do it is face-to-face. I owe you that.'

'There's nothing to explain. You did what you did, and the trust between us is broken, shattered.' She could hear the emotion rising in her voice and the last thing she wanted was to erupt into a fit of anger or, even worse, burst into tears. She risked adding a single word, 'Irrevocably.'

'Listen, Lou, I don't want to upset you any more than I've already done, but there's something you need to know: this wasn't just a fling. I'm in love with Melissa – that's her name – and I've never felt anything like it before. I'm sure that must be hard for you to hear, but you needed to know that I wasn't just playing around. I would never have done that to you. I was all set to tell you about her when we met up but, of course, you came back a day early... This wasn't the sort of thing I could tell you in an email. I knew it needed to be done face-to-face.'

Louise felt almost swamped by a tsunami of mixed emotions. There was anger and there was outrage, there was sadness and no doubt plain good old-fashioned jealousy but, along with all this, there was maybe a spark of compassion. She had loved this man and, at the end of the day, she wanted him to be happy. This glimmer of empathy quelled her rising anger just enough to allow her to get a few final sentences out in a calmer tone.

'I wish you well, Tommy, I really do. Thank you for telling me this but please – and I really mean this now – go off and live your life and leave me alone. All right? Now I have to go back to my boss.' Without waiting for an answer, she turned away. '*Buon appetito.*'

'Thank you, Lou.' He sounded relieved.

Louise started walking back towards Joseph, but she knew she needed a minute or two to collect herself so as she reached their table she didn't stop. She just excused herself briefly in a strained voice as she passed. 'I'd better go and wash my hands, Joseph. I'll be right back.'

She went out into the lobby and ran up the stairs to her room on the first floor. Without bothering to close the door, she went into the bathroom, switched on the light above the mirror and took a long, hard look at herself. Her eyes were unnaturally bright and it would have been easy to let the tears flow. Whether these would have been tears of sorrow, rage, frustration or self-pity was difficult to tell, but she steadfastly refused to let herself cry. She blew her nose and dabbed her face with a warm towel. Another glance in the mirror confirmed that the tears had retreated so she took a few deep breaths and set about trying to compose herself before heading back downstairs.

In the lobby she spotted Calogero chatting to Domenica at the front desk and went over to them. 'Calogero, there's a man having dinner on his own in the dining room. Is he a guest here?'

The maître d' shook his head. 'No, he came in half an hour ago and asked if he could have dinner.'

'Louise, is something wrong?' Domenica sounded concerned. 'Has something happened?'

Reassured by the news that Tommy wasn't going to be staying, so there was no risk of having to face him over breakfast, Louise rallied, reached out and gave Domenica's hand a grateful squeeze.

'No, thanks for asking but I'm fine. I'll tell you all about it tomorrow.'

By the time she reached Joseph she felt reasonably confident she was once again functioning normally – or at least returning to a semblance of normality. She even managed to produce a hint of a smile as she sat down opposite him, her back fortunately turned towards Tommy's table.

'I'm sorry about that, Joseph. It's a bit complicated. I'll tell you all about it some time.'

'I ordered a bottle of champagne. I hope that's all right.' He avoided any mention of what had just happened and she was immensely grateful to him for this.

'Thank you, I'd love a glass of champagne.' He took the bottle from the ice bucket, filled two glasses and passed one across to her. She resisted the temptation to drain it in one – not least so as to avoid a repetition of the embarrassing mineral water up the nose incident earlier in the month – and held her glass out towards him. 'Cheers, Joseph, and thank you.'

'The maître d' tells me the chef's proposing serving a local speciality menu. I said yes. I'm looking forward to it.'

Louise didn't need to struggle to give him an answering smile. It can't have escaped his attention that she had been upset by the Tommy incident, and Joseph's discreet avoidance of the subject was welcome and rather endearing. She embraced the change of topic gratefully. 'I'm sure you'll love Luigino's cooking. He's a very talented chef and he knows all about the local specialities.'

The meal turned out to be another culinary triumph for Luigino. After a seemingly never-ending selection of antipasti, he produced no fewer than three different types of pasta and Calogero put generous spoonfuls of each on their plates to try. There were Luigino's trademark tagliatelle with wild boar ragú, spaghetti with delicate fresh pesto, and broad strips of pappardelle with a cream, mushroom and smoked ham sauce. On top of these, Calogero reverently grated the slimmest slivers of the famous white Alba truffles, named after the town just down the road from here. Sight and taste of these highly prized fungi prompted Joseph to ask about their provenance and Louise was able to tell him what Ernesto had told her a few days earlier. These had been found in the hotel's very own woods last autumn and his little dog had a real flair for rooting out these delicacies. Attila the terrier had apparently acquired a considerable reputation in the area on account of his finely tuned nose that could detect these most valuable delicacies even though they were often buried well below the surface of the ground.

'Ernesto – he's the winemaker here – says he's been approached by people who've offered him mind-blowing sums of money to buy the dog, but he's always said no. Apparently a kilo of white truffles can go for up to five thousand euros.'

'Maybe I should give up the hotel business and take up truffle hunting.' Joseph was sounding relaxed and his calming influence spread across to her side of the table.

'It's a thought, but maybe not just yet.'

After the pasta, Calogero arrived bearing a huge platter on which there was a choice of roast lamb, pork and beef, accompanied by a mountain of what looked like little roast potatoes but which were, in fact, crispy fried polenta slices. By this time Louise was feeling full so she just allowed herself to be persuaded to try a tiny taste of each. Predictably, it was all excellent but by the end, she was having serious doubts as to whether she would be able to handle the chocolate tart that had been promised for dessert. Joseph ate heartily and left her in no doubt that he had become a fan of Luigino's cooking.

'I can't believe a chef of this ability hasn't been able to get himself a Michelin star or three. This is one of the best meals I've had this year.'

'I suppose it's probably because the hotel's barely been ticking over and it just hasn't appeared on the radar of the people who write the guidebooks.'

'Well, we're damn well going to make sure that changes. The man's an artist.'

When Calogero appeared with the cheese trolley laden with lovely local cheeses with little-known names like Castelmagno, Murazzano and Raschera as well as slightly more familiar cheeses like Robiola and Toma, Louise had to shake her head and sit back and watch as Joseph sampled a number of them and washed them down with the remains of the bottle of Ernesto's red that had followed the champagne. Just like the last time they had dined together, Louise had limited herself to little more than a glass of each of the wines so as to keep her wits about her while Joseph had consumed the rest with gusto. When he reached the end of his cheese tasting, he looked across the table at her and smiled.

'Really excellent all round. And the wine's terrific. I must get them to send a few cases over to London for me.' He sat back, wiped his mouth with his napkin, and stretched. 'So, do you feel like letting me in on the big secret now? Who was the guy?'

'What guy?' Louise knew full well, but needed a moment to marshal her thoughts.

'The guy you spoke to at the start of the evening. The one who sneaked out half an hour ago looking furtive.'

'He's left?' Louise swung round and saw that Tommy's table was indeed empty. The sensation this created in her was yet another crazy mix of relief mingled with a twinge of regret. Still, she told herself firmly, that was it now. Tommy really was history. She returned her attention to Joseph. 'I must apologise again, Joseph. He just turned up unexpectedly. He's my ex-boyfriend.'

'Ex? So the two of you split up?'

Louise nodded and gave him a quick, sanitised account of how it had all come to a sudden conclusion, without letting on that this had in fact already happened before their dinner together in London. He appeared shocked and sounded most supportive as he told her what he thought of Tommy's behaviour, but what he said next set her nerves tingling.

'Louise... have you ever had feelings for somebody but been unable to voice them?'

'Um, no, not really.' Although this wasn't true.

'Oh.' There was a long silence before he carried on. 'You see, that's sort of the situation I'm in and I don't know what to do. I wondered if you might be able to help.'

'Of course I'm happy to help, if I can. But what sort of help do you need?'

'By telling me what to do.'

'Um, what's the problem?'

'You see... it's somebody I work with. I like her a lot, I respect her as a person and a colleague, and I'm terrified what might happen if I say something and she's not on the same page as me. I could lose her. She's a very special person and it would be an awful loss.'

Louise hesitated before commenting. Was this his roundabout way of referring to her or was she just imagining things? Surely he wasn't really trying to say he was interested in somebody like her?

'Do you think she feels the same way about you?'

He shook his head helplessly. 'I honestly don't know.'

'And you work with her?' She saw him nod. 'Then I think you need to ask yourself whether it's worth the risk of losing her from your life. Maybe you should wait until she shows some sign of feeling the same way about you.'

'But how do I do that?' For a forty-year-old man he was sounding particularly clueless. Still trying to keep things in the third person and at arms' length, she tried again.

'Talk to her, I suppose. Spend time with her and see if she gives you any signs. Women are normally pretty good at indicating if they're interested or not.' If she hadn't been concerned he might be edging closer to admitting that she was the object of his affections, she would have suggested he invite the woman out for a meal and talk the thing through but, of course, here the two of them were, doing exactly that.

'I've tried talking. I even took her out for dinner a few weeks back…' His voice tailed off again.

'And nothing…?'

'Nothing.'

Louise saw Luigino himself emerge from the kitchens with their desserts so she decided to close the subject. 'Well, my advice would be to give it time. Let her be the one to make the first move and if she doesn't, find yourself another woman.' She couldn't be any clearer than that, surely? 'For a man like you that shouldn't be too hard.'

Joseph looked up and caught her eye. 'I suppose you're right; it's best not to risk losing what I've already got. Thanks, Louise, I needed to hear that.' There was resignation in his voice.

Luigino arrived at the table and deposited plates containing generous slices of deep dark chocolate and hazelnut tart in front of each of them. Alongside the tart was a scoop of smooth rich vanilla ice cream, a pyramid of his homemade baby meringues and a little pot of blackberries conserved by him last summer in honey and liqueur. It all looked and smelt wonderful. Grateful for the interruption, Louise made the introductions and helped Luigino with a bit of interpreting. His English was basic but with her help he and Joseph managed to make themselves understood and Joseph was gushing in his praise.

'I was out for dinner in one of the best restaurants in London last week and I can safely say that the meal you've given us tonight was head and shoulders above that. I've eaten divinely and I want you to know two things: first, you're in for a substantial pay rise and second, if you carry on like this I'm going to do everything I can to see you have a Michelin star certificate on the wall of your kitchen by this time next year. Truly excellent, thank you.'

Luigino went off with a broad smile on his face and Louise was happy for him. She shot a warm look across the table at Joseph. 'You've just made his day, his year. By the way, as far as the other staff members are concerned, my recommendation is that we keep all of them on, give them a good pay rise and I'd like you to give serious consideration to making Domenica the new manager.'

'You think she's up to it?'

'I think she's perfect for it.'

'Then if that's what you think, you have my blessing. I always listen to you, Louise.'

Thinking back on the conversation they had just had, she hoped he really had been listening.

Chapter 11

Joseph was already in the dining room when Louise came down for breakfast and he was looking remarkably bright and cheerful for somebody who had consumed the better part of two bottles of wine the previous night. Louise herself was feeling okay, but she hadn't slept as well as usual, mainly as a result of the surprise visit from her ex-boyfriend. That, and the tricky conversation with Joseph had conspired to keep her awake on and off all night.

She was pretty convinced that the air between her and Tommy had now been cleared and he would respect her wish not to make any further contact, but there was no doubt her feelings were still mixed. True, she now had complete closure; it was just that saying goodbye to him had meant saying goodbye not only to five years of her life but also to the future she had been planning.

Determined not to dwell any longer on the past, Louise focused all her attention on the hotel as she sat down with Joseph. After two hours of hard work, grinding through the list of things to be done, new staff to be recruited and improvements to be made, they arrived at the subject of the grand re-launch to take place the first weekend of July. The intention was to invite movers and shakers of the travel trade to come over for an all-expenses-paid weekend during which they would be able to sample first-hand the facilities of the Grand Hotel. Louise had been involved with similar events in the past and knew how useful they could be – and how exhausting for those involved with organising them.

It was decided that the event should consist of a black-tie gala on the Saturday night with a sumptuous buffet made up of local speciality dishes and wines. There would be dancing in the dilapidated old ballroom at the back of the hotel, and renovation of this was high up on Louise's to-do list. As well as representatives of the travel trade, a number of local notables would also be invited and at the end of the evening there would be a firework display. For the daytime the new outdoor swimming pool would hopefully be in use as long as Louise could manage to get one installed in time. She hadn't included this in her list of improvements because of the considerable cost involved but Joseph had been adamant. A luxury hotel needed an outdoor pool at the very least, and probably in the fullness of time an indoor one as well, with all the bells and whistles of a spa.

On launch day there would also be a treasure hunt and games for any kids, along with clay pigeon shooting and croquet on the lawn for the adults, and the climax of the weekend would be a slap-up lunch on the Sunday outside on the terrace if the weather was fine. Altogether it promised to be spectacular – and a lot of hard work. At the end of the session, Joseph subjected her to a searching look.

'The success or failure of the launch depends on all the works being completed here in good time, new staff being engaged and trained up, all the entertainment booked and everybody knowing exactly what's expected of them. That's all down to you and your team, Louise. Can you guarantee to me that it'll all be done?'

'It'll all be done, I promise, even if I have to fit the new toilets and run the kiddies' treasure hunt myself. You can count on me.'

He gave her a warm smile. 'I know I can, Louise.' And then he raised the stakes. 'And I'll be here to see it myself.'

After the Porsche had snarled off down the drive at just before noon, Louise gave a sigh of relief – tempered with trepidation that the success or failure of the grand re-launch would be witnessed by her boss – and then she walked back into the lobby. Waiting in there she found Domenica and Calogero standing behind the reception desk looking apprehensive so she went straight across to give them the good news.

'Joseph was seriously impressed. I get the feeling he loves this place as much as I do. He's authorised me to institute an immediate pay rise for all staff and he asked me to make sure everybody hears how pleased he is with how things are going here. I completely agree and I can only thank you for what you've been doing. I can't wait to see this hotel back to its glory days. Working with all of you over the next couple of months will be a lot of fun, I'm sure.' She caught Domenica's eye. 'And I particularly look forward to working with the new manager.'

'When does he start?' Calogero and Domenica exchanged uneasy glances and Louise took pity on them.

'She already has.' She smiled benignly as she saw comprehension dawn on their faces, followed by joy.

'You mean…?' Domenica was looking flabbergasted.

Louise nodded. 'That's right, Domenica. If you want it, the position's yours.'

To her surprise, the first to react was Calogero. A broad smile spread across his normally impassive face and he reached out, caught hold of Domenica by the shoulders, kissed her warmly on the cheeks and enveloped her in a bear hug. She instantly blushed the colour of a ripe tomato and Louise studied the couple with new awareness. Could it be that Domenica had feelings for Calogero?

'Thank you so much, Louise.' Domenica disentangled herself from Calogero and came over to Louise. 'This is all your doing, I know. Of course I accept. I don't know what to say.'

'I'm delighted. You and I are going to be busy deciding what needs to be done and the new staff members that need to be hired, so I'm delighted I'll be working through it all with you. Our deadline's the beginning of July and that's only eleven weeks away. We're going to have our work cut out. By the way, Joseph's told me we're going to need a swimming pool. I don't suppose either of you have a cousin in that line of business...'

Calogero tapped the side of his nose. 'Signor Mondrone, the builder who's fixing the drains, also does pools. I'll give him a call.'

'Brilliant.'

Louise left the two of them still standing there digesting the good news and went into the dining room for lunch. She was picking at a simple salad – after last night's feast she was still feeling full – when she got a call. It was Silvana.

'*Ciao, Louise, come stai?*'

The two of them had a friendly chat and Louise related the events of last night involving Tommy and then Joseph. Unsurprisingly she found Silvana still encouraging her to give the multi-millionaire a try.

'By the sound of it he definitely likes you, and it also sounds as though he behaved impeccably last night, being supportive after the scene with your ex and not pressuring you. Why not invent a mini crisis to get him back to the hotel some time soon? I would.'

'I don't know, Silvana, I just don't see him as boyfriend material. Yes, he was kind and diplomatic last night and I'm grateful to him, but that's as far as it goes.'

'Just give him a try? Things can change, you know.' Clearly, Silvana remained unconvinced but she didn't push it and soon turned the conversation to a different man. 'I've had a long email from Paolo. He sounded a bit low. He's back in the US and things don't seem to be going too well with him and his wife.'

'I know, he told me they were going through a rough patch.'

'Anyway, the thing is he asked me for your phone number. What do you want me to do? Shall I give it to him?'

'Yes, of course.' No sooner had she said it than Louise had second thoughts. She had made her mind up not to interfere in another couple's problems because the last thing she wanted was to become 'the other woman'. At the same time, she couldn't put Silvana in the awkward position of having to lie to Paolo so she went with it. 'It'll be good to hear from him again, but I really don't want to get involved with their troubles.'

'You still like him, don't you?'

'Well, yes, but no longer as a life partner. He had his chance and he blew it. He's moved on since then and so have I. No, I hope he and his wife manage to patch things up.'

'No regrets?'

Louise shook her head. 'Not really. I got all that out of my system years ago.'

She still liked Paolo – she couldn't deny it – but she felt increasingly sure that her feelings for him would never go any further than that. Apart from anything else, how could two people with clear career priorities expect to make a go of a relationship? And just to muddy the waters even further, there was the reclusive science professor living down by the river who had been occupying more and more of her thoughts.

'A lot of time's passed, Silvana, a lot of water's flowed under the bridge. I'm a very different person from the girl I was back then and I'm sure he's changed as well. The last thing I would ever want is to give him false hope, maybe breaking up his marriage at the same time, only for the reality no longer to be what it once was. If that happened I'd never forgive myself for screwing up his life – not to mention my own.'

'So might it be better if I don't give him your number?'

'No, give it to him. After all, he knows where I'm living and working at the moment. He could easily call me here at the hotel. I'll just need to be careful what I say.'

Chapter 12

That afternoon she phoned her mum and gave her a rundown of what had happened the previous night and, as always, received massive sympathy in return, along with a few more rude words about Tommy. She assured her mum she was now completely over him and by the time she put the phone down she had pretty well come round to believing this herself. It was a sunny day so later on she went for another walk, as always relishing the peace and quiet of this particular piece of countryside. It was soothing to be out here in the fresh air and she knew she was really going to miss it when she left to continue her job elsewhere. Partway through her walk, just as she reached a fork in the path, she was delighted to find she was going to have company. There was rustling in the bushes in front of her and a big black shape came bursting out, tail wagging, and made a concerted, although affectionate, effort to knock her over again.

'Leo, you great lump, get off.'

She crouched down and stroked him until he began to calm down. She had to admit that it felt good to have another male so obviously pleased to see her – and this time without any complicated amorous intentions or emotional baggage. After a while, by which time the dog was lying on his back in the dry leaves grunting happily to himself, she straightened up and set about deciding which way to go. Seeing the Labrador reminded her of Vito and she wondered if he, too, was out in the woods. She decided to test out the dog's comprehension skills.

'Leo, where's Vito? Vito? Take me to Vito.'

As she said it she realised this was pretty stupid. If the man and the dog lived alone, how on earth would Leo know his master's name? Nevertheless, the dog jumped to his feet and faced her, front legs splayed, tail wagging. She decided to hedge her bets by repeating the command in Italian and, whether it was the change of language or something else, the dog appeared to get the message and charged off down the left fork in the path which led steeply downhill. Louise had to run to keep up with him, jumping over tree roots and loose stones, but she managed to keep him in her sight until he suddenly skidded to a halt and pointed proudly with his nose into the long grass.

It immediately became clear to Louise that her message hadn't been received as well as she had hoped. There, lying on the ground between two clumps of dead ferns was an equally dead rabbit – and it looked and smelt as though it had been dead for quite some time. She came to a halt and caught her breath before looking down at the dog in mock reproach.

'Vito, not bunny, you daft dog.'

He trotted over and nuzzled her while she breathed deeply – not too deeply as the rabbit's carcass was far from fragrant – before trying again.

'Vito, Vito, got it? Vito, your master, where's Vito?'

Clearly puzzled that she didn't share his excitement about the rabbit, he turned and trotted off down the path again, fortunately this time at a more sedate pace. To her surprise, less than a hundred yards further on, they turned a corner and she found herself back on the track leading to his home. The dog stopped and turned towards her as if to say, 'See? Am I a good boy or am I a good boy?'

She was about to go over to pet him when she heard crunching of tyres on gravel and looked round to see a car coming down the track towards her. It slowed and came to a halt and by this time Leo was up on his back legs, pawing at the driver's window. It opened and Vito looked out, and as he did so, her heart gave a little involuntary somersault.

'Ciao, Leo. Stop scratching the car and try to be a good dog for once. And hi, Louise, how are you?' As ever, he was sounding quite formal, but there was a smile on his face this time.

'Hi Vito.' She had to clear her throat before continuing as she was still trying to process her reaction to seeing him. What on earth was going on? 'I met your dog in the woods and he guided me here via a smelly dead rabbit on the way. Are you on your way home from work?'

He shook his head. 'No, I've just been up to Moncalvo to buy groceries. Otherwise there'll be nothing for me to eat tonight.'

'Well, you know you can always come up to the hotel for dinner. Luigino's food's must be tempting.'

'Don't I know it! If I ate up there every night, I'd pack on the kilos and probably explode. I assume you eat there all the time and I'm amazed you look so slim.'

Louise was genuinely surprised. This was the first time he had made any sort of comment that could be construed as personal. Another tiny victory, perhaps. She gave him a big smile. 'All you'd need to do would be to add on a couple of kilometres a day to your regular runs. You look very fit as it is.' The least he deserved was a personal comment in return. She was rewarded by a look of almost embarrassment on his face.

'Um…' She saw him glance at his watch. 'You were asking about conservation… If you don't have anything else you need to do, would you have ten minutes now? Maybe you'd like a cup of tea? I've got some real English tea if you like…' His voice tailed off and she realised that, handsome and hunky as he undeniably was, he was sounding uncertain and maybe even a bit insecure, so she hastened to say yes.

'That sounds lovely, thank you. I'd love to learn more about what you do.'

With Leo leading the way, she followed his car along the track to the old stone gateway. They turned in and Louise had her first view of the old mill and it was gorgeous. It was a delightful ancient-looking building made of hefty blocks of grey stone, and with the river flowing gently alongside it lined by willow trees, the impression was almost magical. If somebody had asked her to describe her dream home, this would have been a pretty close approximation. All right, there wasn't a tower with a flagpole or a pet unicorn grazing in the garden but the rest more than made up for it, and inside was even more perfect.

'Do come in.' Vito ushered her in through what turned out to be the kitchen door. 'You don't need to worry about your shoes. The floors can stand virtually anything. They've seen it all.'

Even so, Louise pulled off her scruffy trainers and padded around in her socks. The terracotta tiles beneath her feet had been worn down by a multitude of former inhabitants over the centuries and she could feel the cracks and indentations beneath her feet that somehow linked her to the history of the house, producing a feeling of familiarity – not unlike the feeling she had got from its owner the first time she had met him. Above her head the ceiling of the kitchen was made of lovely mature rose pink bricks, strung between old beams in a series of vaulted arches. The kitchen wasn't composed of modern units but was built around a collection of mismatched wooden cupboards and dressers, and there was a huge farmhouse table in the middle of the room. Lunchtime's dirty plates were still sitting there and Vito was quick to apologise.

'I'm sorry it's so untidy but I had to finish something I was writing and send it off by mid-afternoon. I only finished half an hour ago and I had to rush out to buy food. I'll get onto the dishes next. Come through to the lounge where it should be a bit tidier.'

In fairness, the only dirty dishes in the lounge were a couple of mugs on the mantelpiece but it could hardly be described as tidy. The two old leather sofas were strewn with books and clothes, while the fine old rug on the floor was in such disarray it almost looked as though some-body had tried, unsuccessfully, to roll it up. As Vito's eyes alighted on it, he turned towards the culprit and addressed him sternly.

'Leo, have you been playing with your ball in here again?' He gave Louise another apologetic look as he reached down to straighten the rug. 'He's got half a dozen old tennis balls that he plays with and one or two regularly get trapped under the rug so he goes burrowing in after them. One time I came in here and almost tripped over him. I only just spotted his tail sticking out at the last moment. Leo, bad dog!'

'Is that short for Leonardo? If so, did you name him after Da Vinci or Di Caprio?' She grinned at him and was rewarded by a little smile in return.

'Neither as it happens. I named him after Galileo, the father of the scientific method. My father was mad keen on astronomy and I know he would have appreciated that.' At the mention of his dead father the smile once more evaporated from his face.

Leo didn't look the least bit repentant and just went across to his master and licked his hand, and Louise was pleased to see Vito's expression soften once more as he bent forward to pet the dog. Domenica was right: getting Leo had been a good idea. Louise studied him closely while his attention was directed elsewhere. He really was a very good-looking man and the sombre air surrounding him just added to his appeal. He was tall, his shoulders were broad, and a couple of days' stubble on his cheeks only added to the fascination. If she had had any doubts before, she now received the confirmation that the sensation she felt when she was with him wasn't so much one of familiarity as one of attraction. There was no getting away from the fact that she liked Vito. A lot. He returned those mesmerising blue eyes of his to her and she felt her cheeks flush. They were only a few feet apart and she suddenly realised she had stopped breathing, in anticipation of what, she didn't dare to think.

'Are you warm enough or would you like me to light the fire?' His voice shook her out of her stupor.

'I'm fine, thanks. I've been running down the hill after your dog.' The dog in the meantime had stretched out on the newly straightened rug and was rolling about on his back, grunting to himself. 'Can I help make the tea?'

'No, just stay there and I'll be right back. Make yourself at home, please.' He was still sounding a bit insecure and she had a hard job not to smile.

He disappeared into the kitchen and she crouched down on the rug alongside the dog and scratched his tummy while slowly recovering from her moment of epiphany. Here she was: a refugee from a recently failed relationship, doing her best to skirt around the possible advances of her boss, and still haunted by thoughts of the man she had loved over a decade ago. Now it would appear that she had fallen for yet another man and, to compound her woes, she had chosen a man who was allegedly the closest thing to a hermit for miles around. For whatever reason, he was one of the most unsociable people she had ever come across – which made this invitation to tea an unexpected surprise.

The good news was that by the time Vito returned with a tray containing mugs of tea and a huge dove-shaped *colomba* cake, she had at least managed to regain some sort of control over her thoughts. He was looking a bit more confident now, so she hoped that boded well.

The traditional dove-shaped Easter cake on the tray was still in its clear plastic bag and she pointed at it. 'There was no need to go to all this trouble, honestly.'

He set the tray down on a low table. 'Hardly trouble.' The smile was back on his face again and it only made him look even more desirable. She swallowed hard. 'All I had to do was to open the box. Besides, it's Easter next weekend and tradition dictates we have to eat at least one *colomba*.'

After cutting the cake and handing a plate to her, but not to the Labrador – much to Leo's chagrin – Vito took a seat on the other sofa across on the opposite side of the coffee table and Louise felt his eyes on her. Doing her best to act like a grown-up, she tried a bit of polite conversation.

'This is a lovely old house.'

'Yes.' At first he didn't appear to have anything else to say but then rallied. 'It's been in the family since the late seventeen hundreds.'

'Wow, so your family, the Dellarosa family, has been here for over two centuries? That's a long time.'

'That's just when they built the mill. The family's been here since medieval times. My earliest ancestors used to have a castle up where the hotel is now. It was razed to the ground by Napoleon and his army in 1795, rebuilt as a villa shortly after and then turned into a hotel in 1902.'

Louise could tell he was feeling more confident talking about history and she managed to keep him going but he was soon flagging, so she steered him onto science. 'You were going to tell me a bit more about what you do. The environment's very topical at the moment.'

'As it should be.'

Almost as if a tap had been turned on, he started to talk about climate change, pollution and the serious consequences of overpopulation. She had always been interested in the subject and she leant forward, delighted that she had found the secret of how to get this uncommunicative man talking. The truth of the matter, however, was that she was only taking in part of what he was telling her as her brain was still coming to grips with the fact that she found him remarkably appealing in spite of her stated intention of staying clear of men for a good long while. She sipped her tea, observing him discreetly as she nibbled the lovely sponge studded with bits of candied peel and sprinkled with roasted almonds and sugar crystals.

As he spoke about the environment it was as though he blossomed and when he finally came to a halt, he was looking far more animated than she had ever seen him.

He gave her an apologetic look. 'Sorry to go on a bit but I'm afraid if you get me started on the environment it's hard to stop me.'

She grinned at him. 'Thanks for the warning, but I think it's a fascinating subject.'

By now she only had a small piece of sponge remaining, and she glanced down at the dog who had been fixing her with an unbroken stare ever since the slice of cake had landed on her plate.

'Is it all right if I give Leo the last bit? I know some people don't give their pets food from the table.'

'That's fine. Any minute now he's going to start drooling so it's probably a good idea. Like all Labs, he could eat himself to death.'

He was smiling once again and Louise mentally added *the dog* to *history* and *the environment* on her list of topics to get Vito talking. She held out the piece of cake rather gingerly towards Leo, hoping he wouldn't take her fingers along with it, but he took it from her delicately before swallowing it whole. In the space of two seconds it had disappeared. She glanced across at his master, but by this time the smile had disappeared again.

'He doesn't exactly stop and savour his food, does he?' Vito gave no response so, sensing that he was once more retreating into his shell, she glanced at her watch and pushed herself to her feet. 'I'd better make a move. Thank you so much for the tea and cake and for telling me all about how we're destroying the world.' She shot him a wry glance. 'Although up here in these gorgeous hills filled with vines and truffles it's hard to believe. I look forward to seeing you again and hearing more about your work.'

'Thank you for coming in.' He was sounding formal and reserved again. 'I don't have guests here very often and you've been kind not to complain about the mess.'

'It's all been lovely, thank you again.' She reached out to lay a grateful hand on his arm but he interpreted it as a handshake and caught hold of it, shaking it politely.

'I hope to see you again, Louise.'

It sounded as if he meant it. This had to be progress. Didn't it?

Chapter 13

The next few days were really busy. On Tuesday morning, Luigino's cousin, the plumber, arrived and together with Domenica they inspected each one of the sixty guest bedrooms before deciding that only eighteen of the bathrooms needed to be completely revamped, while the remainder just needed a few cosmetic touches. Louise queried how long this might take and was heartened to hear that as long as the new bathroom furniture was not too different in size and shape from the old, he and his men should be able to do it in a matter of weeks.

After each room was finished he would get decorators in on the heels of the plumbers until the whole hotel looked like new. He also informed them that his sister company specialised in tiling and Louise was delighted that it sounded as though he and his team should be able to do the whole thing. She had long since discovered that it was almost always best to get a single firm to take responsibility for major works. That way there could be no question of one blaming another for delays. Even better, he reckoned they should be able to start work towards the middle of May which would be well before the new promotional push started to bear fruit, and should be finished in time for the summer bookings which would hopefully start to pour in. She was greatly impressed to see a van arrive containing Signor Mondrone. This was the first time she had met this grizzled elderly gentleman whose firm was going to fix the damaged drains. He had been summoned back to give an estimate for repairing the tired plaster on the outside walls and redecorating the façade, as well as discussing plans for construction of the new pool. He assured her that his men would also ensure that the tree growing on the roof was removed along with any other unwanted vegetation.

Louise walked around with them and was fascinated to hear him talking to Luigino in Piemontese. The heavily French-influenced local dialect of Piedmont was almost indecipherable to Louise, although she managed to pick out a few familiar words from time to time. Once widely spoken by all in this region, it was becoming less common in urban areas and among the young, but out here in rural settings it was still the lingua franca, particularly among older people. Although Signor Mondrone reverted to Italian when speaking to her, she could tell he was more comfortable in the dialect.

Using a mixture of languages, the three of them managed to establish that the new pool would be best situated over on the far side of the hotel, protected from the wind by a copse of trees and a laurel hedge. Signor Mondrone promised to produce estimates before the end of the week and by the time he left, Louise was feeling a lot more confident that the work could indeed all be completed before the early July deadline.

She phoned her mother that evening for a chat and soon ended up talking about Vito. Her mother must have noted something in her voice.

'You rather like this man, don't you?'

'Yes, I suppose I do, but nothing's going to happen there. He's withdrawn into his shell over the past few years and getting him to sit down and chat about anything other than his work is like getting blood out of a stone.'

'And what about Paolo, now that it's all over with Tommy? Is he staying in the US?'

'I have no idea. He told me things weren't going swimmingly with his wife but I'm keeping well out of it. Nothing's ever going to happen there either and I hope he doesn't get ideas. The last thing I want is to find myself in the middle of somebody else's marital problems. Hopefully they'll be able to sort things out.'

She received an update on Paolo's troubled marriage only half an hour later as she was having dinner. Her phone buzzed and she saw it was an unknown number.

'Hello?'

'Hi, Louise, it's me… Paolo.' Although she knew his English to be fluent by now, he was speaking Italian and she wondered if this was to avoid being overheard.

'Hi, Paolo. What's new with you?'

'Not a lot. Katharine and I are still fighting and we don't seem to be getting anywhere. She wants a promotion and I want a wife and a family. But, listen, what about you? I heard on the grapevine you've broken up with your boyfriend. I didn't realise you had a serious partner. You didn't say…'

Louise growled in annoyance and wondered who had told him. Silvana had promised not to breathe a word. 'Yes, I did have but it's all over.'

'That's great… no, I don't mean that. Sorry. I mean that's sad for you but maybe it's a sign.'

'A sign?'

'You know, a sign that perhaps you and I are destined to be together again after all this time.'

Louise had been dreading this and she hastened to pour cold water on any hope he might harbour of the two of them getting back together. From what he had just said it sounded like his wife was following a similar career trajectory to her own and that was what was screwing things up between them, so she decided to concentrate on that.

'It's not a sign and I'll tell you why. You've just told me you want a stay-at-home wife, not a woman who's dedicated to her career, but the thing is that's what I am nowadays. That was one of the reasons, maybe the main reason, why my last relationship broke up, just like it was the reason you chose your career over me twelve years ago. I love my job even though it takes me away so much and you'd just be falling out of the frying pan into the fire. No, you've got your career and I've got mine so the best thing is for you to forget about me. Besides, you're married. Doesn't that mean anything to you? It certainly means something to me. We shouldn't even be having this conversation. You need to try to get your marriage back on track. Do you still love her?'

'I honestly don't know.'

'Do you think she loves you?'

'I don't know that either. Maybe, but who knows?'

'Have the two of you thought about counselling?'

'You must be joking. Have some shrink telling me how to feel? I'm not going down that road.'

Louise was shocked to hear him sounding so dogmatic. Back when they had been a couple, he had always been a pacific, non-confrontational sort of guy. She realised that this was further proof that he had changed since then, but so had she. She made one more attempt at getting him to give his marriage another chance.

'The two of you need to talk. You know that, don't you? If all you're doing at the moment is fighting, maybe you need a referee to give you both a chance to talk things over calmly and rationally.'

'You don't appear to be very keen on getting back together with me.' He was sounding more downbeat now. 'Does that mean you've found yourself another man already?'

Although she was annoyed at his probing, this was a good question and if she had been totally honest, she would probably have had to say yes, although the chances of anything happening between her and Vito in the short time she was going to be here were slim, but she made no mention of him to Paolo. 'No, it doesn't and my personal life's no longer anything to do with you. Like I told you, I'm more interested in my job than in looking for another man at the moment.'

She managed to move the conversation on to less controversial topics like the renovations going on at the hotel and Silvana and Davide's upcoming wedding. Towards the end of the call, Paolo said something that made her sit up and take note.

'I've decided I'm coming over for the wedding. I've got a bit of unused holiday to take so I'll come over before the wedding and stay for a few days just to see how Turin feels after so long away.' There was a pause. 'Besides, it'll give you and me a chance to meet up again and see what develops.'

'For God's sake, Paolo, you haven't been listening to a word I've been saying, have you?' Louise had to stop and take a couple of calming breaths. It sounded ominously as though he still hadn't got the message that nothing was going to happen between them, so she made one last try to get him to understand.

'We're history. Got that? Forget me, Paolo. Concentrate on your wife. I'm not interested in you or any man.' She did her best to sound convincing even though, deep down, she knew there was now someone else inside her head, if not her heart.

And his name was Vito.

—

By the time Easter weekend came, Louise was ready for a bit of rest and recuperation, and she decided to drive down to Turin for some sightseeing and maybe a bit more shopping. Joseph had told her to hang onto her rented car for the full duration of her stay and she was glad of it. Although there were buses up here in the hills, the journey time to Turin by public transport was twice what it was by car and she found she was having to make the trip two or three times a week as decisions on all manner of things from new tablecloths to new toilet brushes kept cropping up.

Today, however, she was free to wander around the centre of this historic city, for many years the capital of the Duchy of Savoy that had spanned the Alps from Nice to Lake Geneva. It was also one of the birthplaces of Italy's industrial revolution, spawning world-famous names like car-makers Fiat and Lancia as well as many other famous brands such as Lavazza, without whom coffee would never be what it is today. In consequence it had always been a wealthy city and the centre was full of imposing eighteenth- and nineteenth-century architecture as well as more ancient buildings like Roman ruins and the medieval castle with its baroque façade.

She spent a fascinating day wandering about, buying more bits and pieces for herself and a big chocolate Easter egg for the staff at the hotel before meeting up with Silvana for another ice cream in the same cafe in Piazza San Carlo. This time Silvana arrived with an invitation, though not to a party, but to a lecture.

'Davide told me to tell you, in case you're interested, that your neighbour, the former owner of the hotel, is giving a public lecture on Tuesday afternoon.'

'Vito?'

Silvana raised an eyebrow. 'Vito, eh? So you and Count Vittorio Emanuele Dellarosa are bosom buddies on first name terms now?'

In spite of the mouthful of frozen yoghurt she had just swallowed, Louise felt her cheeks flush. 'I certainly wouldn't describe us as bosom buddies, but I've met him. He doesn't seem to be a happy man.' She went on to tell Silvana what Domenica had said about him being a changed man since his return from England and about his distinctly reticent behaviour. This came as a considerable surprise to Silvana.

'I didn't know that and I'm sure Davide doesn't either. Vito used to be the life and soul of the party. And he had all the girls running after him as you can imagine. So does that mean he's unattached now?' Louise had a feeling she knew where Silvana was going with this and she wasn't disappointed. 'Unless you've taken my advice and hooked up with your boss, why don't you see about Vito? He must be worth a fortune after selling the hotel, and isn't every girl looking for a prince? All right, he's only a count but still…'

'He's not interested, Silvana, and neither am I.' Deep down inside, Louise knew she was being less than honest with her friend but the last thing she wanted was for her name to be linked with Vito's on the Turin bush telegraph. If it ever got back to him she would be mortified. 'Besides, from what Domenica tells me he's pretty much a hermit these days.'

'Well, the hermit is emerging from his grotto next week to give a lecture on endangered species and the dangers to biodiversity. He's a big name in that field nowadays.'

'And he's giving a talk that's open to the public?'

'That's right. Why don't you go along? I'm going to a conference in Milan for a few days otherwise I'd come with you. Anyway, his talk's taking place not far from here. I'll text you the address if you're interested in going.'

'You know something, Silvana? I think I am.'

Chapter 14

The lecture took place in a large auditorium at Turin University. Louise got there fifteen minutes early and was surprised to find the room already almost completely full, and not just with students. There were elegant Torinese ladies and smart gentlemen in suits and there was even a television crew with all their equipment. By the time of the official start at four o'clock, there were people having to stand at the back of the room and along the side walls and Louise was impressed. Clearly, as Davide and Silvana had said, Vito was a big name in the field of conservation.

An austere grey-haired professor appeared at the lectern to introduce him and Louise noted that he did not mention Vito's aristocratic title. He was simply introduced as Professor Dellarosa, followed by a string of qualific-ations and awards. There was polite applause as the old gentleman left the stage, followed by heartier applause as Vito appeared. He was smartly dressed in a dark suit, collar and tie and looked most professional.

He delivered his lecture in Italian and accompanied it with a selection of maps, charts and graphs on the screen behind him. He spoke clearly and Louise managed to follow most of it, although she got a bit lost when he started reeling off depressing statistics about the impact of climate change on so many endangered species. She also kept losing track of what he was saying when she became too concentrated on his face, his broad shoulders and his unruly mop of dark hair. She wondered if his female students also had the same problem. What emerged from his talk without any possible doubt was that he clearly knew his stuff. At the end of the lecture he took questions from the audience and Louise listened in awe as he answered some in fluent French as well as Italian and English. Professor Vito was a smart cookie all right.

When he finally left the stage to an accompaniment of prolonged applause, Louise let the bulk of the audience leave before she stood up and stretched. She glanced at her watch, saw that it was almost six and toyed with the idea of staying on in Turin for an *aperitivo* followed by dinner, but decided against it. After all, with a hopefully future Michelin-starred chef waiting for her back at the hotel, why bother? Besides, although she had done a lot of it over the past ten years, she had never really enjoyed eating alone.

At last, as the crowds in the gangway began to thin out, she made her way along the now empty row of seats and followed the last of the audience into the lobby. There she found Vito standing beside the austere grey-haired gentleman who had introduced him, being interviewed for the television. They were surrounded by an enthusiastic group of people and Louise couldn't miss the fact that well over half of them appeared to be young women. She wondered how much their presence was spurred by the subject and how much by the speaker – although she was a fine one to talk.

Suppressing what could only be explained as a stab of jealousy, she hurried for the main exit without stopping, hoping he wouldn't see her. If the truth be told, she felt a bit uncomfortable at the idea he might think she had been checking up on him. However, when she was almost at the door she saw him look up and, momentarily, catch her eye. He gave her a hint of a smile, as if to say, 'I wish I didn't have to do this,' before returning his attention to the interviewer. She stepped out of the door, hoping he hadn't seen her cheeks flush.

Back at the hotel she checked her phone and found she had two messages. The first was from Annabelle, the Head of Operations, confirming that she would be coming over at the end of the following week for a night or two. The other was from Tommy and her heart sank. She had heard nothing more from him since their brief encounter in the hotel dining room and she had begun, if not to dismiss him, at least to relegate him to a secondary place in her thoughts. She was relieved to find the message was simply about her share of the deposit money for the flat. He told her he was moving out at the end of May and queried what she would like him to do with her half. She texted him back, telling him to pay it into her current account, and the thought went through her head that maybe this meant he was moving in with his new woman, but she did her best to banish any such conjecture. His life was his own now and that was that… hopefully.

She hadn't had any lunch today so that evening Luigino prepared her a mixed salad with local goats' cheese and hazelnuts from the hotel's own bushes, followed by a helping of his delicious mozzarella and basil agnolotti. She was just finishing her pasta and wrestling with the important decision as to whether or not she should have a panna cotta, when Domenica appeared bearing not such good news.

'I've just had a phone call from Vito. He was involved in an accident on his way home from Turin this evening.'

Seeing Louise's hand shoot to her mouth in alarm, she was quick to reassure her. 'He says he's perfectly fine and he's back home but his car's in the garage and he was asking if one of us could give him a lift down to Turin on Thursday to pick it up again. If Luigino or Calogero can't do it, I can take him in my car if that's all right with you.'

The wave of dismay that had flooded through Louise at the thought of Vito being in an accident only served to confirm to her that he was now irrevocably in her thoughts, if not more. The idea of something terrible happening to him was too awful to contemplate and the sense of relief that had followed Domenica's clarification had been palpable. She was quick to offer her services.

'I'm happy to help out. I'm doing a lot of trips to Turin these days, so it'll be no trouble for me to do it. He and I are friends now.'

Domenica caught her eye and winked. 'And would you say you are *close* friends?'

Once again Louise could feel her cheeks flush. She and Domenica were getting on well and had been growing closer in the last few weeks so she felt she owed her the truth. 'Feel like joining me for a panna cotta and a glass of wine?' She waved to the empty chair across the table from her. 'This might take a while.'

'I'll definitely have a panna cotta, but if I drink red wine in the evening I don't sleep.' Domenica pulled out the chair, sat down and gave Louise a knowing look. 'And as for Vito, he's a good-looking man, isn't he?'

By now, Louise had lost interest in her last couple of agnolotti so she dropped her fork and sat back. 'He's a *very* good-looking man but there's more to it than that. There's something about him. The first time I set eyes on him I felt a real wave of attraction, but I promise it wasn't just a physical thing. It was something far less explicable, almost as if I already knew him. I just felt an immediate connection and, besides, apart from anything else, he's clearly very bright. I've always had a thing for men with a brain.' She grinned at Domenica across the table. 'You'd be amazed how many I've met with frighteningly little between their ears. Do you know where I've been this afternoon? I've been listening to Vito give a talk on conservation.'

Domenica was smiling now. 'So that's why you went to Turin. I'm glad you like him and I'm sure he must like you.' She grew more serious. 'It would be wonderful if you could return him to the happy, friendly, outgoing man he used to be. I'm sure there's more to it than the death of his father but he's never said anything. It breaks my heart to see him so withdrawn and alone.'

'I know what you mean. There's a cloud hanging over him; you can't miss it. On the rare occasions I've seen him smile, it lights up his face but it never lasts long.'

'Well, if anybody can put a smile back on his face I'm sure it's you, Louise.' She lowered her voice in conspiratorial fashion. 'So shall I let you do the driving on Thursday, then?'

At that moment Calogero came over to remove Louise's plate and Domenica asked him for two servings of panna cotta. He gave Domenica the lightest pat on the shoulder before returning to the kitchen and this reminded Louise of something she had been wondering. She and Domenica were getting on really well together now so she decided to risk a direct question.

'Tell me to mind my own business by all means but I can't help noticing that you and Calogero are very close.

It looks to me as if you might even have feelings for him. Am I right?'

For the first time ever, Louise saw the newly promoted manager of the Grand Hotel del Monferrato blush to her roots. Domenica even reached across to a neighbouring table, grabbed a spare glass and helped herself to a splash of red wine from Louise's bottle which she swallowed before setting her elbows on the table and leaning forwards. When she spoke, it was in a hoarse whisper.

'Promise me you'll never tell him what I'm going to tell you.'

'I promise.'

Domenica took a deep breath and lowered her voice to little more than a whisper. 'I've loved him since the first day I saw him, thirty-one years ago. Of course he was married then and there was nothing I was going to do about it but that initial feeling has never gone away. Listening to you talk about your first impression of Vito brought it all back to me. It sounds impossible that a single glance can do it, but you just know somehow, don't you?'

Wow, Louise thought to herself, so Domenica had harboured this secret infatuation for well over a quarter of a century.

'Calogero's wife's been dead for five years now and I've been waiting and waiting, but I've never dared to say anything. Just like I know I fell for Calogero the moment I saw him, he and his wife, Giovanna, were devoted to each other and I imagine it was probably the same for him when he first met her. Maybe he'll never get over losing his her.' Domenica sighed and helped herself to another drop of wine. 'I'd love to tell him how I feel but I'm terrified it'll spoil things between us forever. It's really hard.'

Louise reached across and gave her hand a little squeeze, understanding Domenica's problem but unable to suggest a solution except time. 'I'm sure he likes you a lot and it'll work itself out, you'll see.' She picked up her glass and clinked it against Domenica's. 'Cheers, Domenica. Here's to love – even if it means a long wait.'

At that moment Calogero reappeared with their desserts. After setting them down, he gave Domenica a quizzical look. 'Drinking red wine at this time of night? You won't sleep, you know.' Tut-tutting, he set off back towards the kitchen and Louise smiled across the table at Domenica.

'You really do know each other well, don't you?'

Chapter 15

Louise spent the next morning going through the websites of a number of kitchen equipment suppliers, ordering the extra kit Luigino had told her he would need in readiness for when the restaurant would hopefully leapfrog from a dozen guests a day to a hundred – assuming the big marketing drive went well. She then spent hours trawling through the listings of hospitality employment agencies, checking to see how easy it was going to be to recruit the new staff they were going to need. After that she went out and took photos of the proposed site of the new pool and sent them across to Joseph, hoping he would approve. A lot was scheduled to be done here at the Grand Hotel over the months of May and June and she was keeping her fingers crossed it would all go smoothly.

In the late afternoon she thought of going for a walk – maybe down in the direction of the old mill – but decided against it. She didn't want Vito to think she was stalking him, after all. Besides, she would be seeing him tomorrow anyway as his car was due for collection from the garage.

Domenica joined her for dinner and explained the arrangements she had made.

'His car's going to be ready any time after five, so I've told him we'll pick him up at four.' She gave Louise a grin. 'But I haven't told him who's going to be driving. I thought you might like to surprise him.'

Louise gave a little grimace. 'Just so long as he thinks it's a pleasant surprise. Will he have the dog with him?'

'I doubt it. Leo will probably just be left to guard the house – although he's not exactly what you would call a natural guard dog.'

The following day it was hard to tell if Vito was pleasantly surprised or not, but he was definitely surprised. It had been pouring with rain all day and when Louise arrived at the old mill to pick him up, he came running out with his coat over his head and only realised who it was at the wheel when he slammed the car door behind him and turned towards her.

'Oh, hi, Louise. I didn't realise it was going to be you who'd be driving. Are you sure you can spare the time? I wouldn't want to put you out; I'm sure you're busy.' He sounded polite and grateful but she couldn't read any more into his reaction to seeing her.

'It's no trouble. I'm happy to do it. Domenica told me about the accident. Are you sure you're all right?' Louise could hear the anxiety in her voice and felt sure he couldn't have missed it.

'Absolutely fine, thanks. A delivery van just hit my front wing a glancing blow. I barely felt it but it damaged the disc brake and it needed to be fixed before I could drive it again. According to the man at the garage it was no big deal and it's all ready for me.'

'Well, I'm just relieved you're okay.'

She turned the car and set off along the gravel track back to the road. To fill the slightly awkward silence she queried him about where they were headed and he gave her instructions. It was all very formal and he could have been talking to a taxi driver. Still, she told herself, at least he was talking – although not that readily.

She concentrated on negotiating her way through the potholes and deep puddles until they emerged onto the road and it took a good five minutes before he decided to start talking.

'By the way, thank you for coming to my talk on Tuesday. I didn't realise you were so keen on conservation. That's great. I hope you found it interesting.'

'I thought it was fascinating, although I must confess I got a bit lost with all the technical stuff. You certainly know what you're talking about.'

'Thank you.' He lapsed into silence once more and she was about to throw a few environmental questions at him in the hope of getting him onto a subject with which he felt comfortable when he asked *her* a question. This was progress.

'Are you going to make changes to the staff?'

'What, at the hotel? Definitely not. Domenica, Calogero and Luigino are lovely. In fact they're all lovely and they're all pulling their weight. I've told my boss we're going to need all of them plus, of course, a whole lot more members of staff when bookings start rising again.'

'Good, good. I'm so pleased… and relieved. I think of them as my family in a way. And what about you? Will you stay on and manage the place?'

'No, hasn't Domenica told you? She's been promoted to manager.'

'That's wonderful for her.' She felt his eyes on her and shot him a quick glance. He was looking at her and smiling. 'Thank you, Louise. That was a fine thing to do. Most generous. She's given so much of her life to the hotel. Thank you for having the vision to realise that. I'm sure she must be delighted.' He then produced – unprompted – a genuinely personal remark. 'My mother died when I was young and I've grown up thinking of Domenica as my aunt, sort of my second mum. Sometimes I still find myself calling her *Zia* Domenica even now.'

She could hear the emotion in his voice, and the fact that he was starting to open up to her came as a shock – and a welcome one. Did this mean that their relationship might be changing? 'Making her manager was pure self-interest, I assure you. She'll do a great job. And, don't laugh, but I also sort of think of her as a mother figure. I find I can talk to her about anything. She's a sweetie.'

'I'm so glad you feel the same way about her.' There was a pause. 'So if she's the new manager does that mean you'll be leaving in the summer?' Was that a hint of regret in his tone?

'Early July, immediately after the re-launch party.' She wondered if he would miss her. She knew she was going to miss him. 'That'll be a weekend event for movers and shakers in the travel trade to get to know the place. By the way, you're invited if you fancy it. There's going to be a gala on the Saturday evening with food, music, dancing and fireworks.'

'That's kind but probably not for me, thanks. I can hardly remember the last time I went dancing.' His tone was once more downbeat so she tried to offer a bit of cheer.

'I'll be there on my own and I'll need somebody to dance with.' This was probably a bit too pushy but she had said it now so she just concentrated on the road as he produced a response.

'You'll be on your own? Really? I'm surprised.' She was still digesting the fact that this sounded like another personal remark when he immediately apologised. 'I'm sorry, that's no business of mine… sorry.'

'Nothing to apologise for. I used to have a boyfriend but that ended so I'm just focusing on my job for now.' The moment she said it she immediately regretted it – it sounded like she was telling him she wasn't interested in him – but it was too late.

'I'm sorry.' That was all he said.

She toyed with the idea of putting him on the spot and asking how come a good-looking, intelligent man like him didn't have a partner of his own but decided against it. They still had three-quarters of an hour to go to their destination and that was a long, long time for an awkward silence if he chose not to reply.

The rest of the journey passed not in awkward silence, but without any further personal remarks on either side. In fact, she took refuge in asking him more about some of the endangered species he had mentioned in his talk the other day and this was enough to keep him going without any further questions being necessary. By the time they reached the garage in the industrial suburbs of Turin she knew a lot more about the threats facing the white-cheeked spider monkeys and giant otters of the Amazon basin and the orangutans and Sumatran tigers of South-East Asia, but was no closer to knowing what had caused him to change from the outgoing man everyone said he used to be to the introverted one he was now. Surely there had to be a more personal reason but he gave no hint of what this might be. Still, she told herself, at least she had managed to get him talking.

Before getting out of the car he turned towards her and shook hands formally. 'Thank you, that was kind. Are you sure you know your way back from here?'

'I'll be fine, thanks.'

'Goodbye, Louise.'

'Goodbye, Vito.'

As she drove off, she watched him in her rear-view mirror. He was still standing there, watching her leave. Might that mean something? She had no more time for conjecture as her phone started ringing. After turning the corner she pulled in to the side of the road to answer it.

'Ciao, Louise. It's me, Silvana.'

'Ciao, Silvana, what's new? How was your conference in Milan?'

'Surprisingly interesting but, more to the point, how did Professor Vito's lecture go?'

'Surprisingly interesting.' She smiled as she repeated her friend's words. 'But maybe for all the wrong reasons.'

'What's that supposed to mean?'

'It means I was probably a whole lot more interested in him than in his talk. There's no getting away from it, Silvana: I really like the guy.'

'That's great news.' As usual, Silvana didn't beat about the bush. 'So what're you going to do about it?'

'There's not a lot I *can* do. I'm pretty sure he doesn't see me in a romantic light. He very much keeps himself to himself. I only bump into him every now and then. In fact, I probably see more of his dog than I do of him.'

'Love me, love my dog. Then you need to cultivate the dog. Is he a nice dog?'

'He's a super dog.' She went on to describe Leo and his antics.

'And Leo the dog spends his life just wandering around the estate?'

'Yes, he's friends with the men who work in the fields.'

'Then lure him up to the hotel and Count Vito'll have to come up and get him.'

'I'm sure Leo already knows his way up to the hotel and home again.'

'Then you'll have to lure the man up on his own. Why not ask him to join you for dinner?'

'I'm not sure he'd say yes. Like I was telling you, he's very reticent, very private.'

There was a pause and Louise could almost hear the cogs inside her friend's head turning. 'If you're fishing, you lure the fish with something they like – worms or flies or whatever. With men it's the same. What's he interested in?' The answer was easy and Silvana got to it a second before Louise. 'Science! Of course, that's your intro. He already knows you claim to be interested in environmental stuff – after all you sat through an hour or more of his lecture the other day – so why not? I know, why don't you go down and ask if he can recommend a book for you to read, maybe even lend you one? How about that as an idea?'

'It's a bit Machiavellian, but you're right, it might work. And, besides, I really am quite interested in climate change and all that.' The more she thought about it, the better it sounded. 'Thanks, Silvana, I might just give it a try.'

Chapter 16

In fact it wasn't until the following week that Louise managed to find the time to go down and ask Vito for some reading material. She and Domenica found themselves increasingly busy with visits from decorators to quote for repainting the exterior of the hotel once the building works were finished. There was an inspection by the fire brigade who, fortunately, did not require them to carry out any major works to keep the hotel up to standard, and on the Saturday they had their first wedding of the season and the hotel was suddenly buzzing. Half a dozen local people were roped into service as waiters while ladies from the village were drafted in to help Luigino in the kitchen. A band played in the ballroom and they all found themselves working non-stop until past midnight. A number of the guests had opted to spend the night at the hotel and twenty-five rooms were occupied so Louise and the others were all up again at the crack of dawn to ensure that the dining room was readied for breakfast. Although it technically wasn't her job to get involved with the day-to-day running of the hotel, Louise was more than happy to muck in and help out.

It was mid-afternoon before it all calmed down again and Luigino went off home for a well-earned rest. The bride and groom and many of the guests had expressed satisfaction with how it had all gone and the hotel's bank balance received a much-needed injection of capital as a result. Although the sun was shining brightly as the end of April approached, Louise didn't have the energy to go out for a walk and disappeared up to her room for a well-earned siesta that lasted almost until dark.

Late the following afternoon, seeing as the outside temperature was very pleasant she decided the time had come to put Silvana's plan into operation, so she set off on foot towards the old mill to track down Vito. She walked down through the fields, breathing in the perfume of wild thyme in the air and admiring the myriad little clusters of wild flowers which had popped up in the hedges and verges. Above her a pair of big birds of prey circled, whistling to each other as they soared effortlessly over the hillside. By now the area was beginning to feel familiar and she was starting to know her way around the network of paths and tracks that crisscrossed the hotel grounds. The more she saw of it, the more she loved the scenery, realising that it reminded her of holidays she had spent as a little girl with her grandmother at her thatched cottage deep in the Dorset countryside. Yes, she was going to miss this place when her job moved her on.

She passed Ernesto among the vines and stopped for a chat. The vines, which only a matter of weeks ago had been bare and dormant, were now covered with fresh green shoots and an air of regeneration reigned. He told her he had just started bottling last September's wine and promised to send a few bottles up to the hotel for her and the others to try, indicating by a knowing look and a very Italian rub of his cheek with his thumb that his prediction that it would prove to be a spectacular vintage had come to pass.

As she approached Vito's home, she was surprised to hear splashing. The sounds grew louder and as she walked in through the stone gateway it became clear they were coming from the far side of the house. She knocked on the kitchen door a few times but there was no response so, tentatively, she made her way around to the side and immediately discovered the source of the splashing. Many decades, if not centuries, ago the river had been channelled between stone walls so as to create a large millpond shaded by ancient willows. At the far end of the wide, deep pool, the old wooden waterwheel was visible, still attached to the side of the house. Bobbing about in the water were two heads – one furry, one smooth.

'*Buongiorno, signori.*' Louise saw both heads turn towards her. A wide canine grin appeared on the face of the Labrador while his master's expression was harder to judge – pleased, but somehow wary. Louise was quick to explain why she was trespassing.

'Hi, Vito. I tried knocking at the door but then I heard you out here. I hope I'm not disturbing.' A thought occurred to her as she stood in the shade and the cool breeze rustled through the branches of the willows. 'Are you sure you aren't going to catch pneumonia swimming at this time of year?' Although April had been predominantly fine, it was far from hot and the water in the river must have been freezing.

'It's lovely. You should try it some time. Mind you, I must admit that I'm cheating.' He raised an arm towards her and she spotted that he was wearing a wetsuit. He swam across towards her and climbed out of the water up an old iron ladder set in the stone wall. Without his glasses he looked even more appealing than usual and Louise had to suppress a little growl of attraction. The dog followed

Vito out of the water, scrabbling up a slippery stone slide alongside the ladder with a practised manoeuvre before charging towards Louise in ebullient mood while she was still looking at his master.

She didn't stand a chance.

'Louise, look out…'

Vito managed to shout a warning but it was too late by then as a happy – and soaking wet – Leo launched himself at her. She told herself afterwards it was her own stupid fault for allowing herself to be distracted by the athletic physique of Professor Vito, rather than taking prudent steps to avoid the dog. In consequence she was knocked backwards onto the grass by the enthusiastic Labrador, landing on her back with a thud that almost knocked the breath out of her. But her troubles didn't stop there. The dog, delighted to see her down at his level, immediately decided to climb all over her. Within a few seconds she was soaked to the skin and his tongue licking her face was the least of her worries.

'Leo, you hooligan. Get off her. You're a bad, bad dog. *Via, via!*'

Vito came running across and heaved the dog off her before reaching down and pulling her easily to her feet. Louise could feel icy cold river water trickling all the way down her back as far as her pants and considering she had been lying on her back with the wet dog on top of her she wasn't quite sure how this could have happened but the sensation it produced was far from comfortable.

'Louise, I'm so sorry. You're absolutely drenched.' Vito sounded so concerned she hastened to reassure him.

'It's my own fault. I know Leo well enough by now; I should have thought.' She glanced down at the dog who was now sitting obediently at his master's side, panting like a steam train, with his tail still wagging furiously. 'He's a youngster and he was happy to see me. It's always nice when somebody's pleased to see you. I don't mind, honestly.' What she didn't say was that if it had been the dog's master who had ended up sprawled all over her, she wouldn't have minded in the slightest either.

Vito frowned. 'You look as if you're soaked to the skin. You need to get inside and change before you catch a cold. Would you like me to run you back to the hotel in the car?'

'I'll be fine, really. I wouldn't want to soak the inside of your nice car.'

'Don't worry about that. If you walk home like this you really might catch a cold. I know, there's a tumble drier in the house. I must confess I've never used it but Rosina uses it all the time. I'm sure between us we'll be able to make it work. Maybe you could put your clothes in that while I make you a cup of something hot to warm you up? I could find you a dressing gown to wear while your things are drying out.'

Soaking wet and chilly or not, the idea of stripping off her clothes in this man's house sent a hot flush to her cheeks again. She shook her head – not without considerable regret – and made a quick decision.

'I'll be fine, honestly. I'll just head straight back home to change. It's uphill so if I walk fast or run I won't get cold.'

For a moment it looked as though he wanted to argue further, but Louise was relieved when he let the issue drop. 'Was there something you wanted to see me about?' Clearly, he was wondering what had prompted her visit.

'I just wanted to ask you about books. I'm interested in reading more about all the horrid things we humans are doing to the planet and seeing as I've got my own personal expert nearby, I thought I'd come and ask if you could suggest something for me.' She was still thinking about his offer to dry her clothes and an image of herself wearing nothing but a flimsy gown, with him sitting close by her, flashed before her eyes and she was powerless to stop her cheeks from reddening again. Mercifully, Vito came up with a sensible suggestion before her resolve could crumble.

'I know, if you really won't let me drive you, why don't you jog home and change and then, if you're sure you've got time, come back down here for a glass of wine and we can talk books. I've got loads I can lend you. Come to think of it, I've still got some of that *colomba* in the cupboard as well. Would that appeal?'

It certainly would – and she wasn't just thinking about the cake. 'That sounds lovely, I'll do that, thanks. See you shortly.'

By the time Louise had jogged back to the hotel, taken a hot shower and changed, it was gone six o'clock as she went back down to the old mill in the car. The air temperature had dropped quite a bit by now and she found a fire burning in the large open fireplace in the kitchen and a lingering smell of damp dog in the air. He had obviously been doing his best to dry the dog off and when Leo came over to greet her, she was pleased to find him no longer dripping wet. She dropped down to one knee to pet him.

'Hello, dog, all nice and dry now?'

'I really am sorry for what he did, Louise. Maybe I should sign him up for some training classes.' Vito was looking apologetic – and deliciously casual – in jeans and a check shirt open at the collar to reveal a few inches of his broad hairy chest. Louise had absolutely no trouble in giving him a warm smile.

'Really, don't worry about it. He'll learn and, besides, it was done with the best of intentions. It's nice to feel wanted. And remember dog training classes are really dog *owner* training classes and I'm sure you've got much more important things to do with your time.'

'Well, my job does keep me busy, that's for sure, but Leo needs to be more considerate. Anyway, what can I offer you? Would you like tea or coffee, or some wine maybe? I've got some of Ernesto's local red or there's cold rosé in the fridge. Come to think of it, I could make mulled wine if you're still feeling cold.'

'I'm as warm as toast now, thanks, and a drop of the rosé sounds great.'

'Rosé it is then. Shall we stay in here as there's a table for the books?'

She sat down at the kitchen table and Leo followed her for another cuddle before padding over to his bed near the fireplace ostensibly to snooze, but with his nose strategically trained in the direction of the table just in case food should magically appear.

Vito took an anonymous bottle from the fridge and filled two glasses with cold rosé – the chilled wine sending tears of condensation running down the outside of the glass.

'Here, see what you think.' He raised his glass towards her. 'Cheers.'

She clinked her glass against his and took a sip. It was excellent and she told him so. He looked relieved.

'I'm delighted to hear you say that. I can now confess that this is homemade.'

Louise was impressed. 'Really? That's amazing.'

'Not really when you've got friends like Ernesto looking over your shoulder and giving advice. I don't have a big vineyard here but it should easily keep me supplied with wine and, if it all turns out like this, I'll be well pleased.'

'Does this mean you still own some of the land around here?'

'Yes, a couple of fields down here by the river, the vineyard, and the woods alongside the hotel estate. By the way, if you ever want to extend your walks into those woods, please feel free. Ask Ernesto to show you the gate leading in. It's quite wild in there and I've put up "No Hunting" signs all over the place so not even the hunters go in there nowadays. The only hunting that takes place in my woods is truffle hunting. In the autumn Ernesto and his little dog spend hours ferreting about in there and they usually find quite a few.'

'So are you a country boy at heart?' She was delighted to hear him talking more freely.

'Definitely. I was born and brought up here in the countryside and I was a bit like Leo when I was a kid – I used to roam all over the place. In fact, it was living here that gave me my interest in the environment. Now, would you like some cake or...' He glanced at his watch. 'It's past teatime so why don't I make us some *fett'unta* – you know, traditional garlic bread?'

Louise was familiar with this simplest of dishes – slices of bread toasted over the embers of the fire and then rubbed with raw garlic, dusted with salt and finally drizzled with good, thick, extra virgin olive oil. When she had lived in Turin as a poor student she had almost lived on the stuff.

'That sounds wonderful, I'd love a slice.' She shot him a little grin. 'It's not as if I'm planning on kissing anybody this evening.' Chance, she told herself, would be a fine thing.

He gave no reply but pulled out a hefty round loaf of white bread and cut off one end. By this time he had a black shadow at his feet, nose trained unerringly upwards at the bread. Vito handed him the crust and Leo took it delicately before disappearing back to his bed in triumph where he wedged it between his front paws and crunched it with obvious enjoyment. Louise then watched as Vito cut a couple of generous slices, peeled a little clove of garlic and brought out the salt and oil. He raked the bigger logs out of the way and produced a well-used grill with metal legs which sat neatly in the fireplace over the hot embers. Clearly he had cooked in this way many times before.

While he grilled the bread and then rubbed it with garlic, Louise took another sip of wine, enjoying the taste and the fact that Vito gradually appeared to be opening up in her company. He still didn't sound totally relaxed but she sensed a real softening in his tense exterior. She glanced around the rest of the kitchen and noted that this time it was spotless and there wasn't a single dirty dish to be seen. Maybe the lady from the village had been recently or Vito had been busy clearing up for her sake. He set a slice of the garlic bread and a paper napkin down in front of her and headed back towards the old dresser.

'Start eating while it's still hot. And when you've finished, I've got a couple of books for you.' He brought them over and set them down by her right hand before taking a seat across the table from her and picking up his toast. Clearly he wasn't planning on kissing anybody this evening either. Between mouthfuls he explained the books. 'One's in Italian and the other's in English. Of course it'll be easier for you to read the English one, but I know your Italian's up to making sense of the Italian one and, modestly speaking, I think it's a better book.'

'Modestly speaking?' Louise picked up what was unmistakably a brand-new copy of a book whose menacing title translated as *Apocalypse Around the Corner* and saw that it was written by none other than Vittorio Emanuele Dellarosa. She looked up in admiration. 'Your own work! Well, I have no choice now. I'll have to read this one first.'

'See how you get on with it. It's yours anyway, as a little thank you gift for acting as my chauffeur the other day. Don't worry – the publisher sent me a load of copies. And before you say anything, I didn't choose the title. The publisher did. I think it sounds far too dramatic and even risks trivialising what is without doubt the biggest threat facing the planet.'

'How kind, thank you and I rather like the title.' She opened the cover and saw the blank flysheet. 'In which case would you sign it for me please? It's not every day I get given a book by its author.'

She pushed the book across the table and he took it from her. Picking up a pen, he scrawled inside and passed it back. She opened the cover and saw that he had written: *To Louise. I hope you find this interesting. Vittorio Emanuele Dellarosa.* A nice message but hardly intimate, though she hadn't really expected anything more.

'Thank you so much. That's super. And I'm sure I'll find it interesting.'

She flicked through the pages for a few moments and when she looked up again she found Vito's eyes no longer on the table but on her, the reflection of the firelight sparkling in them. The sun outside had disappeared behind the hills by now and the shadows in the room were deepening, so hopefully he didn't see the colour rush to her cheeks once more. There was no getting away from it – being with him somehow reduced her from a grown woman to a clueless adolescent. She struggled for something to say and hit on the hotel.

'Can I ask why you sold the hotel? It's been in your family for so long, after all.'

'Partly money – the place needs a lot of investment and I just didn't have it, and partly because I have a different life now. I honestly don't know how long I'll be staying here. I gave up an exciting job in Oxford to come back here when my father fell ill and part of me would like to go back to it.'

'And leave all this?' Louise indicated the surroundings with her hands. 'This house, the hills, the vineyards, the woodland, not to mention the food and the wine. It's your very own rural paradise.'

'I know, it'll be tough but maybe it's the right thing to do. Now that my father's gone and the hotel's sold, there isn't anything much to keep me here and my career could flourish elsewhere.'

'No special someone to keep you here?' Louise held her breath, wondering if this had been a question too far. He didn't answer immediately but when he did, she couldn't miss his cold, expressionless tone.

'No special someone anywhere… now.' He picked up his glass and drained it before standing up. 'I'm sorry, I promised you some cake. Would you like some?' He was being polite but she could see he was just trying to change the subject. She hastily finished her own wine and stood up.

'Oh, no, thanks. The *fett'unta* was lovely and ever so filling. I'd better make a move and leave you in peace.' He didn't object so she went round to ruffle the dog's ears and then give his master a formal handshake.

'Thank you so much for the books, and I apologise again for interrupting your swim this afternoon.'

'Thank you for coming. I don't entertain much. It's been good to see you.' He sounded sincere, if deflated, and she was mentally kicking herself for putting him on the spot when he was only just starting to open up.

'Goodbye, Vito.'

Chapter 17

The following days were filled with a series of decisions to be made about colour schemes, signage – starting with a new sign down at the end of the drive – artworks to decorate the walls of the rooms and even decisions about the selection of free toiletries to be put in every bathroom. She specifically chose gold-wrapped Gianduiotti chocolates, the speciality of Turin, to be placed on the pillows by the evening staff who would turn down the bedcovers. Louise knew full well that it was little touches like these that guests in Joseph's hotels had come to expect. She drove down to Turin again twice and by the time Friday arrived she felt reasonably confident she had it all in hand. Of course the crunch would come in two weeks' time when the different tradesmen had promised to start work. She had enough experience of builders and their promises not to feel completely confident until she saw them all turn up with their tools.

At lunchtime on Friday she drove back down to Turin one more time to collect Annabelle from the airport. She and Domenica had decided to give the Head of Operations the same room they had given Joseph, feeling sure the views out across the vineyards to the distant tree-covered hills would appeal. She waited for Annabelle to emerge from the baggage hall, wondering what she would make of the Grand Hotel and sincerely hoping she would like it. Annabelle occupied a senior position in the firm and if she didn't like something, it could mean a lot of trouble.

Annabelle emerged with a smile on her face and shook Louise's hand warmly. The two of them had always got on well.

'Hi, Louise. Thanks for coming to pick me up. I'm pleased to see you looking a lot better than last time I saw you. You looked a bit under the weather then. Knowing you, it was probably because you'd been overworking. Now you've got colour in your cheeks and you look… happier.'

Considering the last time the two of them had met had been only three days after Louise had caught her boyfriend in flagrante, it was no wonder she had looked a bit zonked. Still, Annabelle didn't need to know about that, so Louise just smiled.

'Thanks, I'm feeling fine. I'm sure it's all down to the Grand Hotel and its surroundings. The area around there's great for walking and getting out in the fresh air.'

Annabelle heaved a wistful sigh. 'That sounds like exactly what I need. It's such a fine day, maybe you could show me some of the walks around the hotel. That's the problem with living in London; it would be lovely to get out in the fresh country air and escape, even if it's just for an hour or two.'

'Absolutely. I know exactly how you feel, and the Monferrato's lovely and so calm and peaceful. Let's go for a walk this afternoon and tomorrow we could have a longer one if you like. How long are you staying?'

'Just tonight, I'm afraid. I'm meeting some old friends in Verona for the weekend. Maybe somebody will be able to give me a lift to the station in the morning.'

'I'll do that, no problem.' Louise glanced at her watch. 'It's almost two. Have you eaten?'

'I had a sandwich on the plane so I'm fine, thanks.'

'I can guarantee you a sumptuous meal tonight so it's maybe just as well you haven't had a big lunch.'

On the way back to the hotel they chatted mainly about work matters. Annabelle told her that the hotel on the island of Antigua, Louise's last mission, was now fully booked and complaints had dried up completely. Louise had been in regular contact with the new manager just to keep an eye on things and she already knew this, but it was good to hear that the senior staff were also aware. Annabelle gave her a brief rundown of the rest of the hotels in the chain and it sounded as though all was going well for the company.

'That's great, Annabelle. Joseph must be pleased.'

'He certainly is. Pre-tax profits for last year are well up so hopefully that means our next bonus should be good.' One of the nicest things about working for Joseph was the profit-sharing scheme he had set up so all the staff could benefit from the company's success. 'By the way, he told me to say hi and thank you for your advice, whatever that was.'

From Annabelle's tone it was clear she was intrigued to know, but Louise had no intention of revealing details of what had been a pretty personal conversation. Mind you, she thought to herself, it was somehow strange that he should have asked a third party to pass on his thanks for something so private. She didn't have much time to let her thoughts dwell on the ramifications of this as Annabelle suddenly revealed that there was little that went on in the company that she didn't know about.

'I heard you and your boyfriend split up. I was sorry to hear that. I remember him from last year's Christmas party. He was ever so handsome and a great dancer.'

'Yes, I'm afraid that's all finished.' Louise found herself wondering if it had been Joseph himself who had passed on that titbit or one of the few staff members she had told. She also realised she was thinking of Tommy again for the first time in a good long while. Yes, he was a good-looking man and a good dancer. No sooner did the image of Tommy appear in her head, however, than it was superimposed with the haunted face of a certain solitary Italian academic and for a moment she found herself struggling to concentrate on her driving. By this time they were approaching the motorway exit which would take them onto the quieter country roads so she didn't reply immediately as she made her way off the autostrada through the toll booth. Finally on the long straight road on which the Rolls Royce had boiled over back in March, she replied in level tones.

'It was a pity about Tommy, but I've pretty much got over it now.' Louise realised this was actually true. Whether this was because of another man was something she preferred not to examine too closely although Annabelle homed straight in on it.

'I'm sure it helped being able to get away from it all, even if it was for a work trip. Any new men on the horizon?'

Louise was unused to having this sort of personal conversation with Annabelle – who was her superior after all – so she negotiated it cautiously, not least as she didn't know the answer herself. 'No, not really... maybe... I honestly don't know. The thing is, after the way things ended between Tommy and me, I'm taking a bit of a time out as far as men are concerned.'

It occurred to her that she had no idea of Annabelle's relationship status. As far as she could remember, Annabelle had always been unaccompanied at the staff parties but Louise didn't know her well enough to ask so she changed the subject to the Monferrato. By now they were starting to climb into the hills so she produced a potted history of the area, freshly gleaned from the internet while putting together a welcome pack for guests.

Back at the hotel, she introduced Annabelle to Domenica and then took her on a tour of the building, pointing out all the alterations that would begin in less than two weeks' time. When they reached room 224, Annabelle declared herself charmed with the accommodation and the views from the windows.

'I can see why Joseph bought this place now. I couldn't work out why he'd opted for something so far off the beaten track.'

Louise nodded in agreement. 'That's exactly what I was wondering. It is a bit off the grid compared to the other hotels in the group.'

'He's been telling me his plan is to make it an event hotel, specialising in upmarket weddings, conferences and so on. Because it's in the middle of nowhere we're going to see if we can get it onto the diplomatic circuit – you know, peace talks and the like. They often need to be in places that are easy to secure, depending on who's been invited.'

'Well, there used to be a castle on this site after all.'

After a cup of coffee in the lounge, they both changed into trainers and set off on a walk. Louise took Annabelle though the fields, stopping to show her Ernesto's vines as they walked past.

'I've just tasted last year's red and it's amazing. We can have some tonight if you like.'

'How wonderful! A hotel that makes its own wine. That's got to be a great selling point.'

They had just reached the river when a big black shape emerged from the gates of the old mill and came charging towards them. Hastily, Louise turned to Annabelle. 'Are you okay with dogs?'

'Love them.'

'Great, well, this one's very friendly, but his idea of saying hello is to take a flying leap and he's already knocked me over a few times.'

Forewarned, Annabelle was able to withstand Leo's enthusiastic greeting and they were still petting him when his master appeared out of the gateway in his running gear and started jogging towards them. It was at that moment that something most unexpected happened. No sooner did he set eyes on Annabelle than he stopped dead and she, in return, gave a little cry of astonishment and jumped to her feet.

'Vito? Vito, is that really you?'

'Annabelle, I don't believe it. What on earth are you doing here?'

'You two know each other?' Louise wasn't exactly sure which of the two she was asking but it was Annabelle who replied.

'We certainly do, but I haven't clapped eyes on this guy for years. How are you, Vito?' Annabelle's tone changed from surprise to something more serious. 'Are you all right now?' Before he could answer she ran across the intervening yards and threw herself into his arms. 'God, it's wonderful to see you, but what an amazing coincidence! I only know a handful of Italians and yet I run into you on my first day and in the middle of nowhere.' By this time the Labrador was standing on his hind legs and had joined in, and the three of them were hugging each other with gusto. For Louise's part, along with mystification, she couldn't avoid the realisation that the other sensation coursing through her was jealousy. From the affectionate way they were clinging to each other, they had been close friends. Maybe even more than friends?

'I'm doing better now, thanks.' Vito's mouth was close to Annabelle's ear and Louise could barely hear him.

'I'm so glad.' Annabelle wrapped herself around his arm and turned towards Louise who was still standing rooted to the spot. 'I first met Vito when we were both at Oxford. It's so amazing to see him again.' She reached up to kiss him on the cheek. This did nothing to sooth the suspicion running through Louise, although Annabelle's next remark reassured her. 'It was love at first sight for me, but he only had eyes for one person.' She kissed him again, more tenderly this time. 'And it wasn't me.'

'Are you staying at the hotel?' By this time the cloud that had passed across Vito's face had disappeared and he had managed to recover from his surprise. A bit. Meanwhile Louise was still trying to make sense of what she was hearing.

'Yes, just for one night. Louise and I work for the same company.' Annabelle was still hanging on to him.

Doing her best to recover her composure, Louise explained. 'Annabelle's our Inspector General and she came over to check up on how things are going.'

Annabelle waved the comment away. 'Louise and the others just call me that. I'm actually Head of Operations.

Anyway, what're you doing tonight, Vito? Please say you'll come and have dinner with us.'

Louise studied his face. The uncertainty was all too clear to see. 'I don't do a lot of socialising these days, to be honest…'

Annabelle gave him a pleading look. 'Please, Vito, it would be so good to talk to you again. It's been an awfully long time.'

Seeing that he was still dubious, Louise offered a suggestion. 'I know, why don't you two just have a quiet dinner on your own? I'll be quite happy doing my own thing.' She felt she had to make the offer, although she knew she would dearly love to find out more about him.

He hesitated and then replied, reluctantly. 'I'd be delighted to have dinner with the two of you.' From his expression he was patently anything but delighted, but he had said yes and Louise felt a surge of excitement – although she wasn't sure she was necessarily going to like what she heard.

Annabelle beamed up at him. 'Wonderful. See you later. What time's best, Louise?'

'The restaurant's open from seven. Whatever suits you, Vito. Say, seven thirty?'

'Seven thirty it is.' He stood there for a moment, looking a bit lost, before making a decision. 'I'd better get on with my run. See you both later. Come on, Leo.' And he was off.

The two of them resumed their walk up through the woods, Annabelle still marvelling at the serendipity of her reunion with Vito. Without Louise having to prompt her, she went on to relate the tragic events that had scarred him so deeply and Louise listened aghast.

'I first met him when he was doing his PhD and I was doing my Economics degree. It was at a party. You couldn't miss him. He was the life and the soul of the party and he was oh so good-looking. He still is, of course, but back then he wasn't just drop dead gorgeous but also so full of life. It breaks my heart to see him like this now.' She glanced over at Louise. 'Do you know him well?'

'Only since I've been here. We've met and talked a few times but I couldn't miss the fact that he's reticent, very quiet and reserved. He comes across as an unusually private person. It seems incredible that he used to be such an extrovert. Domenica said the same thing about what he was like when he was younger, but now...? What happened?'

Louise saw Annabelle take a deep breath. 'He fell in love with my flatmate, my best friend, Augusta. She was a stunningly beautiful girl from Portugal – olive skin, green eyes and gorgeous hair. She was doing PPE and was well on target for a first. I'm sure she would probably have ended up running the country.'

'But...?'

'But she died.' Annabelle went silent for over a minute as they continued to walk up through the trees, the silence only punctuated by a pair of noisy cackling magpies high above in the branches. Finally, she picked up the story again, the sadness in her voice only too evident. 'It was four years ago; after they'd been together for quite a while. Augusta and Vito were inseparable. They were living together by then and as she had just completed her doctorate, they'd decided to get married. They were already making plans for the wedding. Then, one night, there was an awful accident. She was hit by a drunk driver as she was walking home. The car crashed into a wall, crushing her and killing the driver instantly. When I heard the news I was distraught.'

'Oh, God, how awful.' Louise didn't know what to say. The horror was just too great.

'I cried for days. And for Vito... for Vito it was totally crushing. Overnight he changed from the cheeriest man on the planet to a mere shadow of his former self. Augusta had been everything to him and it was as if the life had been drained out of him. We all rallied round and did our best to support him but he never got over it. I stayed in touch for as long as I could but I hadn't actually seen him since he came back to Italy. I was vaguely aware that he was living somewhere near Turin but I had no idea he was so close to the Grand Hotel del Monferrato.'

'Not just near it, he used to own it.' Louise gave her an abbreviated version of the history of the Dellarosa family and Annabelle was even more amazed.

'I knew he had an aristocratic background but he never used his title and he never told me about the hotel. Fancy that.' She glanced across at Louise. 'Who would have thought our company would end up buying his hotel?'

Chapter 18

Vito appeared in the hotel lobby at seven thirty accompanied by his four-legged friend. Louise was delighted to see he had brought the Labrador to lighten the mood as she had a feeling it might prove to be an emotional evening. She knew Annabelle, always well-dressed, would appear looking elegant so she had once more pressed her trusty charity shop Dior dress into service, accompanied by the new heels she had bought in Turin. At the last moment she even put her hair up, telling herself this was for Annabelle's benefit while knowing, deep down, that it wasn't.

Vito walked in with the dog and as soon as Leo spotted her he came running, but she was ready for him and started to crouch down. Although it was dry outside and hopefully not muddy, the last thing she needed was a mucky dog climbing all over her nice clean frock. This time, however, she didn't need to take evading action as she heard Vito's voice, sounding remarkably authoritative.

'Leo, no! Come here. Now sit!'

Louise was impressed to see the dog obey and she straightened up again and walked over to greet him as he now sat primly beside his master, tail wagging excitedly.

'*Ciao, bello.*' She could have said the same to his owner who was looking decidedly *bello* in a freshly ironed light grey linen shirt and chinos. He had even shaved and this was the first time she had seen him without a stubbly chin and she wasn't sure which look made him more desirable. She stroked the dog's head and glanced up. 'And good evening to you, Vito. Have you been to those dog training classes after all? That was a masterful bit of canine control.' The slightly apprehensive expression on his face cracked into a little smile and Louise took heart from this small but significant gesture.

'No, no classes, just me trying to be a bit more assertive.' His eyes ran across her and she struggled hard to prevent the inevitable flush from appearing on her cheeks. 'You look stunning, Louise. I've never seen you with your hair up before and it makes you look so...' He was still hunting for the *mot juste* when Annabelle's voice interrupted them.

'Good evening, or should that be *buona sera*?'

Her voice also attracted the attention of Leo who leapt to his feet, ready to launch an enthusiastic canine greeting but Vito's hand shot down to his collar to stop him from messing up Annabelle's stylish light-blue dress. Louise felt sure the label would belong to one of the big-name designers.

'No, Leo! I've told you once and I'll tell you again: no jumping up.' Vito walked the dog over to Annabelle where she gave Leo a cuddle before reaching out and throwing her arms around Vito's neck.

'I'm so glad you could come, Vito. We've got so much catching up to do.'

'Well, I couldn't ask for two more beautiful companions.' Louise was pleased to hear him sounding so complimentary and, just for a few seconds, she thought she had a glimpse of the Vito of old, the man who had been vivacious and loved by all. Louise was beginning to live for these small moments of warmth and happiness from Vito, and she found herself wanting to bring more of these expressions to his face, more joy to his life so he could smile freely once again. But no sooner had it appeared than the cheery expression melted away.

They walked through to the dining room and found that Calogero had given them a table in the far corner, well away from the other half dozen tables that were already occupied. Whether this was to allow them their privacy or so that the dog would be out of the way of anybody who might be allergic was uncertain, but Louise applauded his professionalism. He and Vito embraced like brothers and this only served to reinforce what Vito had said about thinking of the staff of the hotel as his family.

'Ciao, Vito. So you're the thorn between the roses tonight. Some people get all the luck.'

'Ciao, Calogero, what's Luigino giving us tonight?'

There then followed a brief discussion, without the need for a menu, until it was decided that they would all have mixed antipasti – what Luigino was now calling the Piedmontese Platter – followed by *crespelle*. These thin rolled pancakes filled with ricotta, spinach, ham and fontina cheese were one of his specialities and, apparently, one of Vito's favourites. After that, Vito and Louise opted for roast rabbit while Annabelle decided to go for boiled beef with a sauce called *bagnet* in the local dialect. Calogero told them this green sauce was made with chopped parsley, capers, crushed hardboiled eggs and garlic and was a Piedmontese speciality not to be missed, so Louise asked for a little with her rabbit to try it. After Calogero had gone off, Vito explained his choice.

'Growing up, with my father and grandfather working at the hotel, I often used to eat here – or rather I used to eat in the kitchen with Luigino and his wife. She used to help him, and between them she and Domenica became sort of surrogate mothers to me. I could have almost anything I wanted, but my favourites always were *crespelle* and rabbit.'

Annabelle shook her head. 'I'm not a great fan of rabbit, but I'm really looking forward to trying these pancake things.'

To drink there was an unlabelled bottle of Ernesto's new wine with a word of warning from him via Calogero that it hadn't yet reached its full potential. Nevertheless, they all agreed it was excellent and Louise was pleased to hear Annabelle extolling its virtues.

'This stuff's amazing. So is the plan to make this the house wine?'

'Most definitely.' Louise reached for her bag and pulled out a folded sheet. 'Seeing as I've got you both here, I'd like your opinions. I've had a graphic designer produce a few alternatives for the new labels, incorporating the company logo as well as the hotel name. Which do you like, if any?'

The decision was quickly made and they all agreed on the best version which included a fine pen and ink sketch of the hotel with *Barbera del Grand Hotel* across the top of the label. Louise was pleased to see Vito looking and sounding animated and she did her best to keep him that way as the meal progressed. It wasn't until they had finished the assorted antipasti half an hour later that Annabelle finally addressed the elephant in the room.

'So, how've you been, Vito? It's good to see you out and about. Are you a happy man again now?' Seeing his eyes flick across toward Louise and back again, she continued. 'I told Louise about Augusta.' Louise saw that same dark cloud cross Vito's face and his eyes drop, and she felt she had to say something.

'I'm so, so sorry, Vito. It must have been awful.'

They had to wait almost a minute before he replied. 'It was, it truly was.' He reached out and took a mouthful of wine. 'Of course it was a long time ago, but some things you never forget.'

Annabelle reached across the table and caught hold of his hand. 'I'll never forget hearing the news that awful day either, but life has to go on. I'm pleased to hear that you've got a good job at Turin University. I'm so glad to know you're managing to make a fresh start.'

He nodded, but again took his time before replying. 'It hasn't been easy.'

'I can imagine. Oh, Vito, I'm so sorry for you.' The catch in Annabelle's voice probably wasn't doing much to raise his spirits and Louise wondered if she should try to lighten the atmosphere, but decided she didn't know either of them well enough to intrude. All of her instincts were screaming at her to get up and go over to envelop him in a warm, supportive hug, but she forced herself to sit back and observe.

Another long pause then ensued before he looked up from his glass. His eyes caught Louise's and she could read the emotion so near the surface within him. 'Can I ask you both a personal question? Have either of you ever been in love? I mean really in love?'

Louise was taken aback to hear him ask such an intimate question and she waited to hear what Annabelle had to say before speaking her piece. What Annabelle said was fascinating – more for what she didn't say.

'Yes, I think I have, in fact I am.'

'You *think* you are, or you are?' Vito's voice was husky.

Annabelle hesitated for a few moments. 'I am… well, I'm almost certain of it.' She glanced across at Louise. 'What about you, Louise? Did you love your boyfriend before it all went sour?'

Louise was helpless to stop the colour rushing to her face. 'I thought I did but now I'm not so sure, and not just because of how it ended.'

'How did it end?' Annabelle took a big swig of wine and Louise followed suit. This was moving her into sensitive waters.

'I found him in bed with another woman.'

'Oh good lord, how awful.' Annabelle looked appalled.

'Yes, it was but, to be honest, I now realise I didn't love him as much as I loved my university boyfriend from years ago.'

'And how did that finish?'

'He went to America. He chose his career over me.' Keen to get off the sad subject of her heartache of twelve years ago, Louise returned her attention to Vito. 'Why did you ask?'

'I was interested. I'm sure there are many differing degrees of affection from fondness to desire to obsession, but as far as I'm concerned, there's only one love. It's not divisible, it's an absolute: love is love.' There was a catch in his voice, which elicited a movement from underneath the table. Louise saw the dog's head appear, big brown eyes directed at his master as he laid a big hairy paw on Vito's thigh in a sign of support. This didn't quite produce a smile on Vito's face, but it did soften his expression. 'And once you've experienced it, you know you'll never experience it again.' He looked up again as he stroked the dog's head. 'I'm fine nowadays, at least physically, but I know I'll never have that chance again. I know what true love is and it was wonderful, but as far as I'm concerned it can never be repeated.'

'Oh, Vito…' Annabelle was still hanging on to his hand. 'You mustn't think like that. Just because you loved and lost doesn't mean you can't love again.'

'I beg to differ.' He took a deep breath. 'But, look, I really am fine. My career's taken off, I've got a full bank account, I've got my best friend in all the world here with his nose on my leg, I'm in the company of two beautiful women and, in answer to your original question, I'm doing well.'

And that was the most they managed to get out of him. Louise listened as Annabelle gradually got him talking about mutual friends, events they had attended and things that had happened, but all the time she kept turning over in her head what he had said about having experienced true love and knowing that he would never have that chance again. There was something so desperately sad about this – for him of course but also, just maybe, for her as well.

At almost ten o'clock he stood up and excused himself, pointing to the dog who, he said, needed a walk. Leo by this time was sprawled across Louise's feet, snoring noisily, and certainly didn't look in urgent need of a walk, but she knew Vito well enough by now to understand that he had to get away and be by himself. After Annabelle had hugged him again and kissed him on the cheeks, Louise couldn't resist doing the same. If he was surprised, he didn't show it. He just gave them both a hint of a smile and left with his dog. Louise and Annabelle sat back down again and looked at each other. Annabelle was the first to speak.

'I don't know about you, but I could do with another coffee and maybe something a bit stronger than a coffee.'

'They have just the thing.' Louise called Graziella over and asked for two more espresso coffees and two glasses of grappa. After Graziella had gone off, Annabelle raised her eyebrows.

'Grappa? Isn't that firewater? I always thought it was the kind of stuff that can blow your head off.'

Louise gave her a smile. 'That's what I thought, too, and some of it can be, but not Grappa del Grand Hotel. Ernesto has his own still and makes the stuff by hand, the old-fashioned way. He's shown me how he does it. It's all copper pipes and cauldrons. It's like watching a medieval alchemist at work. See what you think.'

They drank their coffees and sipped the grappa – which was met with definite approval from Annabelle – but studiously avoided talking about Vito. They discussed work matters for a while before Annabelle took the conversation in a different direction. The Grappa del Grand Hotel they were drinking probably helped to loosen her tongue.

'Louise, can I ask how old you are?'

Louise looked up in surprise. 'Yes, of course. I'm thirty-two, thirty-three pretty soon. Why do you ask?'

'I've been thinking about what you were saying; you know, about taking time out from men.' She took another sip of grappa. 'You see, that's pretty much what I've been doing. My job's been my life, really.'

This was sounding familiar to Louise. 'You and me both.'

'The thing is, I'm thirty-six now and I think it's time I made a change.'

'You're not thinking about leaving the company, are you? You'd be a massive loss to Joseph and to all of us.'

'That's sweet of you, Louise, but no, I'm not thinking about a change of job. I'm thinking it might be time for a relationship.'

'And does this mean you have a suitable man lined up, the man you said you might be in love with?'

'Yes, but this is where it gets tricky.' She took another sip of grappa and Louise could see she was looking and sounding uncharacteristically insecure.

'Want to tell me what the problem is?'

And that was the moment the conversation took a weird turn.

'You see... it's somebody I work with. I like him a lot and I'm terrified what might happen if I say something to him and it turns out he doesn't feel the same way about me. It could all get awkward.'

This time it was Louise who reached for her grappa. Annabelle had just used almost exactly the same words Joseph had used when talking about his feelings for some unnamed woman. Suddenly she began to see a connection and realised how it all made sense. Joseph hadn't been making veiled advances towards *her* – he really had been talking about somebody else. Of course, Annabelle was a much more logical and suitable partner for him than she was. How stupid she'd been to assume he might be interested in her. She followed the grappa with a sip of coffee and took her time over swallowing it. Finally she decided to take the bull by the horns.

'Don't answer if you don't want to, and I promise not to tell a soul if you do. This man... is it Joseph?'

Annabelle glanced around before answering as if afraid to be overheard 'Yes, but please don't breathe a word of this to him or to anybody else.'

Louise reached across and gave her hand a gentle squeeze. 'I promise. And here's a secret in return. When Joseph was here the other week, we had a conversation.' She saw Annabelle straighten up, ears pricked. 'He said the exact same thing to me. He told me he liked somebody he worked with a lot – he pretty much said it had been love at first sight – but he didn't dare speak to her as he was terrified he might lose her if it turned out she didn't feel the same way about him. I didn't know who he was talking about at the time but of course it now makes sense.' Ever more convinced, she looked across the table at Annabelle. 'He must have been talking about you.'

'There are lots of women in the company, and lots of them are younger and more attractive than me.' Louise could tell that Annabelle was deliberately trying not to jump to conclusions or to get her hopes up.

'I would question that. You're an attractive woman. Seriously, I've always thought that. You're always immaculately turned out and I'd kill to have your lovely hair. I know everyone in the company admires you. You've got so much going for you; the more I think about it, the more convinced I am that Joseph was talking about you.'

To give Annabelle time to get her thoughts in order, she deliberately took another slow sip of coffee, wondering what was going through Annabelle's head. As far as she was concerned, she was feeling more and more certain that Joseph had indeed been talking about his Head of Operations and she hoped it was true. Apart from bringing happiness to Annabelle, this would, of course, remove the doubts she had been harbouring ever since that infamous dinner. Of course, she wasn't the first woman in the world to misinterpret a man's advances, but looking back on it, she should have realised that Annabelle was a far more logical and obvious choice. There was just one big problem – and she had unwittingly caused it.

'The thing is, Annabelle, that bit of advice I gave him – you know, the advice he asked you to thank me for – was to take it slow and wait for the woman to make the first move. So what I've gone and done is to make things even trickier for you. If only I'd told him to go for it, you'd know where you stand by now.'

Annabelle shook her head and even managed a little smile. 'No, please don't worry, I'm sure I'd have given the same advice. Thanks for telling me what Joseph said and I promise I won't say a word to him or to anybody. I'm still not convinced I am the woman he's interested in, which means I'm still faced with the dilemma of whether to speak to him or not.'

'All very Shakespearian. I'll tell you something else in the strictest confidence. The manager here, Domenica, is in a similar situation to yours. She's in love with Calogero.' She kept her voice low and nodded across to where Calogero was standing by the entrance to the kitchen, keeping a weather eye on all the tables, including theirs. 'The thing is, she feels she can't tell him for fear of screwing up a working relationship and a friendship that's lasted for over a quarter of a century.'

At that moment Calogero himself came across to ask if they wanted anything else and inclined his head towards Annabelle. 'Was the meal to your satisfaction, signora?' His English accent was pretty good and Louise gave him an encouraging wink as Annabelle replied.

'That was wonderful, thank you, Calogero. Please thank the chef. It's all been excellent.' She glanced across at Louise. 'I'm not sure I've got the energy to get up from the table.' Once Calogero had gone off to relay the good news to Luigino in the kitchen, she gave Louise a weary look. 'An excellent meal in a lovely hotel but it still doesn't get me any closer to knowing what to do.' She mustered a weak smile. 'Love can be so complicated, can't it?'

Chapter 19

It was as they were driving back down to the station next morning that Annabelle said something that almost made Louise run off the road.

'Last night, you know you asked me if I liked Joseph? Well, can I ask you a similar question? Do you like Vito? I mean *really* like Vito.'

Louise waited until she had got past a tractor and trailer occupying most of the country road before replying.

'You gave me an honest answer so I'll do the same. Yes, I like him a lot. Why do you ask? Was it that obvious?'

'I wouldn't say it was obvious. I mean, you weren't drooling all over the table or anything, but there was just something in the way you looked at him. How well did you say you know him?'

'I suppose the truth is that I don't know him very well at all. I've had a mug of tea with him on one occasion and a glass of wine on another but neither lasted for more than half an hour. I've chatted to him a couple of times when we've met up while walking in the woods, but up until last night I probably hadn't spent more than an hour or so in his company.' She glanced across at Annabelle. 'Sort of the opposite of you and Joseph. If you add it up, you've probably spent weeks if not months one-to-one with Joseph, haven't you? But tell me, this attraction you feel for Joseph, has it gradually crept up on you or did you know from the start?'

'I've been asking myself the same thing, ever since you told me he said he'd known from day one that he was in love with this mystery woman.'

'The mystery woman's you. The more I think about it, the more convinced I am.'

'Whatever… but the answer to your question's probably yes. I think I did know from day one but, because he was my boss, the last thing I wanted was for things to become awkward between us so I've stifled it for years now. Anyway, returning to you and Vito, do you think he likes you?'

'I'd like to believe he does, but I don't think there's any more to it than simple friendship as far as he's concerned.'

'Well, if it helps, I think you're wrong. When I wasn't watching you last night I was watching him and, for my money, I think I saw something there.'

'Says the woman who can't tell if the man she's worked with for years loves her or not.'

'Touché. I may be wrong but I don't think I am.'

'You know something, Annabelle? I'm beginning to get the feeling you and I have more in common than either of us thought.'

When Louise dropped her off at Turin's main Porta Nuova station she was genuinely sorry to see her go. Would Annabelle have the courage to talk to Joseph or would their feelings just lie dormant? As a backstop, she suggested Annabelle should come over for the re-launch party at the beginning of July so that both she and Joseph could be together in a more social setting. Maybe a few glasses of Barbera del Grand Hotel might be enough to get them talking. Mind you, she thought to herself as she drove back to the hotel through the Saturday morning traffic, she wasn't that different: knowing she was developing feelings for Vito but not wanting to voice them as he had made it clear the only woman for him was dead.

Back at the hotel, after a stop to confirm the order of the tiles for the bathrooms, she was greeted by a call from the man himself. She came in through the front door to see Domenica at the reception desk, beckoning with one hand. In her other hand was the phone.

'It's Vito. He wants to speak to you.'

Louise took the phone. 'Ciao, Vito. I've just come back from taking Annabelle to the station. It was good to see you last night.'

'Louise, yes, it was…' He sounded troubled, quite abrupt. 'Listen, have you told anybody what we were talking about last night… about what happened to Augusta?'

Louise glanced up and saw that Domenica had gone off to do something in the back office. 'I've only talked to Annabelle.'

'Good.' There was relief in his voice. 'Look, if you don't mind, would you just keep that to yourself?'

'Of course, I promise.' She was tempted to ask why, but he supplied the answer for her.

'Thank you… You see, like I said, I think of the people up there at the hotel, particularly Domenica, as family and I know she'd be upset to hear what happened. It's all in the past now and it'll serve no purpose apart from saddening her if you tell her, so thanks for keeping it a secret.'

'You can count on me. And, Vito, once again, I'm so terribly sorry for you. If you ever want a shoulder to cry on, you only have to shout.'

'Thanks, Louise.' His voice almost cracked. 'You're a good friend. Ciao.' And he rang off.

Louise set the phone back down and went up to her room, her mind filled with thoughts of this unfortunate man who should have had it all – brains, good looks and a fortune – only to find himself plunged into deep depression by the deaths not only of both his parents but of the woman he truly loved. She couldn't help reflecting on his choice of vocabulary. He had called her a good friend but she knew she would like to be more to him than that.

–

The next day, at Domenica's suggestion she drove down to Casale Monferrato for the monthly antiques fair. This bustling commercial town was situated at the foot of the Monferrato hills, alongside the river Po, and it was swarming with people. She parked in the centre, close to the massive defensive walls of the old castle, and followed the crowds to the antiques market. Her main reason for coming was to see if she could find a couple of nice old paintings for the hotel lounge but her eye was immediately drawn to a number of stalls selling vintage clothing. Among the whalebone corsets, hats with veils, moth-eaten furs and lace-trimmed blouses, she discovered an absolutely charming long evening dress. It was made of shot silk and shimmered between red and black, depending on the light, and she loved it.

She had just one long dress that got brought out each year for the staff Christmas party, but she had left it back in London. Since Joseph had specified the re-launch party on the Saturday night should be a formal black-tie event she decided to buy this dress and hope it would fit. She held it up against her body, thanked the stallholder but rejected his offer to go and try it on in the back of his van, fairly certain it was going to be close to her size. If it didn't fit, she felt sure Domenica would be able to point her in the direction of a good seamstress to make the necessary alterations.

Altogether she spent two hours and quite a lot of money at the market and had to make several trips back and forth to the car to deposit her purchases. Finally, just before lunchtime, she decided enough was enough and went for a stroll through the town. Although the outskirts had been quite industrial, here in the narrow streets of the centre it was most pleasant. The architecture was more baroque than medieval but she knew from her research on the internet that hundreds of years ago Casale had been far more important than its present incarnation. She wandered around, stopping off to visit the cathedral with its two tall, slim bell towers, before entering the main square which was a charming mix of styles and colours.

After a while she started to feel hungry so she found a seat at a table outside on the cobbles, looking across at the magnificent statue of one of the early kings of Piedmont on his horse. May was starting out warmer than average and she was glad of the awning to keep the midday sun off her head as she nibbled a focaccia sandwich and sipped her ice-cold mineral water. A few minutes later her phone started to vibrate.

'*Pronto.*'

'Hi, Louise, it's me.'

'Paolo? How are you?' He was speaking English this time and she hardly recognised his voice at first. Once upon a time her heart would have skipped a beat, but not now. Was this just a question of the passing of the years or was it because somebody else now occupied the top spot in her affections?

'Okay, I guess.' His American accent heightened the sense of unfamiliarity. 'Katharine and I are taking a break.'

'What does that mean? Just a few days apart, or full-blooded separation?'

'Trial separation I guess you could call it. I've moved out.' Apart from the accent, his voice was sounding strange.

'But not permanently?'

'Who knows? What do you think? Would you like it to be permanent?' He sounded exhausted and was slurring his words together.

Conscious that she might be running the risk of getting sucked into the middle of their marital strife, she searched for a way of staying out of it without making him any more unhappy. From his tone, he was obviously feeling low. 'This is nothing to do with me, Paolo. It's a matter for the two of you. You need to get yourselves sorted out. I presume you didn't go for counselling like I suggested?' She heard him snort with derision but she persevered. 'You should, you know. It might help.'

'But it's you that I want…' The plaintive, whining note was so unusual the penny suddenly dropped and made her realise what was wrong with his voice – he sounded drunk.

'Paolo, have you been drinking?'

'You're damn right I have.'

Louise glanced at her watch and did a bit of quick calculation. It was lunchtime here but Denver was something like eight or nine hours behind which meant it was the small hours of the morning over there. 'Have you been up all night?'

'Mmmh…'

She took that as a yes. 'Then you need to get some sleep. Where are you?'

'Motel.'

'Then turn the light off and go to sleep. Things will look a lot better after you've had a good rest.'

'It's you I want, Louise… really.'

'Just get some sleep. We can talk another time. Go to bed. Right?'

'Right… love you, Louise…'

Mercifully the line finally went dead and she dropped her phone back on the table, picked up her glass and took a big swig of her drink, rather wishing she had opted for something alcoholic. To say her thoughts were swirling was to understate the confusion she felt. Part of her felt genuinely sorry for him, while part was still processing the fact that he had been drinking. Hearing him like this and imagining him in a seedy motel room aroused a feeling of pity, but along with it was something else and she struggled to analyse what this might be.

It took her a while before she realised it was something approaching disdain. This man was very different from the boy she had once loved. Of course he was going through a hard time, but she didn't like the thought of what he had become. One thing was for sure; Vito or no Vito, she no longer felt that same powerful attraction to Paolo. He had sounded like a completely different person and even if he were to emerge from his unsuccessful marriage somehow unscathed, one thing was for sure: he was no longer the man for her.

She sat there alone for some time, finally remembering her sandwich and picking it back up again. While she finished her lunch she looked around and breathed deeply, feeling surprisingly happy in spite of everything. There was something about being back in Italy. The sun was shining, she was sitting in a charming spot, she was living in a delightful place in the midst of countryside that was becoming ever more familiar to her, and she loved all of it. She watched a couple of little kids chasing a poodle who, in turn, was chasing a flock of pigeons across the square. People strolled past arm in arm, cycled across the piazza on battered old bikes, pushed prams, walked their dogs, or just stood and chatted. There was a warm, friendly atmosphere here and, for the first time she really began to have serious doubts about her hitherto unswerving career path. Maybe a life that saw her jetting off all over the place wasn't the be all and end all. Maybe what she needed was to settle down and escape to the country. Why not put down roots somewhere like this?

Chapter 20

Over the next days she received several phone calls from Paolo; at first to apologise for calling her when he was drunk, but then attempting to convince her that she should consider getting back together with him. As tactfully and kindly – but also firmly – as possible she did her best to get the message across to him that that ship had sailed. She had moved on and the best thing for him and his wife to do would be to seek professional help. He still didn't appear to get it but at least the calls dried up. The recurring thought going through her head was that Silvana's wedding was coming up in little more than a month. He had said he might come over for the event and, if he did, she had a sinking feeling his presence might spoil it for her.

May wore on and she found she had less and less free time as the various builders and tradesmen began to appear as promised. Soon the front of the hotel was festooned with scaffolding and a digger was excavating a trench all the way along the length of the building. At the side of the hotel an even bigger digger was preparing the site for the swimming pool while indoors the whole of the second floor was closed off while plumbers, tilers and decorators set about the renovations. She managed to fit in a quick walk most days but saw no sign of either Vito or his lovely dog and she knew she was missing them.

Then, one Friday night, she was surprised – and delighted – to see the two of them walk into the dining room as she was sitting down to eat. Only two other tables were occupied – Domenica had been right about May being a quiet month – and Louise was planning on having a peaceful dinner while reading the final chapters of Vito's book. She waved to attract their attention and gained an immediate response, not so much from him as from his dog. As Leo spotted her he came charging over and did his best to climb onto her lap, emitting little yelps of delight. He was followed by his master who did not, however, attempt to climb onto her lap.

'Leo, get off. I'm sorry, Louise. He obviously likes you.'

She looked up from the dog and beamed. 'And I like him too. How are you, Vito? I haven't seen you for a while. Have you come to eat? Would you like to join me? I'm just reading some random book I found.' She saw his eyes register what she was reading and a hint of a smile appeared on his face.

'I hope you aren't getting too bored with it. I've just been talking to Domenica about a problem that's come up and, yes, I have come to eat, but I don't want to disturb you.'

'You aren't disturbing me in the slightest, either of you.' By this time Leo had finally calmed down and was sitting at her side, his big hairy head resting on her lap. 'Do join me. I'd like that a lot.'

'Well, if you're sure…' He sat down opposite her and she did her best not to flush as she felt his eyes on her.

'Did Domenica manage to sort out your problem?'

'Yes, with the help of Calogero and Luigino. It's about a formal dinner. I've been asked to give an after-dinner talk to the Piedmont Conservation Society.' He gave her a little smile. 'There really is such a thing. This year's spring dinner is scheduled for the twenty-third of this month and it was supposed to take place in a lovely old castle just on the other side of Turin but there's been a disaster. Part of the ceiling of the banqueting hall has collapsed and all events have been cancelled. I've been asking Domenica if it might be possible to do it here. It's in just ten days' time so it's very short notice but they've all said yes and I'm mightily relieved, as is the president of the society. I've just come off the phone to him now.'

'Excellent. I'll put it in my diary. How many people are you expecting?'

'Around a hundred or so. The president will confirm final numbers next week.'

'That's great news. It'll provide a valuable rehearsal for our big re-launch event at the beginning of July.' She smiled at him. 'I'll sneak in and listen to your talk if you don't mind. What's the subject going to be?'

He smiled back and she was delighted to see him looking and sounding quite relaxed. 'The end of the world.' Seeing the expression on her face, his smile broadened. 'I know it's not exactly a cheerful after-dinner topic but unless we can cut right back on the use of fossil fuels, by the end of the century the global temperature will have risen by between three and five degrees. That may not sound like much, but the ensuing rise in sea levels will kill off animals, plants and humans all over the globe and destroy many low-lying islands forever. It's already happening in places like Fiji and the Solomon Islands...' He suddenly stopped in mid-flow. 'I'm sorry, Louise, when I get started, it's hard to stop me. Just give me a slap next time.'

'I wouldn't dream of it. I think it's fascinating. I'm really looking forward to your talk.'

At that moment Calogero came over with the news that although there weren't any *crespelle* tonight, there was rabbit stew, and they both chose that along with a simple starter of *prosciutto* and melon. After he had gone off with their order, they sat in silence – but not an uncomfortable silence – for a few moments before Vito broke it.

'It looks as if the builders are getting on well.'

Louise was pleased to hear him restart the conversation unprompted and this emphasised the impression she had already got this evening that he was more relaxed in her company now. Maybe the meal with Annabelle had been a cathartic moment. She reeled off a list of all the refurbishment works currently being undertaken and answered his questions before settling back, relaxing and savouring the fact that he was opening up towards her. The food was excellent as ever and the meal was going well right up until just before the end. It was only as he set down his fork after a helping of Luigino's rabbit stew and polenta that the mood of the evening took a less hopeful turn.

'By the way, Louise, I'm going away for a while when this term ends.'

'Really, where to?' Suddenly the idea of losing him from her life was very real, and very unwelcome.

'To Brazil.'

'Brazil?' She was just finishing her last mouthful of stew and she almost choked, having to take a big swig of water before she could carry on. 'What on earth for?' Although she felt sure she already knew the answer – his job. She was right.

'To join an international team of scientists who're working to try to stop the destruction of the Amazon rain forest. Over the last fifty years, twenty per cent of the jungle has disappeared and many of its indigenous plant and animal species – and human inhabitants – with it. An area the equivalent of thirty football fields of rain forest is disappearing every single day.'

'That's terrible for the whole planet. And how long will you be away?'

'The second half of June and the whole of July – six weeks. I need to be back in August to prepare for the autumn term.'

She took a mouthful of Barbera del Grand Hotel and let it run slowly down her throat. The middle of June was barely a month away. She was going to miss him a lot. 'And what about Leo? You can't take him with you. He might get eaten by an anaconda or something.'

She saw him smile. 'More likely by piranhas. You know him – he'd head straight for the river. No, he's staying here. I'm going to start asking around to see if I can find somebody to come and stay in my house and look after him. If not, then I know Domenica will take him.'

'I wonder…' It occurred to Louise that she would be here in June anyway and, as far as July was concerned, she actually had quite a bit of unused holiday entitlement. She had been saving it up since last year as the original plan had been for her to go off with Tommy for a long break together this summer. Clearly that wasn't going to happen now, and she did a bit of quick thinking. She might just be able to manage it. It all depended on what plans Joseph had for her when she finished here. 'If you can give me a couple of days to talk to my boss, I think I might be able to do that for you. I just need to check that there isn't some urgent job for me straight after this but I think I should be able to take the month of July off and look after Leo for you. I know I'll be here for all of June and the first few days of July so I can definitely move into your house when you go off and I'd be happy to keep an eye on that plus the dog until our big re-launch event, but the more I think about it, I reckon I should be good for the full six weeks.'

'You'd do that for me?' He sounded quite touched.

'For you, for Leo, and for myself. I've grown to love it here and the idea of a few weeks lazing about with your lovely dog in the middle of the countryside really appeals. I mean that.' The only downside to this arrangement would be the thousands of miles that would be separating her from the dog's master.

'Well, that would be great, thank you so much, but I don't want to put you to any trouble...'

'You won't be and I can't imagine a nicer place to spend my summer holiday. It's been a tough year... for all kinds of reasons.'

'I was sorry to hear about your break-up. That must have been brutal.'

'It was tough, but not as tough as what you've had to go through.'

She saw his face fall but, fortunately, at that moment Calogero arrived with their desserts of zabaglione with crushed amaretti and provided a welcome interruption. After clearing away their dishes he revealed that the chef tonight had not been Luigino after all.

'I hope everything was up to standard.' He smiled in response to their enthusiastic nods. 'You see, Luigino couldn't come in today as he and his wife had to go to a funeral in Pisa, so tonight's meal has been cooked by my daughter.'

'Graziella made dinner?' Louise was surprised and impressed. 'I knew she helped out in the kitchen but I hadn't realised she was such a talented chef.'

'Since her mother died, Graziella's done all the cooking for Rodolfo and me at home and she's always up here at Luigino's side, learning from him – and he's a wonderful teacher. He wouldn't have left her in charge if he hadn't been confident she was up to the task.'

In spite of her concerns over Vito's impending departure from her life, Louise switched back to business mode for a moment as she realised that this might solve a fairly fundamental problem she and Domenica had been facing. With the anticipated increase in guest numbers, Luigino was going to need sous-chefs in the kitchen. If one of these could be somebody he knew and trusted – and who could produce such excellent food – it would be a terrific solution and she resolved to talk it over with Domenica in the morning. She glanced down at the dessert.

'And did she make this?'

'She did indeed. I hope you enjoy it. *Buon appetito.*'

Louise didn't look up until she had tried a couple of mouthfuls of zabaglione. It was exquisite.

'This is a really good dessert. What do you think, Vito?'

She was relieved to see him once more looking quite relaxed.

'Absolutely excellent. I knew Graziella could cook but I didn't realise she was this good.'

'I think a position in the kitchen might just be about to open up for her.' As Calogero went back to the kitchen Louise swallowed her food and took a mouthful of Barbera del Grand Hotel before returning to the subject of his upcoming trip.

'So tell me about Brazil. Will you be camping in the jungle or living in a hotel?'

'A bit of both, I believe. Part of what we're doing is trying to support the indigenous tribes and I'm sure that'll involve a certain amount of travelling around.'

'Well, you just be careful. I wouldn't want you to be eaten by an anaconda either.'

This actually brought a twinkle to his eye. 'And neither would I. They say most snakes are more afraid of you than you are of them, but try telling that to a constrictor the length of the Rolls Royce.'

'Ugh!' Louise shivered at the thought. 'I'm going to miss you.' No sooner had the words come out of her mouth than she regretted yet again making a comment that had come out sounding way too personal. To her relief, however, he appeared untroubled and, to her even greater surprise, produced an unexpected response.

'I'm going to miss you, too.'

After which he dropped his eyes and concentrated on finishing his dessert while she struggled to work out the extent to which this might have been any sort of declaration of affection from him. Unfortunately, he then went on to spend the remaining minutes talking about endangered species and disappearing biodiversity and steadfastly kept the conversation off anything of a personal nature.

Until right at the end.

He swallowed the last of his espresso, glanced down at the sleeping dog for a second or two and then surprised her with an invitation. 'You were saying you might quite like to listen to the talk I'll be giving at the Conservation Society dinner. I was wondering – if you aren't going to be working that evening – maybe you might like to join me at the top table.' For such a handsome man he was looking and sounding remarkably insecure. 'But only if you'd like to.'

'Are you sure? Won't I be in the way of all you environmentalists?'

'No, of course not. Most of the others will have their partners with them...' Before she had a chance to reflect on his choice of vocabulary he threw in a hasty addition. 'Or friends, of course.'

Doing her best not to sound too eager, she accepted willingly. 'Then I'd love to, thanks.' A thought occurred to her. 'What should I wear? It's not long dresses and diamond tiaras, is it?'

This drew a little smile from him. 'Whatever you like, though I suppose I'll have to wear a suit or maybe a tuxedo.' She saw him hesitate for a moment. 'If you turn up dressed like you were when Annabelle was here you'll be the most beautiful woman in the room.'

Now that, surely, sounded like flirting.

Didn't it?

Chapter 21

'That sounds to me like flirting.'

'I'm not so sure, mum. You should have seen him. No sooner had he said it than he jumped up and disappeared into the night with his dog. It was almost as if he regretted saying it. He didn't even shake hands with me.'

'Well, all right, maybe not outright flirting, but it's a pretty clear sign he likes you, isn't it?'

'I suppose so...'

Louise had phoned her mother shortly after Vito and Leo left and, with the help of a small glass of Ernesto's grappa, was still trying to get her head around the implications of his invitation to the dinner as well as his trip to Brazil. She had yet to contact Joseph to check that he would be happy to let her stay on here for the month of July, but she felt quietly confident that the answer would be yes. Living in the beautiful old mill with the lovely dog promised to be a wonderful way of spending her holiday – and her birthday which was coming up on the seventeenth of July – although the knowledge that Vito would now only be here for a few more weeks had come as a definite blow. Nothing had happened between them, apart from a budding friendship and an invitation to the conservation society dinner, and the mid-June deadline would be upon her before she knew it. Her mother was quick to point that out.

'It's such a pity he's going off so soon. I suppose that means the chances of you two developing a meaningful relationship are looking less and less likely.'

'Afraid so. I know he's still hung up on his poor fiancée, but there was probably a part of me that was hoping against hope he might change.' She gazed blindly across the now empty dining room. 'To be perfectly honest, I've been having a recurring dream about him turning up unexpectedly at the re-launch party in his tuxedo, looking amazing. I'm there in that antique silk dress I told you about, feeling like a princess, and there's a Cinderella moment on the dance floor with him, but of course that's now a forlorn hope.' She did her best to rally – as much for her mum's sake as for her own. 'That was only a pipedream. It was never going to happen.'

'If you say so, dear. Maybe this dinner date with him will be the shove in your direction he needs.'

'It's not a date, mum. It's just so I can listen to his talk. Besides, in a matter of weeks we'll be separated and that'll be that.'

By the time Louise put the phone down she was no nearer knowing whether he had intended it as a date but it had been reassuring to be able to talk to her mum about it. Two days later she was also able to recount recent developments to Silvana and receive more reassurance, accompanied by a call to action. They met again in their regular cafe in the centre of Turin and Silvana listened impassively to Louise's account before responding.

'It's a date, I'm sure of it. After all, why ask you to sit at the top table with him when you both know you could come and listen from the back of the room anyway. No, it's a date.'

'I'm not so sure…'

'Well, I am.' A glint appeared in Silvana's eye. 'Listen; Davide and I've been talking. We've just had a reply from Paolo, saying he'll be coming to our wedding on his own.' Spotting the expression of horror on Louise's face, she was quick to offer a solution. 'After what you've told me, I'm assuming you don't want to be partnered with him, so how would it be if we invited Vito?' Seeing the expression of surprise on Louise's face she was quick to elaborate. 'Like Davide told you, he and Vito used to be close friends and it's only since Vito went off to London that they lost touch. Anyway, we were thinking that maybe if we invited him, the two of you could come together and that would provide you with a bulwark against Paolo but also would throw you and Vito closer together. And you know what they say about weddings…' She added a knowing wink just in case Louise might have failed to catch her drift.

Louise couldn't help grinning. 'It's no coincidence that Machiavelli was Italian. Have you ever considered giving up medicine and taking up full-time scheming and plotting? I reckon you could have world domination sewn up in a matter of months.'

Silvana looked undeterred. 'Well, what do you think of that as a plan? Like I say, this would kill two birds with one stone by keeping one man away while bringing you closer to the one you want. Weddings are romantic events so maybe it might provoke some sort of reaction in him…'

Louise swallowed a mouthful of delicious *stracciatella* and white chocolate ice cream before beaming across the table at her friend. 'I think it's a great idea but only if it isn't going to throw your planning out.'

'No, it'll be fine. In fact, if we can sit you with him rather than on your own it'll make for an even number on your table and the seating plan gets easier for me. As for

Paolo, my cousin Loredana will be coming on her own and she's got a track record of drinking too much and groping whoever she's sat beside, so If I stick her with Paolo, that should help your cause even more.' Louise saw her reach into her bag and produce an envelope. 'I was hoping you'd agree so I'm one step ahead of you. Here's the invitation for Vito. I thought it might be a good idea if you were to deliver it to him in person.'

'You're wasted as a surgeon, Silvana. Thank you so much.' Louise took the envelope but then had a sudden thought. 'I just hope he'll still be here. He said he was going off to Brazil for the second half of June and your wedding's on the fourteenth. That's cutting it pretty fine.'

With that thought in mind, the next day Louise picked up the invitation and set off through the fields to the old mill. Although it was late afternoon, the sky was clear blue and the May sun hot enough to make her grateful she had thought to apply sunscreen. By now there were wild flowers everywhere and the edges of the recently ploughed fields were laced with bright red poppies. Birds were nesting in the trees and somewhere a cuckoo was calling. She breathed deeply, delighted to have received confirmation from Joseph that she would be able to take the month of July off – immediately after the re-launch party – and enjoy a few weeks of R&R here in these charming surroundings. Yet again she couldn't help reflecting that this place was growing on her and it would be a real wrench to leave – not just because of the people she would be saying goodbye to.

Down by the river she met Beppe mending a hole in the perimeter fence, and sprawled in the long grass alongside him was a familiar black shape. Leo spotted her, jumped up and came charging over to say hello. Louise greeted him warmly, knowing that it wasn't just the place and the people she was going to miss. She made a fuss of the dog and then looked up at Beppe.

'Hello, Beppe. Isn't it a beautiful day?'

He smiled. 'On a day like this, Louise, who needs to fly halfway around the world for a holiday? I love it here.'

'And so do I.' Louise glanced down at the dog who was now stretched out on his back at her feet, paws in the air as his tail swept the leaves beneath him. 'Is Vito about?'

'I'm pretty sure he's at home. I heard the sound of somebody chopping wood down at the old mill.'

'Great, I've got a letter for him. *Arrivederci.*'

Louise, now accompanied by the dog, went out through the side gate onto the track and headed for the mill. As she got closer, she started to hear the unmistakable sound of an axe on wood. She went in through the gateway and followed the dog around to the back of the house where she was presented with the spectacle of Vito splitting firewood. He was stripped to the waist, the sweat glistening on his naked torso, and she genuinely had to stop and swallow hard before approaching. She also had to struggle to restrain herself from jumping all over him like his Labrador as a wave of what could only be lust swept over her.

Clearing her throat, she announced her arrival. 'Hi, Vito, I've got something for you.' She waved the envelope at him.

'Louise, ciao. It's good to see you.' With a practised movement he swung the axe in a glittering arc so that it thudded firmly into the chopping block, and then walked across to greet her, apparently unaware of the effect his appearance was having on her. 'What's this? Are you acting as postman today?'

'It's from Silvana and Davide. I saw her yesterday and she gave it to me to pass on to you.'

'You know them?' He took the envelope from her and opened it. After reading the card he looked across at her. 'Can I ask how come you know them?'

Louise told him about how they had met while she was doing her year abroad and she saw him nod.

'It's a small world, isn't it? I've known Davide ever since we were kids. I'm so happy they're getting married. I don't know Silvana quite so well but she always struck me as a bright girl.'

'Oh, she's bright all right.' Louise didn't go into details – without Silvana's machinations she probably wouldn't be standing here now. As it was, she had to make a concerted effort to tear her eyes away from a drop of perspiration she had been watching as it ran slowly down over the muscles of Vito's hairy chest towards his ribbed stomach. She refocused, blinked a couple of times, and did her best to sound normal. 'Are you going to be able to come? I'm invited and I thought maybe we could sort of go together… you know, just for company.'

Maybe he picked up something in her tone or maybe it was just natural modesty but he turned and reached for a T-shirt, pulling it on before replying. She couldn't help feeling disappointed.

'I'd like to but I need to double check my flight times. Have you got time for a cup of tea or a glass of wine?'

'I'd love a cup of tea if I'm not dragging you away from your work. By the way I also came to say that I've heard back from my boss and it's okay for me to stay on until the end of July, so if you still need a house- and dog-sitter, I'm all yours.' The better she got to know him, the more convinced she was becoming that she really meant those last three words.

'That's wonderful.' It was clear that he was simply referring to her offer to look after the house and the dog and she repressed a little sigh as he carried on. 'Thank you so much.'

The kitchen was once again cluttered with dirty dishes so, when he disappeared off to look for the air ticket, she set about washing them. When he returned he looked embarrassed and remonstrated with her but she shook her head. 'You make the tea. I'll do the dishes. Besides, it's a good idea for me to familiarise myself with where everything is, seeing as I'm going to be staying here. And I need to know all about Leo and his diet, although I somehow get the impression he isn't a fussy eater.'

'He's a Labrador, what do you think? He'd eat himself to death if he had the chance. Believe it or not, he's a vegetarian. He may not realise it, but the food I give him is plant-based.'

'He doesn't eat meat?'

'Don't get me wrong; if I gave him a joint of beef he'd wolf it down, but I try to keep him on a sensible diet that's good for him, and for the planet.' He smiled at her from close range as he leant across her to fill the kettle. He was so close she could smell him and she did her best not to let a gormless, dreamy expression appear on her face. 'He's at an age when he needs to think of his figure. Like me, for that matter.'

'You've got a super figure… I mean body… shape. You know what I mean.' Even the dog was probably aware of her glowing cheeks by the time she stumbled to the end of this little speech and she could have snorted with frustration. Talk about behaving like a teenager…

'Thank you for the compliment. Coming from you that means something.' She glanced across at him and caught his eyes on her body. This did nothing to reduce her blushes. 'You look amazing, Louise.'

Fortunately he then disappeared from her view as he prepared the tea and she had a chance to get her head down, concentrate on the dirty dishes, and reflect that her schoolgirl comments appeared to have resulted in a positive reaction from him after all. His voice interrupted her musings.

'My flight to Brazil departs from Rome on Monday the sixteenth in the late afternoon and I'm on the lunch-time flight out of Turin airport that day to pick up the connection.'

'So you'll still be here on the fourteenth. Does that mean you'll be coming to the wedding?' She waited anxiously for his reply, fearing yet another comment along the lines of 'I don't socialise much'. To her delight, he didn't prevaricate this time.

'If you're going to be there to keep me company, I'll go.'

Louise felt her heart soar. 'That's great news. I was dreading being on my own.'

'Will you know many of the other guests?'

'Some of them, yes. I met up with a number of them again shortly after I first arrived here before Easter.' Louise had a sinking feeling. Although several weeks had passed since the last time Paolo had called her from the US, the fact that he would be at the wedding on his own, like Silvana had said, meant she was going to find herself with both men in the same room at the same time. It was a daunting prospect, to say the least. Her voice tailed off lamely. 'It'll be nice to catch up with everybody again.'

Chapter 22

The Piedmont Conservation Society dinner was unexpectedly glitzy and Louise was glad she had pressed her faithful old Dior dress into service once more. She stood alongside Domenica at the reception desk watching the guests arrive, calculating that if even half the sparkling jewels on display were real, the event would present a tempting target for a gang of opportunist thieves — assuming they could navigate their way through the tortuous lanes to get here and away again.

Vito had arrived half an hour earlier in the company of two other men and had barely had time to give her a little smile and a wave before being led into the lounge where he was still deep in conversation with a group of what were presumably fellow conservationists. It had not escaped Louise's attention that a number of these were young, female and clustered suspiciously closely around him. She glanced over at Domenica.

'I wasn't expecting to see so much opulence. I thought conservationists would be more rough and ready.'

Domenica smiled back at her. 'And I'm sure a lot of them are. The thing is, Vito told me this is really intended as a fundraising event, so a good number of the people you see here have been invited more for the thickness of their wallets rather than for their commitment to the cause.'

At that moment the clock struck eight and the sound of a gong reverberated through the building as Calogero emerged from the dining room to summon the guests to dinner. People gradually made their way through to their seats and Vito finally arrived at Louise's side. He was looking and sounding apologetic.

'Hi, Louise, sorry I haven't been able to stop and talk before but I've been rather monopolised. Anyway, hi, you look wonderful.' And then, to her considerable surprise – and no little pleasure – he leant forward and kissed her on the cheeks. '*Buona sera.*'

'*Buona sera a te, Vito.* You're looking very smart yourself.' She could have added a number of other adjectives from handsome to desirable but she didn't. Instead, she reached out and ran her hand down the sleeve of his dinner jacket, enjoying the feel of his arm within. 'Is this silk? It looks amazing.'

A thrill ran through her when he didn't pull his arm away. 'This, silk? I don't really know. Maybe, yes, I think so… I've had it for years. Anyway, ready to head in for dinner?'

'Lead the way.'

The dining room was filling up fast and the there was a hubbub of conversation all around. Up at the top table at the far end of the room Vito introduced Louise to various notables, including no fewer than three mayors of nearby towns sporting sashes of office, several regional councillors, the local member of parliament and even a distinguished-looking old gentleman with a mass of immaculately styled silver hair who was addressed as *Senatore*. After all, conservation was a hot political potato these days. It came as no surprise to find that nobody was introduced to her as *Signore* or *Signora*… Everybody was either *Dottore* or *Professore* or *Onorevole* or some other title. Vito introduced her to the assembled dignitaries and their partners as *Dottoressa* Rhodes – the normal Italian title for any female with a university degree – but did not specify their relationship. Louise hoped she wasn't going to be asked, because she didn't really know either.

Calogero himself was looking after the top table while Rodolfo and the usual extra helpers from the village were serving the other guests. He saw Louise sitting beside Vito and gave her a surreptitious wink and she felt her cheeks colour. The man sitting on the other side of her turned out to be the same august-looking professor who had introduced Vito to his audience at the talk she had attended some weeks back and he was soon chatting to her. He told her he was the head of the faculty and he had a high opinion of Vito.

'He's one of the university's rising stars. He goes off to conferences and events all over the world and does wonders for the prestige of the university. And what do you do, signora? Are you an academic?'

Louise explained her role in the company and their plans for the Grand Hotel and he appeared interested – not as interested, however, as the lady with the red hair sitting directly opposite. Unlike most of the other diners, this lady – maybe twenty years older than Louise – wasn't decked out in anything extravagant, wearing instead a simple, if attractive, dress with no jewellery.

'So does this mean you'll be living here now?'

Louise shook her head ruefully. 'No, I'm afraid not. My job takes me all over the world. I must say, though, the more time I spend here in the Monferrato the more comfortable I feel. Considering we're so close to Italy's industrial heartland it's remarkably natural and unspoilt here and the air's so fresh and clean.'

Particularly now that the dodgy drains had been fixed.

The lady across the table nodded in agreement. 'I was born just down the road in Asti and I've always loved this area. I knew I had to come back. I used to work for Greenpeace and that meant an awful lot of travelling. My work took me all over the globe from the Himalayas to Antarctica, but I finally felt the need to slow down and settle. Travelling the world's great, but so is putting down roots.' She caught hold of the hand of the bearded man alongside her. 'We all need to settle down sooner or later.'

This was striking a familiar note in Louise. To her surprise, before she could respond, Vito demonstrated that he had also been listening.

'Do you think you'll ever settle down, Louise?'

'I'm pretty sure I will. To be honest, I've been thinking about it more and more over the past few months.' She looked across the table at the redhead. 'I know exactly what you mean by putting down roots. The question for me is where? I was born and brought up in London and my parents still live there but, deep down, I'm beginning to think I might be a country girl at heart.'

'So why not stay on in the Monferrato?'

'It's a lovely thought. A little cottage and a dog and I'd be happy.' Although a certain man and a new job would also help...

The meal – deliberately locally sourced – was another triumph for Luigino and his recently appointed sous-chef, Graziella. After the usual half hour of antipasti, there were *pappardelle al cinghiale* in a rich brown wild boar sauce for the meat-eaters, and for the vegetarians there were his trademark gnocchi – this time served with pesto. This was followed by a selection of boiled and roast meats with a vegetarian alternative of roast aubergine, chickpeas, peppers and courgettes covered in an aromatic tomato sauce. Although Louise liked meat, she opted for the vegetarian main course and found it excellent. When asked, Calogero described it as a *pasticcio*, which translated literally as mess, but was anything but.

Finally, after fresh cherry tart with homemade hazelnut ice cream for dessert, Louise sat back as the president of the society stood up to introduce *Professore* Vittorio Emanuele Dellarosa. While the audience applauded, Louise shot him a sideways glance and whispered. '*In bocca al lupo*.'

This traditional Italian way of wishing somebody luck – 'into the wolf's mouth' – resulted in a little smile flitting over his face in return.

His talk on the threat of an impending apocalypse was convincing and moving and Louise hoped there would be a number of sizeable donations as a result. When he finally sat down again – to considerable applause – she saw him take a long draught of cold water and give a heartfelt sigh. She leant towards him and lowered her voice.

'Great talk, Vito. Everyone was hanging on your every word, including me. Really well done.' To reinforce her point, Louise gave his free hand a squeeze and saw him shrug despairingly.

'Thanks. The thing is: I've been giving these talks to students, academics, politicians, business people, journalists and Joe Public for years now but it's only recently, as people begin to see the resulting forest fires, floods and famine that the world seems to be waking up – a bit. There are still some big global players who refuse to accept the fact that unless we take drastic action now, we're on a collision course towards extinction.' He glanced at her and smiled. 'Anyway, I'm glad you found it interesting.'

'Fascinating and scary.'

At the end of the evening Louise once again lost contact with him as he was led off around the tables to shake hands and answer questions. It was almost midnight when the last of the guests finally left or retired to their rooms and silence once more descended on the hotel. There was no sign of Vito, and Louise wondered if he had also gone home – without saying goodnight – but that turned out not to be the case. She wandered into the entrance lobby and saw Domenica leaning on the reception desk looking drained. On closer inspection, Louise realised her expression was more troubled than tired and went across to see if she could offer some help.

'Everything okay, Domenica? Has something happened?'

Domenica looked up and ran a weary hand across her face. 'I'm afraid so. Calogero's just had some terrible news – his father's died.'

'I'm so sorry. Was he sick? Was it unexpected?'

Domenica nodded. 'Totally unexpected. All right, he was in his eighties, but he was as fit as a flea. I've got to know him well over the years. He always used to come up from their home in Sicily to visit Calogero and the kids at least once a year. Maria, his wife, doesn't travel. She has heart and respiratory problems that mean she has to live down there by the seaside and away from the winter chill.' She lowered her voice. 'To be honest, I never thought for a moment that it would be Calogero's father who would go first, he always looked so healthy. We were expecting him to come back up here this summer, but the doctor said he had a massive heart attack a few hours ago and that was it.'

'And where's Calogero now?' Remembering how Domenica had said she felt about him, she risked asking, 'Wouldn't you like to be with him? I'll take over here – although it looks as though everybody's gone.'

'Thanks, but it's all right. Vito's gone in to see him; they've always been close. And of course there's Graziella and Rodolfo as well.'

At that moment the door to the back office opened and Vito emerged with a sober expression on his face. Domenica caught his eye.

'How's he doing, Vito?'

'He's okay. He's just worried about his mother. She's all on her own now down there in Sicily and she's not terribly well.'

'Domenica's just been telling me.' Louise knew what needed to be done. 'Calogero should go to be with his mum as soon as possible.' She glanced across at Domenica. 'We've not got any big events scheduled for a few weeks, have we? Pretty soon we've got new staff starting so we should easily be able to cope without him for a while. Why don't you tell him to go straightaway and stay as long as he needs to? As long as he's back in time for the re-launch we should be able to cope. Does that sound like a good idea?'

Domenica nodded. 'That sounds like a wonderful idea. Thank you, Louise.'

Louise shrugged off her thanks and indicated the door to the back office. 'Why don't you go and say that to him? That way he can call his mum and tell her he's on his way. And you know I'll happily muck in and help out if there's ever a need.'

Domenica disappeared through the door, leaving Louise alone with Vito. Unusually, he was on the inside of the reception desk while she was out in the hallway. He gave her a little smile.

'That was a very generous reaction. Are you sure your boss would approve?'

'He'd be the first to agree. He's a caring sort of guy.'

'Domenica told me he's also a good-looking guy. She said he came over to see you a little while back. Do you think he's interested in you?'

Louise could hardly believe her ears. Not only was Vito bringing up a personal matter but it almost sounded as though he might be jealous of Joseph.

'I would like to think he's interested in what I do for the company, but that's as far as it goes.'

Was that relief on his face? Now would have been an excellent opportunity for him to pick up on her words and ask what kind of man she liked, but he didn't. Instead he straightened up and came out from behind the counter.

'I'd better get home to Leo. I left the TV on for him but the movie will have finished by now and he might be getting bored. I wouldn't want him to start chewing things again like he did as a puppy.' There was a gentle smile on his face.

'And what kind of movies does he prefer: *One Hundred and One Dalmatians*, I imagine?'

'Romance, mainly. It's probably for the music, but maybe he's got a romantic streak.'

This would have been her opportunity to pick up on *his* words by asking if the dog's master also had a romantic streak but she didn't. Instead she reached up and kissed him lightly on the cheeks.

'Be sure to give him my love.'

Chapter 23

Louise didn't see much of Vito or his dog over the next few days. As the end of May arrived, she concentrated on keeping a close eye on the builders and helping out in the restaurant in place of Calogero who had flown straight off to Palermo the morning after the conservation society dinner. There were relatively few guests as the big advertising campaign had not yet started and there was little that needed to be done. One morning she had a bright idea. It came to her as she was chatting to Domenica who had just received a regular update from Sicily.

'Domenica, when do you usually take your holidays?'

Domenica looked almost embarrassed. 'To be honest, Louise, I only really take a day off here and there. I haven't had a proper holiday for years.' She caught Louise's eye. 'I find that holidaying on my own's not much fun.'

'Am I right in thinking that we've only got a handful of guests booked for next week?'

'Yes, slim pickings for the month of June, I'm afraid.'

'Hopefully that will all change at the beginning of July. The new advertising campaign's just starting but I can't see any big increase on the way until July. Anyway, I was thinking, seeing as things are quiet here for now, why don't you fly down to Sicily to give Calogero a bit of moral support for a week or two? Do you think he'd like that?'

She was unsurprised to see the hotel manager's cheeks flush. 'To be honest, he asked me the same thing a day or two ago, but I told him I had to work.'

'Well, why don't you go? I can cover for you.'

'Yes, but the builders… the new staff…'

'I can easily cope. Why don't you give Calogero a call and see what he says. Tell him you could fly down as soon as tomorrow. I'm sure he'll be delighted.'

'Well, if you're absolutely sure… That's most kind of you, Louise.'

'Go and make the call.'

The result of the call was that the next day Luigino drove Domenica down to Caselle airport in the newly serviced Rolls Royce and she jetted off to Sicily. Over the next few days Louise took over the duties of hotel manager and enjoyed herself more than she had expected, making decisions on everything from the menu to cleaning supplies. The plumbers and decorators were making excellent progress and had completed the renovations on the second floor which was looking good. They had now moved down to the first floor, while another team of decorators was making an excellent job of breathing new life into the old ballroom on the ground floor in readiness for the big re-launch scheduled to take place in less than a month's time. The drains were now working properly once more, while the swimming pool was nearing completion and the first of the new staff had begun work under Louise's supervision.

Although she managed to pop out for a quick walk from time to time, she didn't get down as far as the river and she only glimpsed Vito's car on one occasion in the distance. She had been heartened by his attitude towards her at the conservation dinner and had sensed a distinct thaw in him. The trouble was that time was fast running out for her. She outlined the problem to Silvana when they met up for coffee one afternoon after Louise had spent several hours dress-shopping in readiness for the wedding.

'The thing is, it's already June. Your wedding's in what, ten days' time, and then two days later Vito goes off to Brazil. I suppose I might see him for a day or two when he gets back, but otherwise, that's that. I'll go my way and he'll go his and that'll be the end of it.'

'That still gives you twelve days. You can achieve a lot in twelve days. Look what God managed to do in just six?'

'In fairness, God had a bit of an advantage over me. The only supernatural power I seem to have is the ability to get myself involved with unsuitable men.'

'But Vito's eminently suitable. I can't think of a better partner for you.'

If she were honest, neither could Louise, but there was one insuperable hurdle to be crossed. 'Even assuming he manages to get over the grief of losing the love of his life, the fact remains that he lives and works here while I could find myself shooting off to goodness knows where. It's no good – as relationships go, this one's destined for disaster.'

'Well, you could always get a different job, couldn't you?'

'But I love my job – and I'm good at it. Besides, what happens if I chuck in my job only to find that he doesn't think of me as anything more than a friend.'

There was a pause during which she could almost hear the cogs turning inside her friend's head. 'I can see the problem. You need to know exactly where you stand before you start making big decisions. I suppose the direct approach would be to turn up at his door stark naked and make an apeal to his animal instincts.'

Louise couldn't help giggling. 'Apart from any other considerations, the thought of what a cold wet Labrador nose could do puts me off that course of action. No, if I'm going to find a solution it'll have to be with my clothes on.'

'Um... I hear you.' There was another pause. 'Well, the first thing you've got to do is to see him. Every day that goes by without contact is a day wasted. You say you thought he was thawing the other night. You mustn't give him the chance to freeze up again. Why don't you just ask him out? We live in the twenty-first century after all and you're both adults. Who says a woman can't take the initiative? That's what I did with Davide.' Louise saw her grin. 'Although I was wearing a microscopic bikini at the time.'

'You're determined to get me out of my clothes, aren't you?'

'That's it! Of course.' Silvana was looking much more animated. 'Is the new pool finished?'

'Not for another week, they said. And then it'll need to be filled with water. No, no way I can get him stripped down to his Speedos.'

After a momentary hesitation, Silvana demonstrated that she didn't give up easily. 'Wait a minute... didn't you say you found him swimming in the river some time back?'

'Yes, wearing a wetsuit. I don't have a wetsuit.'

'You don't need one. Wait for a sunny afternoon and then all you have to do is turn up in your most alluring bikini and dive in. There's something about a gorgeous woman emerging from the water in a wet bikini. Look what it did for James Bond.'

'The water in the river's probably still freezing. What if I pass out with the shock?'

'Then he'll have to rescue you and give you the kiss of life. Imagine waking up to find his lips on yours.'

'Imagine the water being so cold my heart stops and I don't wake up.'

'Well, either way your problem would be solved. Anyway, listen, the forecast's for a heat wave over the next few days. Give it a try. Have you got a skimpy bikini?'

'Silvana, I'm not going to parade myself around half naked. I'm not that sort of girl.'

'Twelve days, Louise, twelve days...'

–

The predicted hot weather started the very next day and by lunchtime the outside temperature was well over thirty degrees. That afternoon Louise had to drive back down to Turin to pick up new staff uniforms from the tailor – along with her freshly laundered, mended and reshaped silk ball gown – and she took the opportunity to stop off while she was in the centre to buy herself a new bikini. Although she drew the line at anything too skimpy – in spite of her friend's exhortations – she had to admit that the one she finally chose looked pretty good on her. Now all she had to do was to put Silvana's plan into action.

The opportunity came the following day – V-day minus ten as Silvana would have called it. The temperature was, if anything, even higher today and the prospect of a refreshing swim in cool water would have been appealing had it not been for the fluttering nerves in the pit of her stomach. She changed into the new bikini, pulled on shorts and a T-shirt, packed her little backpack with a towel and a change of clothes – just in case Leo knocked her over again – and set off on foot. On the way down the hill, sinister rustling noises in the long grass at the sides of the path probably only indicated the presence of lizards, but she hurried past all the same. Although Beppe had told her the only snakes around here were harmless grass snakes, reptiles of any description had never been high on her list of favourite species.

The Labrador clearly had no such scruples as she found him snuffling about in a patch of dry leaves and brambles. He came rushing out to greet her and she then spent a couple of minutes crouching down, removing twigs, thorns and burrs from his fur before setting off along the track towards the old mill with him bouncing happily along at her side. When she got there she went to the back door and knocked. The dog, not to be outdone, also scratched at the woodwork with his paw as well. A few moments later, Vito appeared. He was also wearing shorts and a T-shirt and there was a moment when she distinctly felt his eyes on her while her eyes were checking him out. He looked good.

'Hi, Louise. You're looking summery. Want to come in? I'm just putting the finishing touches to a paper. I won't be long.'

'Hi, Vito.' She reached up on tiptoe and kissed him on the cheeks. 'I don't want to disturb you. It's so hot today and the pool up at the hotel won't be ready for another week or two, so I was wondering… would you mind if I had a swim in your millpond?'

'You're most welcome. The water's still cold though – and I mean, cold.'

She gave him a smile. 'Don't forget I'm English. I'm used to cold water.'

'Well, don't say I didn't warn you and I hope enjoy yourself. Come in for a cup of hot chocolate afterwards to warm up. English or not, I think you might need it. I'll be out in a moment to check you're doing all right.'

Louise left him to it and went round to the side of the house accompanied by the Labrador. Slipping out of her clothes and leaving her towel to heat up in the sun, she walked across the sun-warmed grass to the equally warm stone walls of the millpond and sat down, dipping her feet gingerly into the water. After the heat of the sun the immediate impact was absolutely freezing. She sat there for several minutes, psyching herself up, before deciding she had to stick to Silvana's master plan and go for it. At that moment she heard movement behind her and saw Vito appear around the corner of the house. Conscious of his eyes now on her, she reached for the iron ladder and slowly began to lower herself backwards into the icy water, steadfastly resisting the urge to give up and climb back out again. Just as the water level was lapping at her thighs and she was steeling herself to duck her bottom into the pool, there was a massive splash behind her and a shower of freezing water drenched her, almost taking her breath away. She looked down to see the happy dog resurface after his inelegant belly-flop and doggy-paddle towards the foot of the ladder.

'Sorry, I should have warned you about Leo. Splashing people is his favourite trick.'

Louise twisted her head back round and looked up to see Vito outlined against the sun above her, his strong, brown legs right in front of her face. By now she was so wet it hardly made any difference so she released her grip on the ladder and let herself fall backwards into the river. The impact of the ice-cold water made her gasp. Somewhat to her surprise her heart didn't stop and she kept breathing, so she rolled over onto her front and swam a few strokes, accompanied by the happy dog, before stopping and treading water, turning to look back at Vito.

'Cold enough for you?' His tone was a mixture of concerned and impressed.

'It's bloody freezing.' Louise had to struggle to stop her teeth chattering. 'I had no idea it could possibly be this cold. I think I'd better get back out again before I turn to a block of ice.'

She swam back over to the ladder and started to climb up it again. Towards the top she felt his hands on her arms, gently helping her up the last few rungs until she was able to step onto the warm stone again. She found herself torn. On the one hand, Silvana's plan had worked and he had been there to watch – and indeed help – her emerge from the water, but on the other, her teeth had now started chattering so much she was almost unable to speak.

He must have noticed.

'Here's your towel. Come and stand in the sun. You look positively hypothermic.' He stretched her now blissfully sun-warmed towel around her shoulders and followed it with his hands, rubbing her arms briskly to warm her up as she hugged the towel to her body. 'You English are crazy, you know.'

Gradually she stopped shivering and regained the power of speech. 'Wow, that water really is cold.' She looked up at him as his hands continued to rub her, his face barely a foot from hers. Acting purely on instinct she reached up and kissed him softly. She hadn't consciously been aiming for them but the kiss landed on his lips and felt good – to her at least. 'Thanks, Vito, my knight in shining armour.'

She was delighted to find that he didn't recoil and, indeed, a smile spread across his face. 'Full marks to you for bravery. I was sure that once you'd felt the temperature of the water you'd have given up on the idea of going in. At least you look as if you're a bit cooler than when you arrived.' And he kissed her in return – also on the lips but just the lightest peck, but still a kiss. Then he released her and stepped back. 'Now, how about that mug of hot chocolate?'

'I can't think of anything I'd enjoy more.' In fact she could, but she left that idea unspoken. For now.

Remembering Silvana's master plan once more she let the towel slip off her shoulders and bent over to dry her legs, enjoying the warmth of the sun on her back and the feel of his eyes on her body. However, as she straightened up again and turned, it was to find that he had disappeared – presumably back to the kitchen to make her a hot drink. Taking advantage of his absence she slipped out of her bikini, towelled herself dry and put on fresh clothes. By the time she was dressed, she had warmed up pretty well, and when she got back round to the kitchen she was able to speak in a normal-sounding voice without shivering.

'Well, I can tick off swimming in the river from my bucket list. I don't think I'll be doing that again in a hurry.'

'I should have told you a bit more about it. The river only emerges from the ground a few hundred metres further up the hillside and the water's the same really low temperature all year round – hence the fact that I wear a wetsuit. I assume they built the mill here because the water never freezes, even in the most severe winter weather, but the trade-off is that it doesn't warm up much either. But, congratulations, you did it. Here…' He pressed a mug of hot chocolate into her hands and she sat down opposite him at the table. The dog sauntered over and rubbed his damp head against her legs but his master called him away.

'Leo, leave the lady alone. Come and have a biscuit.' The magic word had an immediate effect and the dog abandoned her and went round to claim his prize.

'What's new with you, Vito? All well?'

'Yes, thanks. I'm just getting everything finished off before my trip to Brazil. By the way, I haven't forgotten that I'll need to show you where everything is and how everything works before you move in, but you'd better give me a few more days to tidy up first. It looks like a bomb's gone off upstairs.'

'Take your time but don't worry about tidying up for my sake. I don't need much more than a bed and the use of a bathroom.' She sipped the hot chocolate and felt it warming her. 'This is lovely, thank you. It's just a bit hot. I promise I'll drink it as fast as I can and leave you alone as I'm sure you must be busy.'

'There's no rush. It's nice having you here.' He gave her a long, appraising scan and she felt sure she would have started blushing as usual except that her cheeks were already burning in reaction to the cold bath she had just taken. 'You're looking better and better, you know, Louise. The country air must agree with you.'

'I love it here and can't wait for my holiday next month. I'm already planning on doing a lot of exploring with Leo.'

'And you're sure you don't mind looking after him while I'm away? I'm most grateful.'

'Like I say, I'm really looking forward to it.'

'And are you going to be all on your own? If you've got friends or family to invite, just go ahead. There are five bedrooms upstairs.'

'That's kind but I don't think anybody'll be coming. My mum was talking about maybe coming over for my birthday but now they're off to Spain with my uncle and aunt so that's going to be too tricky. To be honest, I'll enjoy a bit of peace and quiet on my own – with Leo to keep me company.'

'When's your birthday going to be?'

'July the seventeenth and, before you ask, I'll be thirty-three.'

He looked genuinely surprised. 'I thought you were still in your twenties.'

'Thank you, kind sir, but it'll be thirty-three in a month's time.'

'Well, that makes you five years younger than me. I'm almost thirty-eight and then forty'll be just around the corner.'

'You don't look that age. And if you don't mind me saying so, you seem more cheerful than when we first met. It must be the prospect of your trip to Brazil coming up.'

'I don't think it's that.' She waited with bated breath for him to elaborate, but without success. Finally, he just smiled across at her. 'Whatever the reason, you're right – I do feel more cheerful these days.'

Chapter 24

Over the days that followed Louise made several more attempts to see him but his car was often absent. No doubt he was rushing around trying to get ready for his trip to Brazil. Then, the following Wednesday afternoon, only three days before Silvana's wedding, she received a phone call from him as she was working in reception.

'Hi, Louise, are you doing anything this evening?'

'Nothing special. We've got a few guests but Luigino and Graziella can easily cope. Why do you ask?'

'I was wondering if you'd like to come down so I can show you around the house and tell you about Leo and so on. I thought I could do a little barbecue, if that suits you.'

'Don't go to any trouble for me. I can eat here first. Or you could come up here and eat with me.'

'No, I've got it all planned. I've bought a nice-looking bit of steak if that appeals to you.'

'That sounds lovely, but only if you're sure.'

That evening Louise left the reception desk in the increasingly experienced hands of Graziella and drove down to the old mill. The moment she climbed out of the car she immediately smelt the barbecue. Following her nose around to the side of the house she found Vito getting the meal ready while the Labrador scrutinised his every move. Although Leo wagged his tail as

Louise appeared, he didn't budge. Clearly his number one priority was the steak. She went over to them, patted the dog and then kissed his master – but only on the cheeks. He was looking particularly appealing tonight – but that might just be because she hadn't seen him for a few days. It was still warm after a cloudless day and he was wearing shorts and a smart pink polo shirt. Or at least it would have been smart if there hadn't been a big splodge of something brown on the front. She pointed to it.

'I didn't realise you were a messy eater.'

He shook his head. 'There's only one really messy eater round here and that's Leo. No, this was the result of my deciding to marinade the steak before grilling it. It's been in a garlic, red wine and ginger sauce in the fridge all afternoon and as I was lifting it out of the dish, it slipped and… splat!'

'I'll have to get you an apron for your birthday.'

'Funnily enough that's today.'

'Today's your birthday? You should have said. The least I could have done was to bring you a present.' Although a couple of other ways she could help him – and herself – celebrate his birthday did occur to her.

'There's no need for presents. Besides, in a way you already have given me a present. Would you believe me if I told you this is the first time in ages I've even owned up to anybody that it's my birthday? I just haven't felt like celebrating, I'm afraid.'

She caught hold of his arm with both her hands and looked up at him. 'You really have had a tough few years, haven't you?'

'You can say that again but, like I said, I'm finally coming out of it – and I know who I have to thank for that.'

'Leo?'

'No, well, yes, to an extent. But the real person I need to thank is you, Louise.'

'Me? What have I done?' She felt her heart give a little leap.

'Just being here and being you. It's been great.' This was sounding very promising indeed and she almost reached up to kiss him again but she suddenly felt him pull away.

'Where are my manners? Let me get you a drink. Champagne okay?'

In truth champagne, however good, wasn't what she wanted right now but she produced a smile and a nod of the head. 'Sounds wonderful. Where is it? In the fridge? Give me your glass. I'll refill it and get one for myself while you get on with the cooking. Just try not to mess your lovely shirt up any more.'

'Yes, miss.' He swallowed the last of the champagne in his glass and handed it over to her.

She went back to the kitchen, located the champagne in the fridge and filled the glasses. By the time she got back outside she could see the steak already sizzling on the barbecue.

'Steak and salad, if that's okay. Here's a little starter to soak up the champagne. Cheers!'

He clinked his glass against hers and took a sip before setting it down alongside the barbecue and proffering a plate loaded with little squares of freshly toasted bread, some topped with goats' cheese and some with chopped tomatoes in olive oil. Louise took one of the cheesy ones and perched on an old bench to nibble it. It was delightful.

'Local cheese?'

'From just on the other side of the valley.'

'And the tomatoes?'

'From the same guy. And before you ask, the steak's from the farmer just down the valley from here.'

'That's excellent. How lucky you are to be able to source such good, genuine produce so close to home.'

'I'd love to get everything locally if possible. Transporting food all over the globe only increases carbon emissions and pollution. If I stay here I'd like to get some chickens, maybe a few ducks seeing as I've got the river nearby.'

'And do you think you *will* stay here? You were saying you thought you might like to go back to Oxford.'

'I'm still trying to make up my mind. As far as my career's concerned, Oxford makes a lot of sense, but I do love this place.'

'Me too. The longer I stay here, the more I find myself falling in love with it.' And not just the place...

They ate outside in the light of the setting sun, sitting on the old wooden bench and resting their backs against the still warm stone walls of the mill. Vito had set up a folding table in front of them and the dog installed himself beneath it and spent his time moving from one to the other, resting his nose on their knees and subjecting them to his most pitiful 'I'm starving' look. Forewarned by Vito, Louise hardened her heart and only gave him an occasional bit of bread but his perseverance was finally rewarded when Vito gave him the hefty T-bone at the end. The dog's eyes opened wide and he took it reverently before settling down under the table and producing horrific crunching and cracking noises. Louise hoped his teeth would be up to the task.

She felt completely at ease here with Vito and his dog, listening to the burbling of the water and looking up over vines and maize fields to the tree-covered hills around them. It was peaceful and it was romantic. However, just as she reached the end of her strawberries and ice cream, the romantic atmosphere was interrupted by her phone. She was sorely tempted not to answer but as she was still sort of on duty, she glanced over at Vito.

'I'd better take this. It's a local number but I don't recognise it.' She pressed the green button. '*Pronto.*'

'Hi, Louise, it's me.' His voice was unmistakable and her heart sank.

'Paolo, ciao. Are you back in Italy?'

'Yes, just got in today. I'm at my parents' place. How're you doing?'

'I'm fine thanks.' She shot an embarrassed look across at Vito but he was sitting back, eyes half-closed, looking miles away. 'I'm kind of in the middle of something here. Can I call you back?'

'No need. I thought I'd come and see you tomorrow. Can I take you out to lunch?'

'I'm afraid I'm working all day every day this week. The manager's on holiday so I'm filling her shoes.'

'Dinner, then? Surely you aren't working in the evenings…'

'Afraid so. But, listen, I'll see you on Saturday at the wedding, won't I? We can catch up then.'

'Well, yes, but…'

'I'm sorry, Paolo, but I really have to go. See you on Saturday. Ciao.'

She tucked the phone back into her pocket and took a big swig of wine – the champagne had now been replaced with homemade rosé – before turning towards Vito.

'Sorry about that.'

'Somebody pestering you?'

Louise did a bit of quick thinking. Seeing as Paolo was going to be at Silvana's wedding and so was Vito, it was probably best to be open. 'I'm afraid so, sort of. He's my old boyfriend from a long time ago. I'm afraid he wants us to get back together.'

'And you don't?' His tone was casual, but she felt sure she could hear a note of interest all the same.

'And I don't. But getting the message across hasn't been easy.'

'Is this the guy you mentioned that you felt you had once loved?'

Louise remembered the talk they had had that evening with Annabelle. 'Yes, the same man.'

'And you no longer love him?'

Louise shook her head. 'No, and the more I think about it, the more I realise I never really loved him after all. It's like Domenica – and you for that matter – said: you just know somehow.' What she didn't say was that her opinion of the nature of true love had been irrevocably altered as a result of meeting the man sitting beside her.

'Good luck for Saturday. I promise I'll be alongside you to offer moral support if you need it.'

'Thanks, Vito, I know I can count on you.'

She took another sip of wine and leant back against the wall, doing her best to return to the lovely somnolent, romantic haze in which she had been falling but it was no good, the atmosphere had changed. Vito must have felt it as well as he set down his glass and turned towards her, adopting a businesslike tone.

'Well, if you've had enough to eat, I need to give you the guided tour. Shall we go?'

Louise nodded reluctantly and stood up. 'Lead on.'

Vito took her inside and talked her through everything from the dog's diet to the heating controls – although central heating was certainly not going to be needed here this summer. Apart from the kitchen and the lounge, there was also a dining room and a study on the ground floor. Vito made sure she had the Wi-Fi code and showed her how to use the printer before leading her upstairs. Although his attitude was practical rather than seductive she couldn't help a little shiver of excitement as she followed him up the old wooden staircase and saw him stop and point through the first door on the right.

'My room's here and you can take your pick of any of the others. Rosina has made up two of them but there's loads of bedding if you suddenly decide to invite people. Rosina comes in on Tuesday and Friday mornings by the way, from eight to eleven. She'll do all the washing and ironing, as well as general cleaning.'

'There's no need for her to come and look after me, Vito. I'm quite self-sufficient.'

'I'm sure you are, but Rosina's been looking after the place since I was a teenager and it would probably take barbed wire and land mines to keep her out. But be warned – if she sits down with a coffee and starts talking, you may never escape.'

The house was delightful and the room she selected for herself looked out over the river and the rows of willows lining the banks. Beyond that, the view was of vineyards, fields, woodland and hills. She couldn't see a single sign of human occupation and it was wonderfully remote. As a relaxing escape from her busy life, it was just right. Vito must have been reading her mind.

'Now, are you sure you aren't going to be lonely? I imagine it might feel a bit isolated to somebody from the big city.'

'It's perfect. I'm looking forward to a bit of alone time, and if I feel the need for company I can always go up to the hotel. Besides, I'll have your faithful guard dog to protect me.'

'He's not much use as a guard dog, but he is good company. By the way, his bed's in the kitchen and he knows he's not supposed to come upstairs so if you find him up here, send him off with a flea in his ear.'

Back downstairs again she followed Vito into the kitchen and watched as he made coffee while she thought wistfully about how things had been going so well right up to the moment Paolo had chosen to call. It had been a lovely meal and a delightful evening but her erstwhile boyfriend had managed to throw a spanner in the works. She had a sinking feeling that Silvana's wedding on Saturday might turn out to be a disaster for her – although hopefully not for the bride and groom.

After a quick espresso, she saw Vito glance at his watch.

'I suppose I'd better get back to work. Now that people know I'm leaving in a few days' time I've been deluged with last-minute requests from students and colleagues and it's taking me forever to work my way through them. I'm really sorry.'

'I quite understand. Thank you for a wonderful evening. The food was super and the company even better.' She reached up and kissed him, chastely, on the cheeks. 'Ciao, Vito. I'll see you on Saturday.'

Chapter 25

Vito picked her up from the hotel on Saturday afternoon. He had insisted on doing the driving as he said he was staying off alcohol in view of the long journey ahead of him over the next forty-eight hours. He was clean-shaven and wearing a smart light grey suit. For her part, she chose the new dress she had bought a few days earlier in Turin. This was a light sleeveless summer frock in a charming, predominantly pink and white, floral pattern. Although her taste in dresses – like her taste in bikinis – was far more conservative than Silvana's, this one exposed quite a bit of skin and she was glad the spring sunshine had done its work in giving her complexion a healthy glow. The moment Vito set eyes on her he gave her the ultimate accolade.

'Wow.'

'Thank you, Vito. A girl likes to hear a "wow" every now and then.' She went over and kissed him – just on the cheeks. 'Who's looking after your dog this afternoon?'

'He's out in the woods with Ernesto and Attila, looking for early porcini mushrooms. I'll pick him up from Ernesto when we get back.'

During the drive down to Turin they chatted – mostly about his upcoming trip – but the conversation never strayed into anything particularly personal or intimate. Louise was acutely conscious that by this time on Monday he would have left the country and all she could expect would be a few hours or maybe a day or two with him when he returned at the end of July. Silvana's master plan had failed and Louise had little option but to accept the fact that she was going to lose him from her life.

As a result she was in melancholy mood by the time they reached the little church in a village in the hills to the north of Turin and took their seats. She spotted a few familiar faces in the congregation but saw no sign of Paolo – at least for now. Beside her she saw Vito acknowledge the greetings of a number of different people and was pleased to see him smiling and looking distinctly more cheerful than just a few months ago. Certainly, whether she had been the catalyst or not, the dark grey cloud she had seen hanging over him ever since the first time she had met him appeared to be clearing. Although she was to be separated from him, she could take heart from the fact that she was leaving him in better condition than she had found him. Nice as this thought was, it did little to cheer her.

The service took almost as hour and they all emerged from the church into the late afternoon sunshine smelling of incense. Seconds later, Louise's mood took another nosedive as she heard a familiar voice in her ear.

'Ciao, Louise, it's good to see you again.'

She turned to see Paolo standing behind her. He, like Vito, was looking smart and the expression on his face was animated.

She automatically answered him in Italian. 'Ciao, Paolo. Can I introduce you to Vito, Vittorio Emanuele Dellarosa.' She saw an interrogative expression on Paolo's face and hoped he wouldn't say anything embarrassing.

Her hopes were immediately dashed as he shot a suspicious glance across at Vito.

'Are you two together?'

Louise felt the colour rush to her cheeks and she was about to blurt out something, anything, when Vito stepped in. 'Here, today, yes, but we're just good friends. We both know the bride and groom so it made sense to come to the wedding together.'

'I see.' Relief washed over Paolo's face and Louise's hopes took another hit as he returned his attention to her. 'Well, I'm going to be staying in Turin for a few days so I'll give you a call and hopefully we can meet up. I'll see you at the reception. Ciao.'

The other guests were all starting to make their way back to their cars to drive to the restaurant where the reception was to be held so Louise and Vito left Paolo and returned to their own car. As they walked, she caught hold of Vito's arm.

'I'm sorry Paolo put you on the spot like that. I hope you weren't embarrassed.'

'No worries. Do I presume that was your ex? He's a good-looking guy.'

'Yes, I suppose so…' What else could she say? 'But I wish he'd stayed away.'

'Never mind, there must be a hundred guests at this wedding. You don't need to spend time with him if you don't want to. I'll stick by your side if you want.'

She shot him a grateful look. 'Thanks, Vito.'

'And if you decide you'd prefer to be with him, just say the word. I've already spotted some familiar faces, so I'll be fine on my own.'

She added her other hand and intensified her grip on his arm, pulling him to a halt. 'I'd prefer to be with you, really, so please don't go off and leave me. Please.'

He gave her an encouraging smile. 'I'll stick to you like a leech if that's what you want.'

'That's what I want. Thanks.'

They climbed into the car and set off in the midst of the convoy of vehicles following the wedding cars, many festooned with ribbons and everybody honking their horns, making a terrible racket. No doubt the owners of the houses around the church were familiar with having their afternoons interrupted in this way. The noise made it almost impossible for Louise and Vito to talk and this gave her more time to reflect on Paolo's arrival. If she had been in any doubt, the fact that the first thing she had felt as she saw him again had been annoyance spoke volumes.

The restaurant had a large car park and the guests all flooded into a big function room, collecting glasses of sparkling wine or soft drinks as they walked in. Louise gave the place an appraising look. It wasn't as big as the ballroom at the Grand Hotel and it was a lot more modern. What it lacked in old-fashioned character it made up for with the brilliant sunlight flooding in through a series of French windows opening onto a patio. She and Vito mingled with the crowd and were soon chatting to mutual friends. Louise had been half expecting him to abandon her so he could go off and talk to people he knew, but he didn't, staying firmly by her side as promised. Either he was being gallant or he was enjoying her company. She hoped it was the latter. For her part, she was definitely enjoying having him alongside her and the fact that she spotted Paolo some way away alongside a woman with suspiciously blonde hair – the sort that comes out of

225

a bottle – with a laugh that could probably shatter glass made things even better. Presumably this was Loredana, Silvana's cousin with the wandering hands.

When the time came to sit down, Louise discovered that Silvana and Davide had pulled off a miracle of planning as she not only found herself at the opposite end of the room from Paolo and the blonde, but she and Vito were seated with four other couples, all of them known to each other to some degree. They were soon reminiscing, as well as talking about their different careers. After a while the inevitable question about Louise's future plans came up. It came from Ines, one of the girls she had been closest to back in her student days.

'But don't you want to settle down, Louise? You can't spend your whole life on the move, surely?'

'I honestly don't know what to say. I love my job but I know that it's been screwing up my personal life. I'll have to do something about it before too long.'

'When the right man comes along.' Ines shot an affectionate glance at her *fidanzato* beside her. 'Just you wait and see.'

What Ines didn't know, of course, was that the more Louise thought about it, the more she was coming round to the realisation that she had in fact already found the right man. The problem was that circumstances, ranging from his grief over his former great love's death to the nomadic nature of her job, seemed destined to make a proper relationship a non-starter. And if that wasn't enough, there was the minor inconvenience of him disappearing off to the southern hemisphere in two days' time. She was still mulling all this over in her head when Ines put Vito on the spot – accidentally or on purpose.

'And what about you, Vito? Davide said there always used to be a long queue of girls who would have liked nothing better than to get together with you. How come you're still single?'

Louise risked a surreptitious sideways glance at him and couldn't miss the momentary flash of sorrow on his face. It only lasted a fraction of a second before he mustered a smile and replied.

'All sorts of reasons, but I'm quite happy as I am. I like my job and I love my dog and I've got some lovely friends.' He turned towards Louise and she felt his hand on hers for a second or two. 'Like Louise here; she's been a ray of sunshine.'

Louise couldn't help reflecting on Vito's choice of vocabulary. Being a ray of sunshine was a nice description, friendly for sure, but not necessarily anything more. Somehow this just served to reinforce the fact that theirs was destined to remain just friendship – hopefully a close friendship, but that was all.

The meal was good – although, if she were being critical, not quite up to Luigino's standard – and the wine flowed, along with the conversation, but the focus now turned towards the others around the table. As far as Louise was concerned, this was a relief as she had been dreading some sort of intrusive matchmaking by Ines, and she was sure that this would only serve to make Vito – and herself – uncomfortable. By the end of the meal she knew a lot more about the goings-on of her old friends and could see that Vito had relaxed and was even enjoying himself. It had been impossible for the two of them to speak privately and it was only after the meal, once the tables at the end of the room had been cleared, and the band had started to play, that she managed to get him to herself. Once the others had got up to dance, she turned towards Vito, hoping he wasn't finding it too stressful.

'How's it been for you?'

'Far better than I thought it would be. This is the first proper social occasion I've been to since… you know, and I've been dreading it. But I've had a much better time than I expected – and without the help of any alcohol either.'

'That's great to hear.' She glanced across at the dance floor where the band was producing a rather shaky medley of Elvis Presley numbers. 'Which is more than can be said for the band. Still, if you feel like dancing, just say.'

'That might be a step too far – if you'll excuse the pun. No, I'm very happy sitting here with you.'

'And I'm very happy sitting here with you, too.'

At that moment she felt a tap on her shoulder and looked up to see Paolo's smiling face. 'Hi, Louise, feel like dancing?'

Louise had been bracing herself for something like this and she didn't hesitate, preferring a white lie to confrontation. 'That's a kind thought, but I've got a sore ankle so I'll just stay here, thanks.'

For a moment it looked as though he was on the point of pulling up a chair alongside her when salvation, in the shape of a visibly tipsy blonde with dark roots, appeared and draped herself all over him. 'Paolo, I want to dance. Dance with me, Paolino…'

Louise watched as he made up his mind. After a few seconds checking Vito out, he nodded in resignation, murmured 'ciao' and turned away, allowing himself to be dragged away to the dance floor.

'Sore ankle, eh, Louise?' She turned to see Vito grinning at her. 'I've had that one used on me a few times. I hope you aren't in too much pain.'

'Yes, I know it was the cowardly way out, but I hardly want to cause a scene at Silvana's wedding, do I?' She took a mouthful of wine, reached over and gave his hand a little squeeze. 'I'm sorry you're going away on Monday.'

'So am I.' He caught her eye. 'Really. I'm sure the Brazil trip will be interesting and hopefully valuable from a conservation point of view, but in many ways I wish I was staying here.'

'It's your job, I suppose, and you've just got to accept that. Just like I've got to accept that my job sends me off all over the place.'

They sat in silence – not an awkward one by any means – until the band decided to take a break and the DJ took over. The wonderful slow intro to Marvin Gaye's *I Heard it Through the Grapevine* washed over the room and she glanced at Vito.

'This is one of my favourites. Feel like giving it a go?' She waited for his response for a few seconds before she saw him nod.

'Let's give it a try. I love this tune as well.' His eyes twinkled. 'As long as your poor sore ankle holds up...'

She led the way onto the dance floor and turned towards him, holding out her arms. He caught hold of her hands and pulled her close, transferring his grip to her waist while she stretched her arms up to his shoulders. They danced slowly in time to the beat and she gradually relaxed against him. It felt really good to be here with him and in his arms. She was close to purring when she heard his voice, sounding strained.

'I think I'd feel happier if we sat down again, if you don't mind too much.'

'Of course, whatever you want.' She did her best to keep the disappointment out of her voice as she took his hand and they headed back towards their table. Four of their companions had also returned and were chatting animatedly but, on an impulse, Louise gave them a little wave and pointed towards the French windows. 'Bit hot... going out for some air.'

Once outside, she and Vito headed for the shade provided by an old oak tree. The sun was low on the horizon by now but it still packed a real punch. A wooden bench had been constructed round the base of the broad tree trunk and she took a seat, tugging him down alongside her. She kicked off her shoes and stretched.

'A step too far?' She kept her tone light.

'I'm afraid so.' He was sounding uncertain and she gave him time to marshal his thoughts. She had to wait a couple of minutes. 'It was really nice dancing with you. It felt good, but it didn't feel right.' He raised his eyes from the ground. 'I honestly don't know how to explain to you – or indeed to myself – what went through me but I felt almost as if I was being unfaithful. Can you understand what I mean?'

'You mean unfaithful to your fiancée?' He just nodded and dropped his eyes again so she gave him another couple of minutes before deciding to say something herself. 'We were just dancing, Vito, that's all.'

He nodded again but this time managed to find his voice. 'I know, I know. It was just that it felt so right being with you but it shouldn't have. Don't you see?'

'Time passes, Vito. We have to move on.' For a moment she wondered if she had overstepped the mark. When he made no reply, she carried on. 'There's no need for you to think of it in terms of being unfaithful. We were just dancing. I was thoroughly enjoying myself and I would happily spend the whole evening dancing with you but I get that you feel awkward. Anyway, listen, you and I both know that you're leaving on Monday and no sooner do you get back home again than I'll be on my way God knows where, so you don't need to worry about things moving too fast between us.' She was impressed at how level she was managing to keep her voice. 'I've loved getting to know you and I hope we can always be friends.'

At that moment Ines and her *fidanzato* appeared on the patio and waved, before heading over towards them. Louise caught hold of Vito's hand and gave it a little squeeze. 'Here comes Ines. It's show time, Vito, so slap on a smile.' She leant over and deposited the lightest of kisses on his cheek. 'Right?'

'Right.' He didn't look convinced.

Chapter 26

They drove back to the hotel in silence. The only words they exchanged were when she offered to give him a lift to the airport on Monday morning and he told her he was being picked up by a colleague. Finally they swept up the gravel drive to the hotel and he pulled up outside, switched off the engine and turned towards her.

'I'm sorry I haven't been such good company today, Louise.'

'You've been great. Besides, I'm the one who should be apologising for the appearance of my ex.' As it had turned out, Paolo had left her alone right up to the end when he had appeared – blonde in tow – and kissed her on the cheeks, telling her he would be in touch, but that had been that.

'No apology necessary.'

'I'm so pleased for you, Vito. I was genuinely afraid you might not last the distance but you did and I heard you chatting and laughing more often than I had hoped, so well done. If that really was your first attempt at socialising in years, I think it went very well.'

'Yes, I have to admit it went better then I was expecting – and, as ever, that was down to you. I can't explain it but when I'm with you I manage to relax and all my cares and woes just somehow melt away. I don't know what I'm going to do without you.'

'You'll manage, you'll have to. Just like I'll have to manage without you.' She was genuinely surprised at how she was managing to keep her voice so level. 'The good news is that you're well on your way to a return to how everybody says you used to be.'

'Maybe we can meet up one more time tomorrow night, just to say goodbye?'

Louise couldn't miss that he had used the word 'night' instead of 'evening' – a slip of the tongue or a glimpse of things to come? She couldn't reply fast enough. 'I'd love that.'

'I've got a load of stuff to finish so I'll give you a call tomorrow afternoon. Okay?'

'Definitely.'

There was an awkward silence for a few moments before she saw him make a sudden move, reaching forward into the glove compartment.

'Here, I almost forgot to give you the spare set of keys to the old mill, just in case it slips my mind tomorrow. Thank you once again for being prepared to look after Leo for me. It's a great comfort to know he'll be with you.' He handed over a little bunch of keys and she tucked them safely into her bag.

'Thank you for trusting me with your best friend.'

'Somehow, I have a feeling he may have been relegated to second place.' He sounded serious. 'Louise, we need to stay in touch. Promise me you won't forget me.'

'I couldn't forget you, Vito. Never.' She leant across towards him, caught his face in her hands and kissed him gently and lovingly on the lips. 'And that's a promise.'

She was already reaching for the door handle when she felt his hand on her shoulder, turning her back towards him. His other hand ran across the side of her face and he pulled her close and kissed her in return – a real kiss. The effect it had on her was almost overwhelming and she was glad she was sitting down. He finally drew back and she could see his eyes glistening in the porch lights.

'I'll hold you to that promise, Louise.'

'I hope you do.' With a considerable effort she pushed the door open and climbed out into the warm night air. 'See you tomorrow, and let's make sure we have a happy time.'

'I'll call you, and I promise I'll do my best to be cheerful.' He started the engine and drove off, leaving her standing there at the bottom of the steps, watching the tail lights of the car disappear down the drive. She was still standing there several minutes later, mildly surprised that she wasn't crying her eyes out, when she heard a voice behind her.

'So has he gone?'

Louise swung round with a gasp of surprise and delight. 'Domenica, you're back. It seems like only yesterday you went off to join Calogero. How did it go?'

Domenica came down the steps and gave Louise an affectionate hug. 'Considering the sad circumstances, it went well, really well. Apart from the funeral, this was my first real holiday in goodness knows how many years and I loved it. That part of Sicily is so beautiful, so unspoilt, and I was with Calogero.' There was a dreamy note to her voice and Louise was happy for her. 'It was wonderful.'

'I'm so glad. And things between you and Calogero... did they go well?'

'Things went very well. It was so good to be able to spend time alone with him. His mother's sweet but she isn't well at all and she's more or less housebound, so

Calogero and I went for long walks, just the two of us, and he took me to visit all sorts of beautiful places.'

'That sounds wonderful. So are you and he...?'

'I'm not sure what we are, but we're definitely closer than before. I could ask you the same question – are you and Vito...?' There was a smile on her face.

'He's off to Brazil on Monday for six long weeks, so we'll only have tomorrow evening together. Then, when he comes back it'll be my turn to leave, but it's been lovely getting to know him.' She did her best to sound positive, even if she was feeling anything but. 'Who knows? Maybe our paths will cross again some time.'

Domenica must have caught something in her tone. 'Oh, Louise, I'm so sorry. Maybe things will change for you or for him.'

'Maybe they will.' She couldn't help a little sigh. 'But I'm not holding my breath.'

–

Next morning was busy, going through with Domenica everything that had happened while she had been away. The decorators had finished – apart from the ballroom which would be completed over the next few days – and the pool was being filled with water this week. The new staff members had been starting to arrive and Louise was happy to share the rest of their training with Domenica.

Vito was never far from her thoughts, a bittersweet mix of sadness at his imminent departure and excitement at the thought of one last evening – or night – together before he flew off to the other side of the Atlantic. By mid-afternoon she still hadn't heard from him so she decided to go down and see if everything was all right. By now, walking through the fields in the sunshine filled her with a wonderful feeling of familiarity – not so different from the feeling of familiarity she had experienced the first time she had met Vito. The paths and tracks were well known to her now and she had even identified a few precious locations where mushrooms might be found. Ernesto had told her not to uproot them as she picked them but, if possible, to cut them at the base and leave some of the root in the ground so more could spring up. Whether this was founded on solid scientific fact was something she didn't know, but since then she always carried a little pocket knife with her on her walks and used it if she found any of the precious fungi.

She was approaching the track leading to Vito's house when her increasingly expert eye suddenly spotted a familiar little brown dome poking out of the long grass right at the foot of the perimeter wall of the hotel estate. She left the path and went along to see if it might be a porcino but was disappointed to find when she knelt down that it was nothing more than a shiny rock at the base of the stone wall. Slipping her penknife back into her pocket, she reflected that if Vito were going to suggest dinner at his place, she could have provided the antipasti. The naughty thought that, even if there were no porcini, she might be able to provide the dessert flashed through her head and she felt a smile forming on her face. To her surprise, as she was still kneeling there, she suddenly heard voices from the other side of the stone wall. One was unmistakably Vito's while the other was a woman's voice.

'Vito, Vito, there you are, I've been searching all over for you…' The woman sounded flustered.

'Ciao, Bianca, what's the matter?' He was just on the other side of the wall, probably only a few yards down the track from where Louise found herself. She was about to jump to her feet when the woman said something that kept Louise firmly glued to the ground.

'Darling, Vito, you can't go. I haven't slept for two nights, ever since you told me you're leaving. If you go, I'll kill myself. I mean it, I'll kill myself. I can't live without you, my wonderful, darling man.'

'Bianca, *tesoro*, I'm only going away for a few weeks. I'll be back before you know it.'

Louise was stunned. '*Tesoro*' was a very affectionate way for a man to address a woman and, of course, her words had been anything but casual. This woman sounded as though she was totally smitten by him. But who on earth was she? A long-lost sister, maybe?

Louise was still crouched there, doing her best to try to work out what was happening, when she heard running feet in the gravel on the other side of the wall, followed by the unmistakable sound of somebody kissing somebody else with passion. It sounded like Leo slurping up his food. The slurping sounds were interspersed with snippets of increasingly emotional dialogue.

'Vito, darling, Vito, don't leave me, I beg of you.' It sounded as though the woman was in tears.

Slowly and carefully, Louise risked getting to her feet. The top of the wall was just above her head but there was a tree trunk lying on the ground a few metres away and she made her way towards it as silently as she could. She gave it a tentative push but it felt solid so she stepped onto it, first with one foot and then the other. In the meantime the woman on the other side was keeping up a constant litany of protestations of love, punctuated by sobs. She sounded desperate. Slowly and carefully, Louise straightened up until she could peer over the top of the wall, her head well hidden by the hanging branches of a willow. The scene that was presented to her almost took her breath away.

The woman was an attractive brunette – if you ignored the lines of mascara running down her cheeks – and she was all over Vito like an octopus. She was clinging onto him for dear life and he was stroking her hair affectionately. No sooner did she come to the end of yet another tearful outburst than she reached up with her lips and started kissing Vito's face from his earlobes to his eyelids all over again. One thing was immediately apparent: this certainly wasn't his long-lost sister.

Louise ducked back down again as silently as she could – although the chances of being heard over the constant babble of the brunette were almost non-existent – and lowered herself until she was sitting on the fallen tree. She felt absolutely devastated. Never even once had Vito – or anybody else for that matter – so much as hinted at his being involved with another woman, but the evidence before her eyes and ears was indisputable. This woman was not only in love with him, but truly, madly, deeply in love with him, and he didn't appear in any way surprised or offended. Clearly these two knew each other – intimately. Following on from this conclusion came a crushing feeling of disappointment and betrayal. Just like Tommy, Vito had been revealed as a cheat. Louise felt tears stinging in the corners of her eyes and wiped them away angrily. How could he have been so false?

She heard more footsteps in the gravel on the other side of the wall and rose to her feet, stepping onto the tree trunk so as to take another look. What she saw was crushing. Vito had caught the woman by the hand and was leading her back towards the old mill. By the time they reached the gateway, the woman had relinquished his hand and had draped both arms around his waist adoringly while his arm stretched around her shoulders. After they had disappeared from sight Louise stayed there, balancing on the tree trunk, until common sense kicked in and she stepped back down again. In a daze, she returned to the path and started to wander back up the path towards the hotel, her mind completely occupied with the ramifications of what she had just witnessed.

She was almost halfway back up the hill when her brain started working again. The fact of the matter was that Vito hadn't really lied or cheated. She had never asked him if he was involved with another woman and he had never mentioned any such connection. Yes, he had said there was no special someone since the death of his fiancée, but 'special' was open to many possible definitions and didn't necessarily include hook-ups of a purely physical kind – and from the way the brunette had been mauling him, theirs was definitely a relationship of the physical kind. If he had sinned, it was a sin of omission. Maybe she was being too hard on him. After all, both he and she knew full well that nothing lasting could ever happen between them – hadn't she said exactly that to him last night? He hadn't made any improper moves – much to her chagrin at the time – and he had always behaved politely and correctly in her regard. How could she accuse him of being a cheat if there hadn't been anything to cheat over?

Still, one thing was for sure: she couldn't bear the thought of seeing him tonight.

Chapter 27

Vito called her a couple of times later that afternoon but she refused to answer. In the end, dreading him suddenly turning up at the hotel to look for her, she sent him a text message.

> Sorry I won't be able to meet up with you tonight. Something's come up. Buon viaggio for tomorrow and have a wonderful time in Brazil. Louise.

She did not add any little Xs.

She steadfastly refused to look at her phone again until almost bedtime and saw a text from him.

> Hi Louise. Hope nothing too serious has happened. So sorry not to see you before I go. Hope you have a wonderful time at the old mill and thanks again for looking after Leo. I'll see you when I get back and, please, don't forget me. Vito xxx

Unsurprisingly she didn't sleep too well that night.

Next day it was almost lunchtime before she managed to get away and head down to the old mill with her stuff.

As she drew up outside the kitchen she heard barking from inside and hurried across to open the door.

'*Ciao, bello.*' She crouched down and gave the dog a hug as he did his best to bury himself in her arms, tail wagging furiously. Vito had told her he would set off for the airport at ten and he would leave Leo indoors. By now it was almost one o'clock so Louise decided to give the dog a walk before getting herself settled in. 'Fancy a walk?'

Although the invitation was delivered in English, this produced an immediate reaction and the dog made a beeline for the door. Clearly his linguistic talents were almost as good as his master's. He set off along the path beside the river and as she followed, she found herself thinking, yet again, about his master.

Yesterday had been a real kick in the teeth especially after Saturday had gone so well. She had loved being with Vito at the wedding and seeing him make real strides in his gradual return to positivity after four long years of grieving. But the best and the worst part of the day had been that final all too brief kiss he had given her in the car. The effect of his lips upon hers had been overwhelming. Even back in the days when she had believed herself to be in love with Paolo, or in happier times with Tommy, she couldn't remember such a simple kiss ever having such an effect on her. It had been soft and gentle and yet it had cut straight to her heart.

And then Sunday had come along and everything had changed. If only he hadn't added that kiss after the wedding on Saturday, she would still have been gutted, but she wouldn't feel this crushing sense of betrayal that now hung over her.

Before the kiss she had liked him a lot and had probably been well on the way to falling in love with him, but he hadn't really demonstrated anything more than friendship towards her. That kiss had changed everything for her. And then, of course, the events of yesterday afternoon had turned everything on its head and she felt bereft. He had gone to Brazil and all she was left with was a broken – or at least seriously bruised – heart and a Labrador on loan. Still, she told herself as she watched Leo trotting along in front of her, tail wagging happily without a care in the world, she couldn't blame this lovely dog for the duplicity of his master.

She wandered along the riverbank, thinking wistfully of the recurring dream she had been having over the past few weeks involving a dramatic appearance by Vito at the grand re-launch party which was now less than two weeks away. In the dream he would sweep her into his arms and whisk her onto the dance floor where they would dance the night away. Of course it was never going to happen in reality – she could hardly expect him to take a twelve-hour flight just to see her – but his encounter with the emotional brunette had knocked that little scenario on the head once and for all.

A splash interrupted her daydreaming and she saw the Labrador paddling about in the river. It was pretty clear what he wanted her to do so she picked up a stick and threw it into the water for him to fetch. While he swam off, she sat down on a tree trunk and reflected on the scene. It was charming, beautiful and welcoming. Even in spite of the upset plaguing her as a result of yesterday's drama, she could feel a sensation of peace settling upon her and that had to be down to this oasis of calm. Forgetting for a moment about Vito – if she could – there was no getting away from the fact that she had developed a deep and lasting love for the Monferrato and for this little chunk of it in particular.

What if she were to contact Joseph, give up her job and settle somewhere around here? She now had six weeks rent-free in the old mill and enough in her savings account to allow her to rent a place over here when that period came to an end while she hunted for a new job. This was the sort of wild romantic gesture a Shakespearian character or a Hollywood heroine might make.

The problems she had with doing something as radical as this were threefold. First, the sad fact was that she now knew that nothing was going to happen between her and Vito, so did it make sense to plonk herself down so close to his home? Would seeing him regularly – maybe even with the clingy brunette – be too tough to bear? Second, she loved her job and she knew it would be hard, if not impossible, to find a satisfactory alternative, especially in a foreign country. And third – and most importantly – she was neither a Shakespearian heroine nor a character in a Hollywood romcom. Doing something as impulsive and rash as that just wasn't the way she was made.

That afternoon, after moving her things into the old mill and giving Leo his lunch – which disappeared at supersonic speed – she walked back up to the hotel with him. En route she spotted Ernesto in the vines with his little dog and left Leo in his care while she had another session with Domenica. She found her at the computer with a broad smile and this even brought a little smile to Louise's own face. The big promotional push had already started with some expensive advertising, and bookings for the summer were pouring in as a result. More to the point, Domenica had just received an email from the company's central booking office with a host of confirmed accept-ances for the re-launch weekend, including many of the big names in the travel trade. All sixty guest rooms were now freshly decorated and ready to go and it looked as though they were going to need them all.

Louise had already decided that there was nothing to be gained by telling Domenica what had transpired the previous day. Vito had left the country and that was the end of it. Although she was sorely tempted to ask Domenica if she knew the identity of the mystery woman, she knew it wouldn't help. Best to just let the whole sorry event fade away with the passing of time and move on. At least that was what the pragmatic part of her brain told her. Her heart wasn't convinced.

Later that afternoon she walked back down to the old mill, picking up her four-legged friend from Ernesto on the way. She stopped to chat to him and he gave her a precious present.

'Are you making your own dinner tonight, Louise?' She nodded and he reached into his bag to retrieve a stunning porcino mushroom, its bulbous cream-coloured stem perfectly unblemished and the broad brown cap the size of her fist. 'Here, I found it only an hour ago, quite by chance.'

'Wow, Ernesto, it's magnificent. I thought I'd found one myself yesterday, but I was mistaken.' She had been mistaken about a lot of things, not just mushrooms. 'But don't you want it yourself?'

He gave her a grin and a knowing look. 'I also found these, see…' He opened his bag and she saw half a dozen beautiful mushrooms resting there. 'I have a few favourite places where I find porcini every year but this was a new spot.' His grin broadened. 'I could tell you where I found them but then I'm afraid I'd have to kill you.'

'Well, thank you so much. Tell me, how should I cook it?'

'Any way you like. Speaking personally, as this is a perfectly unblemished mushroom without any bugs or animal tooth marks, I would eat half of it raw, just sliced and drizzled with olive oil and maybe with a bit of squeezed lemon. Then you can chop the other half and make an omelette. Should be perfect.'

It was. Louise followed his instructions that evening and sat outside on the bench by the millpond to eat the mushroom feast accompanied by a glass of Vito's homemade rosé from one of half a dozen bottles he had left in the fridge for her. She gave the dog the crusty end of a loaf of bread and he settled happily at her feet as she ate. Sitting here brought back memories of the barbecue with Vito that had been interrupted – and ultimately ruined – by Paolo's phone call. Seeing Paolo again at Silvana's wedding had only reinforced her conviction that what she had had with him had not been the real thing and that had made saying goodbye all the easier. Saying goodbye to people seemed to be what she was best at. In spite of the gorgeous surroundings, she felt a shiver of regret for what might have been with Vito.

She was just finishing her meal when her phone rang and she saw that it was her boss.

'Hi Joseph, all well with you?' She did her best to sound positive and animated.

'Hello, Louise. Yes, thanks, all good here. I'm delighted to see we should have a full house for the big launch. You will keep a room for me and one for Annabelle, won't you?'

'Of course. Domenica's already taken care of it. You'll be in the same room as last time – number 224.' What she didn't tell him was that Annabelle would be in room 222, right next door to him. He could find that out for himself when he got here.

Chapter 28

Her first night alone in the old mill wasn't completely uneventful. In spite of what had happened and the fact that Vito's bedroom was only a few feet away from hers, she managed to get off to sleep quite quickly – no doubt helped by the fact that she hadn't slept well the previous night. However, at just after three in the morning she was woken by a cold wet nose prodding her arm. She rolled over and looked down to see a pair of big canine eyes staring at her, glowing a spooky green colour in the moonlight. After her initial surprise, she waved an admonitory finger at the dog but the smile on her face probably didn't help.

'Leo, you aren't supposed to be upstairs. We both know that. Now, be a good dog and go back downstairs and let me sleep.' In reply he just wagged his tail and gave her elbow a lick so she had another go, doing her best to make her voice sound more authoritative. 'I said no, Leo! Go downstairs... downstairs to the kitchen, got it?'

To add weight to her argument she provided a translation, but he just kept wagging his tail and staring at her. In the end she had to get out of bed and march him back down the stairs to the kitchen. As she stood there in just her old T-shirt and bare feet she saw him pad over to his food bowl and wag the end of his tail hopefully, but she shook her head. 'No food. It's the middle of the night and we both need to go to bed. Go in your bed, Leo. *A cuccia!*'

He still made no move to lie down and she had a sudden thought that maybe he needed to go outside for a canine comfort break, so she went over to the back door and unlocked it. She pulled it open and he trotted out into the remarkably bright moonlight.

It was a gorgeous quiet night. The moon was almost full and there wasn't a single light to be seen anywhere around. It was far from cold but the oppressive heat of the past few days had relented somewhat and the night air was refreshing. She stood there, watching the dog wander around the courtyard, sniffing at interesting scents, and realised that it wasn't completely silent out here after all. A chorus of frogs down by the riverside was punctuated from time to time by the high-pitched cry of a night bird, presumably some sort of owl, no doubt hunting for those same frogs, while the musical flow of the water provided a soothing background to this life and death struggle. She breathed deeply and reflected, yet again, that this whole area had an almost magical attraction and she felt herself drawn ever closer to the place – but a fat lot of good it was going to do her.

Her musings were interrupted by the unmistakable whine of a mosquito by her ear so she decided it would be wise to retreat inside. She gave a low whistle and Leo trotted obligingly across to her.

'Come on, dog. It's time for bed.'

By the time she had once more locked the door, she turned to find he had finally taken the hint and was lying in his wicker basket. She went over and stroked him affectionately for a few moments before returning to bed.

When she woke at six thirty next morning she made two discoveries. One was a big black Labrador sprawled out on the wooden floor beside her bed, snoozing contentedly, and the other was a text message from Brazil.

> Hi Louise. Arrived safe and well. Very hot.
> I'm going to miss you. xx

Well, she thought to herself, nobody could accuse him of being excessively verbose. She said good morning to the dog and then perched on the side of the bed while she composed her reply.

> Hi Vito. Glad you arrived safely. Leo is fine
> and happy. Look after yourself.

Once again she omitted inserting any little Xs.

After giving Leo a biscuit and then making herself a cup of coffee with Vito's swish coffee machine, she went out for an early morning walk with the dog. The sun was up, but its rays still had to reach the bottom of the valley and she relished the refreshing feel of the air under the willows alongside the river. They had only been walking for ten minutes or so when her eyes were drawn to something in the bushes alongside the path. On closer examination it turned out to be a little family of what looked like porcini mushrooms, but she knew she wasn't going to risk eating them unless she could be sure. She was bending down to see if they had the familiar mushroom smell when she heard a yappy bark and, seconds later, she was joined by Ernesto and Attila, also on the hunt for mushrooms.

'Louise, good morning. What have you got there?'

'Hi, Ernesto, I think they're porcini but I need your expert eye. I wouldn't want to poison myself or anybody else.'

While the two dogs renewed acquaintance, he squatted down beside her and gave her find his seal of approval. 'Definitely porcini, definitely edible and they look wonderful. Well done.'

'Then the first thing I need to do is to repay your generosity yesterday by returning the favour. I only need one for myself, so please would you take the other three?'

'That's most kind, but only if you're sure… Luigino asked me to see if I could get him some as he's planning to do a mushroom risotto tonight.'

After dividing the spoils, Louise arranged to deliver Leo to him for the day while she returned to work and then she and Leo went home for breakfast. She was sitting there eating a slice of toast with the dog sprawled at her feet when her phone started to ring. When she saw it was Paolo, her heart sank.

'Ciao, Paolo, where are you?'

'Ciao, Louise. I'm still here in Turin, but just for two more days. Can we meet up?'

Louise stared blankly at the screen for a few moments. The last thing she felt like was another session with Paolo, with him going on about how they should get back together again. Although Vito was now out of the equation she knew for sure that this didn't change the way she felt about Paolo after all these years. He was no longer the same man and she no longer the same woman. She probably owed it to him – if not to herself – to spell out to him in words of one syllable that she and he were irrevocably separated, so she made a decision. 'I'm coming down to Turin tomorrow. Why don't we meet up, say tomorrow afternoon?' At least if they met in a public place there would be less likelihood of him doing anything stupid.

'Or I could come and see you today? Are you still at the hotel?'

'No, I've moved in with a friend.' She shot a glance down at the dog. 'So there's not really anywhere for us to meet up. Let's make it Turin tomorrow.'

Grudgingly, he agreed, and they arranged to meet at Turin's famous Caffè Fiorio at three o'clock the next day. This old cafe had been a well-known meeting place for intellectuals and politicians ever since the end of the eighteenth century and Louise had only been in there once, twelve years ago. Although she was dreading meeting up with Paolo, she was rather looking forward to seeing the stylish old coffee house again.

No sooner did she put the phone down after talking to him than it started ringing again. It was her old schoolfriend, Viv, back in London; Louise hadn't seen her since that fateful weekend when her relationship with Tommy had bitten the dust. It soon turned out that Viv's call today also involved Tommy.

'Hi, Lou, have you heard the news?'

'No, what's happened?'

'It's Tommy, he's getting married. It's all over his Facebook page.'

'Wow!' Louise had unfriended him on Facebook straight after the break-up and this certainly came as news. 'He hasn't wasted any time. It's only a few months since we split up.'

'It must be serious.'

'Certainly sounds like it.'

They chatted for five minutes and Louise told her about the hotel but, for some reason, avoided mentioning Vito, apart from saying that she was house- and dog-sitting for a friend. After the call had ended, she reflected on what she had just heard and it was fairly depressing. Here she was, a month away from her thirty-third birthday and all alone – apart from the temporary loan of a Labrador. All around her she could see happy relationships from Silvana and Davide to maybe Joseph and Annabelle and Domenica and Calogero. And now it looked as though her ex was also happily shacked up. It was an uncomfortable feeling to be the odd one out.

Grey clouds were massing in the sky over Turin the next day as she drove down to meet Paolo. Although she knew that country folk like Beppe and Ernesto would welcome some much-needed rain, the impending deluge rather matched her mood. Not even the sight of the extravagant marble bar inside the entrance to Caffè Fiorio or the red velvet-clad walls of the narrow rooms beyond served to cheer her much, although the selection of cakes, biscuits and ice creams did look tempting. She found Paolo already in there, sitting at a corner table. He jumped to his feet as he spotted her and kissed her on the cheeks.

'Ciao, Louise, it's so good to finally have some time alone with you.'

She took a seat opposite him and was bracing herself to launch into the little speech she had been rehearsing in her head when an immaculate waiter dressed in a tight white military-style tunic with gold piping on the shoulders appeared and asked what they would like. Paolo ordered the cafe's speciality coffee – a syrupy mix of coffee and chocolate – while she just opted for a glass of cold mineral water. On Paolo's insistence she agreed to share a slice of chocolate cake with him and waited for the waiter to leave before making a start on what she knew she needed to say.

'It's good to see you again, Paolo, and I do hope we stay friends, but you have to realise that there will never be any more to it than that. Those days are long gone.'

'But, Louise…'

She held up her hand to interrupt him. 'Let me say my piece. We've both moved on with our lives. Things are no longer like they were twelve years ago. I've changed and you've changed, and, above all, you're married. I refuse to let myself get embroiled in somebody else's marital problems. You need to understand that.'

To her surprise he nodded in agreement. 'I get that, Louise, I really do, but what if I wasn't married? What if Katharine and I get a divorce? Surely then you couldn't have any objections, could you? I still think the world of you and I know I made a huge mistake all those years ago, but please give me a second chance.'

At that moment the waiter reappeared and deposited their drinks on the table along with a thick slice of sticky chocolate sponge cake and two spoons. After he had left, Louise gave her reply.

'No, I don't want you to convince yourself that we're going to get back together and use that to push ahead with getting a divorce.' She made sure she caught and held his eye. 'Listen carefully – it isn't going to happen. *Hai capito?*'

He sat there in silence for almost a minute, taking a sip of the hot coffee before setting the cup down again and looking up. 'You really mean that? Does this mean you've found yourself another man? The one you were with at the wedding? Vittorio?'

'No, not him.' Realising that her reply had come out a bit too fast and a bit too adamant she hastened to cover her tracks. The last thing she wanted was to find herself telling her former boyfriend about yet another failed relationship. 'It's not that I've found somebody else, it's just that I know that you and I are no longer meant to be together.'

There was a long pause before he responded. 'Not ever?'

She shook her head. 'Never. Let's stay friends but that's all we'll ever be. If you want my advice, you should go back to your wife and try to get that relationship back up and running.'

Chapter 29

On Friday the first of July the specially invited guests started arriving from lunchtime onwards for the gala relaunch weekend and the Rolls Royce was repeatedly called upon to shuttle people from the airport. The old car was now driven by one of the newly recruited staff, seeing as Luigino was fully occupied in the kitchen. There were so many arrivals they also had to employ the services of an airport transfer firm to help out.

It was a scorching hot day and the new pool was soon very popular but Louise could only gaze longingly at it, knowing she would be far too busy to use it herself this weekend. She spent her time meeting and greeting the new arrivals, recognising a good number of familiar faces from previous launches. Among these was tall, good-looking Martin, from the biggest tour operator in Switzerland. He had made clear his attraction to her in the past and she had politely rebuffed him as she had been in a relationship with Tommy. Although she was now a free agent, she knew things hadn't changed.

As Martin caught sight of her he came striding over and kissed her on the cheeks. There was nothing particularly abnormal in this. At these events there always tended to be a lot of kissing as old alliances were reinforced, new deals struck, and commercially inspired friendships formed. She gave him a big smile and welcomed him to the hotel. He smiled back.

'Great to see you again, Louise. You're looking fabulous.' Nothing out of the way here either. In these circles, compliments were the order of the day.

'And you look as good – and prosperous – as ever.' She was quick to get him onto more formal matters. 'How's business been this year?'

They chatted for a few minutes before he was escorted off to his room and she moved on to greet other new arrivals. His parting words to her were, 'I hear there's dancing tomorrow. Make sure you save a few dances for me.' He blew her a kiss as he disappeared into the lift.

Joseph arrived in another rented Porsche – this time a white one – with Annabelle alongside him. Both of them were looking cheerful and both greeted her warmly. Joseph disappeared into the lounge to press the flesh with the assembled travel trade glitterati and Louise accompanied Annabelle up to her room, taking the opportunity to quiz her on the progress of her relationship with Joseph. The answer didn't come as much of a surprise.

'I still haven't had the nerve to say anything to him and he hasn't so much as dropped a hint. We went out for a lovely dinner together a few weeks back but the conversation never got beyond business. He's always caring and friendly, but I just can't read him.'

Louise hastened to reassure her. 'I'm still convinced he's the one for you and I'm sure you'll find out this weekend.' She stopped outside room 222. 'He's next door in room 224. I'm afraid we don't have any interconnecting rooms otherwise I would have put you in those.' She grinned. 'But I'm sure you'll find a way. *Amor vincit omnia* and all that…'

Annabelle flushed and then turned the conversation back onto Louise. 'And what about Vito? Have you seen much of him? How are things progressing? Will he be here for dinner tonight or for the dance tomorrow?'

'I'm afraid not. He's in Brazil.' With the passing of the days since his departure, Louise had been working hard – if unsuccessfully – at banishing him from her mind, although living in his house with his dog had provided constant reminders. She really didn't feel like talking about him to anybody so she had adopted a firm policy of non-disclosure as far as he and his emotional lady friend were concerned.

'Brazil?'

Louise went on to explain that he had already been in the Amazon region for two weeks and read sympathy on Annabelle's face.

'So does that mean nothing has developed between you two?'

Louise took a deep breath. 'We're friends, but that's about it.'

'Oh, Louise, I'm so sorry. You would have made a perfect couple.'

Louise just nodded and shrugged. She, too, had believed that… once.

The rest of the day passed in a flash as Louise flitted from place to place, greeting new arrivals, helping out at the reception desk and in the bar, as well as doing her best to big up the hotel to anybody interested in taking a look around. She barely had time to exchange more than a handful of words with Joseph who was fully occupied with a charm offensive aimed at the great and the good – and the not-so-good – of the travel trade.

At the end of the afternoon she hurried off to collect Leo from Beppe and give him his supper before leaving him in the house – with the TV turned on – while she drove back up to the hotel again. That evening's dinner, with tables outside on the terrace, was predictably excellent and she heard nothing but compliments for Luigino's cooking. Martin came along to talk to her at one point, ostensibly to tell her how good the meal had been, but it was pretty obvious he was sniffing around to see if her reaction to his approaches might have changed since they had last met at the World Travel Market the previous year. She couldn't help drawing parallels between his tentative approach and the similar way Leo surveyed a dead bird or an aromatic bag of rubbish. This even brought a smile to her face and reinforced her confidence as she tactfully made sure Martin got the message that she had no interest in him.

After he had disappeared she found herself mulling over why she had turned down a good-looking, successful guy who was clearly interested in her. The answer wasn't hard to find. Ten thousand kilometres away or not, Vito's presence was still with her, hanging over her like the branches of the willows down by the river. And like the branches casting shade over the water, his memory darkened her mood. One way or another, there was no man she could trust so she would do better to forget men and concentrate on her life.

That night Louise was so tired she slept like a log – untroubled by thoughts of Vito or by Leo who had finally got the message that his place was in the kitchen, not in her bedroom – and she was back on duty by seven thirty next morning, checking that breakfast went without a hitch and helping Domenica with the numerous bookings that continued to pour in. The fortunes of the Grand Hotel were rapidly changing for the better.

The day went smoothly and she found herself supervising the treasure hunt for the dozen or so kids who had come with their parents, followed by a guided walk through the grounds for anybody interested in seeing the full extent of the estate. To her surprise almost twenty people chose to come with her and the dog. She had fetched Leo so as to give him an outing and he appeared delighted to have so many new faces to greet, mercifully without knocking any of them over. She could hear a constant battery of shotgun blasts behind them as Beppe's clay pigeon shoot offered the guests a chance to demonstrate their talents. It was another warm afternoon and most of the remaining guests had headed for the pool. As far as her walk was concerned, she had arranged with Ernesto for it to include a tour of the hotel's vineyards, finishing with a wine-tasting in the *cantina* behind the hotel. Everything went to plan and by the time she returned home that evening to get ready for the ball, she was feeling confident that the launch was going to be a success.

She showered, put her hair up and changed into the lovely old silk dress she had found at the antique market in Casale. After stepping into her new heels, she checked herself out in the mirror and had to admit that the seamstress who had modified the gown had done a super job. It fitted like a glove and the overall effect was sleek and smart.

After giving the dog his dinner she found herself thinking of her recurring Cinderella dream of Vito turning up unexpectedly tonight to sweep her off her feet. She glanced down at Leo who by this time had vacuumed up his food and was pushing the empty bowl around the room with his nose as he licked it scrupulously clean.

'Some Cinderella, me! All dressed up and somewhere to go, but no Prince Charming in sight. I'd take you with me if I could, Leo.'

He glanced up at the sound of his name and for a second it looked as though he winked.

She sat outside with him for ten minutes while he wandered about, sniffing and marking his territory, before she returned him to the house and left him in the kitchen. Before closing the door she turned the TV on again and gave him one of his special big dog biscuits, told him to be good, and went out into the warm evening air. She drove up to the hotel in her bare feet – her rental car, like the hotel van, hadn't been designed for people wearing three-inch heels – and parked around the back. Slipping her shoes back on, she climbed out of the car, straightened her dress and took a deep breath. It was time to go to work.

On the way in she stuck her head around the door of the ballroom and was heartened to see the band already setting up. Further along the corridor there was a hive of activity. In the restaurant, tables had been lined up all along the far wall where the buffet was already in the process of being set up. She spotted Graziella and went over for a progress report.

'Hi, Graziella, how's it going? How are you chefs coping?'

'Fine, thanks, Louise. We'll start serving at eight.'

'*In bocca al lupo.*'

She found Joseph in the lounge, sipping a glass of mineral water and bracing himself for a long night of socialising. She ordered an espresso from the bar and went over to join him.

'Hi, Joseph, all well?'

'Hello, Louise. Yes, it all seems to be going well. Everybody I've spoken to sounded positive and we've already signed deals with Swedish, Danish and Japanese firms. Fingers crossed.' He stopped in mid-flow and surveyed her. 'Wow, that's a lovely dress. What amazing colours.'

Louise thanked him and was just explaining where she had found it when they were joined by Annabelle, looking ravishing in a sheer, cream-coloured gown, her lustrous dark hair cascading to her bare shoulders. Louise couldn't miss the look of wonder that spread across her boss's face as he saw her and this only served to reinforce her conviction that Annabelle was indeed the one for him.

'Hi, Joseph.'

'Hi, Annabelle.'

There then followed a few seconds of awkward silence which Louise hastened to break.

'Annabelle, that dress is gorgeous. Don't you think so, Joseph?'

'Um, yes, absolutely.' Louise struggled to conceal a smile at the sight of his obvious discomfort which, in her book, was final confirmation – if it were needed.

'And Joseph always looks so elegant, doesn't he, Annabelle?' She was rewarded by the sight of two little red spots appearing on her cheeks.

'Yes, indeed, very smart…'

Louise was just about to scamper off and leave them to it when a voice from behind her interrupted proceedings. She turned to see it was Dieter Gruber, CEO of one of the biggest travel companies in Germany.

'My compliments on another wonderful addition to your portfolio of hotels, Joseph.' He smiled affably at Annabelle and Louise as Joseph greeted him, looking almost relieved to have been rescued from the increasingly intimate conversation.

'Dieter, I'm delighted you approve. I think it's a charming spot. You know the plan is to make it a secluded – and discreet – conference centre. Come and let me show you what we've got planned.'

With a smile and a nod to Louise and Annabelle, he led the German away. Once they had receded into the distance, Annabelle turned back towards Louise and confessed.

'Thanks for helping out. I've never felt so nervous. I was like a cat on a hot tin roof.'

'A beautiful cat. You look gorgeous and even I could see he thought the same.' Before Annabelle could object, she hurried on. 'Honestly, I have absolutely no doubt. Make sure you get to dance with him and when you're out there with his arms around you, just tell him.'

'Tell him what? That I think I'm in love with him and I hope he feels the same way about me? What if he laughs or, even worse, if he's offended or embarrassed? I love my job and I can't bear the thought of losing it.'

'You won't. I know I'm not wrong about this.'

Over the course of the evening, Louise alternated between acting as hostess, waitress, receptionist, guide and dancing partner. The buffet was excellent with a fine selection of antipasti as well as cold cuts, seafood, and a massive dish of risotto made with lovely smoked ham and Ernesto's porcini mushrooms. For dessert there were finger-sized bites of chocolate cake, strawberry tartlets and a wonderful fruit salad with every conceivable ingredient, accompanied by Luigino's homemade ice cream. Louise helped herself to a little bowl of fruit salad and took it out onto the terrace where she spotted Joseph, for once on his own. She made a beeline for him, determined to help Annabelle's cause.

'Enjoying it so far, Joseph?'

'It's going well. I'm just hoping my voice will last out. I feel as if I've been talking non-stop for thirty-six hours.'

'On the subject of talking, do you remember that conversation we had that time you came over to visit? About how you had feelings for somebody you worked with?'

She immediately had his full attention. 'Yes, of course.'

'Well, have you spoken to her yet?'

He shook his head. 'No, I decided to follow your advice and let her make the first move.'

Mentally crossing her fingers that she had read the signs correctly, she took the plunge. 'Well, I'm changing my advice. I think the time has come for you to tell her how you feel.'

'You do?'

'Yes, I do.' Louise waited a few seconds just in case he might be about to launch into a declaration of love aimed at her but it didn't come and she breathed again. 'Am I right in thinking she's here tonight?'

He looked up sharply. 'How did you guess it was her?'

She smiled at him, finally relieved. After all he had just said 'her', not 'you', hadn't he? 'I think you two will make a perfect couple.'

'But what if she doesn't feel the same way? What if she never wants to speak to me again?'

'That's a risk you just have to take, but I want you to know that I formally retract my previous advice. Promise me you'll tell her...'

It was a long night but she did manage to enjoy herself a fair bit, particularly on the dance floor. As midnight approached and the lights dimmed she glanced over the shoulder of Mr Takahashi from Tokyo with whom she had been dancing and spotted Annabelle and Joseph clinging together, their faces only a few inches apart, hopefully having their talk at long last. Finally, as midnight struck, the music dropped and the noise of loud explosions echoed in through the open French windows. People made their way outside onto the terrace and stood in the clear night air, watching the firework display.

Louise stood by herself in the shadows, her eyes following the flashes and sparks, while her mind was far away. Not only had Silvana and Davide found love, so had Tommy and his woman, and now, hopefully, Joseph and Annabelle. That just left her. Yet again she was reminded of her recurring dream which, as so often with dreams, hadn't come to fruition. On a wonderful balmy night like tonight it would have been wonderful to feel loved. Her cosy reverie was suddenly interrupted by a touch on her shoulder and a voice at her ear.

'Louise, I've been looking for you.'

She turned to see a tall figure standing behind her in the shadows and – in spite of everything that had happened – her heart leapt. There was a movement as he stepped into the light and she saw that it was Martin from Switzerland.

'You promised me a dance, but every time I came looking, you seemed to be avoiding me. Is it something I've done?'

Regaining a semblance of composure, she reached over and gave his arm a little squeeze. 'Of course not. It's just that for some reason the whole Japanese contingent decided they wanted to dance with me. I'm exhausted.'

'Does that mean you're ready for bed?' He sounded hopeful.

'It certainly does. Leo's been expecting me for ages. He's probably getting worried by now.'

'Leo, your boyfriend?'

'He's a close friend. I'm living with him.'

'Ah, I see.'

Chapter 30

Next morning there was no sign of Annabelle or Joseph at breakfast – although, in fairness, Louise was back at the hotel early – and they didn't appear until almost nine o'clock. The broad smiles on their faces were all Louise needed to be sure that her machinations had worked. She resolved to give Silvana a ring one of these days to boast of her success – her doctor friend wasn't the only one who could give Machiavelli a run for his money.

A couple of hours later she found herself acting as temporary lifeguard at the swimming pool while Carla, one of the new staff members, went in for a coffee. Louise was sitting high up on the raised chair alongside the pool, keeping a weather eye on the gaggle of kids in the water, when her phone bleeped. It was a text from Vito.

> Hi Louise. Sorry for lack of communication but we've been deep in the rainforest. Your big event was this weekend, wasn't it? Hope it's gone well. Thinking of you. Don't forget me. xx

Louise sat there and stared down at the screen, vaguely aware of the shouts and splashes of the children in the pool. Somehow it would have been easier if she and he had just broken off relations but she was, after all, living in his house and he would only worry if she didn't reply. How should she reply? What should she say? In the end, after a quick glance around to check that the swimmers were all doing fine, she opted for short and sweet...ish.

> All going well here. Leo sends his love.
> Look after yourself.

She still didn't add a kiss and she didn't mention the fact that, like it or lump it, she would never forget him.

Around mid-morning Joseph gave an illustrated talk to the guests about his plans for the future of the hotel including 'secure and discreet conferences' and 'top-end private functions'. Louise stood at the back and listened with interest. A few minutes later she was joined by Annabelle who reached across and gave her hand a surreptitious squeeze.

'You were right, Louise. I don't know how to thank you.'

'How did it go? Did the reality match up to your expectations?' She kept her voice low.

'"Surpass" is the word you're looking for. It was amazing; he's amazing.'

'So are you two a couple now?'

'We certainly are.'

When the presentation came to an end, Annabelle went off to socialise, while Louise, aided by Federico, the newly appointed assistant manager, escorted the guests out onto the terrace for drinks before lunch. It was another brilliant day with a cloudless sky and the lunch tables had been set up out there, shaded by umbrellas. Birds were singing and all that was missing as far as she was concerned was Vito, but she knew he was a forlorn hope.

After another excellent meal from Luigino and his team, people started to leave and a regular procession of vehicles headed off down the drive in a steady flow until the hotel was quiet once more. Once the last taxi had ferried the final guests to the airport, Louise walked wearily back up the steps and into the lobby where she found Joseph and Annabelle thanking Domenica, Calogero and Luigino, congratulating them on a job well done. Joseph then walked over to Louise and gave her a warm smile.

'And the same to you, Louise, plus a thank you of a more personal kind.' He lowered his voice. 'I took your revised advice and it worked.'

Louise smiled back. 'If I helped in any way, I'm pleased, and I must say I think you really are perfect for each other.' She ran the back of her hand across her brow. 'And now, I need to sleep for a week.'

'Well, from tomorrow you're on holiday, aren't you? Have a wonderful time. Are you doing anything special?'

'It depends what you mean by special. I'm staying here in the country, just down the hill from the hotel, looking after a friend's lovely old house and his dog. I'm going to do a lot of sleeping, a lot of walking and maybe a bit of mushroom hunting. It should be sheer bliss.'

'Well, enjoy yourself and thanks again.'

After Joseph and Annabelle – who embraced Louise warmly – had left in the Porsche, Louise went over to the reception desk and rested against it. On the other side of the desk Domenica and Calogero looked equally weary. She gave them both an encouraging, if weak, smile.

'That's it. Everybody's left and from tomorrow the new regime begins. How many rooms are occupied tomorrow night?'

'Thirty-eight so far, rising to over fifty by the end of the week. It hasn't been like this in twenty years. It's wonderful.' Domenica pointed to the door. 'Now why don't you go off and start your holiday right now? You've earned it.'

'Well, if you're sure, I think I'll collect Leo from Ernesto and take him for a walk to clear my head. It's been quite a weekend. But I'll look in tomorrow to see how everything's going, and you know where I am if you need me.'

Domenica reached over and patted her arm. 'You go and enjoy your holiday.' She smiled. 'And thank you for everything you've done. You've revolutionised the old place and we all thank you from the bottom of our hearts.'

'It's been a real pleasure. See you tomorrow. Ciao.'

–

Leo was delighted to see her and to accompany her on a walk down the river to the nearby village where she knew Luigino and his wife lived. She had driven through it before but this was the first time she had walked there and seen it close up. It wasn't a big place, the build-ings mostly fairly typical plain Piedmontese smallholdings and cottages, some with gardens or courtyards and many with dogs that barked at Leo as he passed. In the centre there was a similarly undistinguished church, its walls a faded beige colour almost without ornamentation and its doors firmly locked. Just beyond it, however, was a more welcoming sight – a cafe with three tables outside on the street – and Louise headed straight for it.

An old gentleman was sitting at one table, reading a well-thumbed copy of the *Gazzetta dello Sport*, its pink pages unmistakable. She took a seat at a neighbouring table beneath the shade of an umbrella that had once advertised a *digestivo* called Cynar, but which now had been so bleached by the sun it was barely legible. The old man looked up and nodded a greeting. It was almost certainly in the local dialect and sounded roughly like '*Bon Dee.*'

She smiled back at him. '*Buongiorno, signore.*'

Registering the fact that she wasn't from these parts, he set down the paper and addressed her in Italian.

'Are you here on holiday, signora?'

'I've been working up at the hotel and now I've got a few days off.'

'I hear it's been returned to its former glory.'

'I hope so.'

At that moment the face of a man with one of the bushiest beards Louise had ever seen poked through the gaudy plastic fly curtain hanging at the entrance to the cafe.

'*Buongiorno, signora. Cosa desidera?*'

Ordering herself a cold beer, Louise relaxed and stretched her legs under the table where Leo had slumped down in the shade, his bright pink tongue hanging out as he panted in the heat. She resolved to find him some water to drink but the bearded barman got there first, reappearing with a bottle of beer in one hand and a plastic bowl of water in the other which he put down alongside the dog who wasted no time in slurping half of it up. Louise gave the man a broad grin.

'Thank you so much. That's most kind.'

'You're welcome, signora. Can I ask, is that one of Luciano's Labradors?'

'I'm afraid I don't know. He's not mine. I'm just looking after him for a friend. Who's Luciano?'

'He has the farm just on the outskirts of the village. He's been breeding Labs for years.'

Clearly it was either a quiet afternoon or the appearance of an Englishwoman was sufficiently rare here as the two men then spent the next ten minutes telling her all about the area, the abundance of good-quality mushrooms this year and, of course, the local wine. Louise listened entranced, fascinated to find the locals so enthusiastic about their own little part of the world. For somebody from the big city, it was wonderful to find people who still had such a sense of identity and she knew she would love to feel something similar. Yes, she knew London pretty well and she liked it, but she couldn't really say she felt an emotional tie to the city, while these two men were completely invested in their homeland.

Not for the first time she found herself wondering whether the time really had come to take a leap of faith, escape from globetrotting and put down roots. Of course Vito was no longer in the mix but, even without the handsome Italian, she could feel a real connection growing inside her for the Monferrato. And, of course, if she were to settle here, there would always be Farmer Luciano with his Labrador puppies as an added incentive. After all, she told herself, with everything that had happened with Tommy and now Vito, maybe the best thing for her would be the simple, uncomplicated love of a faithful pet.

She enjoyed listening to the two men and was genuinely sorry to leave after finishing her beer. On her way back up along the narrow village street she passed a cottage with a handwritten sign pinned to the door marked *Affittasi* – To Let – and a phone number. On impulse she took a photo of it. If she really did decide to take the plunge, she would need somewhere to live. The trouble, of course, was that there wasn't likely to be any work for her anywhere around here, and an hour or more commute into Turin and back every day might prove to be too much.

Chapter 31

After a good night's sleep and a late breakfast she took Leo for a long walk next morning and then went up to the hotel in the afternoon as promised, just to check that all was going smoothly. She was delighted to see several dozen cars already in the car park. Guest numbers were definitely looking up. Sounds of splashing from the side of the building indicated that the new arrivals were taking full advantage of the facilities. Inside there was a busy feel to the place with the new staff much in evidence. She found Domenica at the front desk looking cheerful.

'Ciao, Louise. Another thirty bookings overnight. August's filling up fast and we're getting a lot more for the autumn as well.'

'Excellent news.' Louise looked around and nodded to herself. 'It's all looking good here. Are the new staff bedding in well?'

They chatted for a few minutes but it was patently clear to Louise that Domenica was in full control and didn't need her interference so she soon left her to it and went back outside into the heat of the July sun.

Over the next few days she extended the range of her daily walks – apart from Wednesday when a monsoon-like deluge kept her hemmed in at home – and felt all the better for spending time in the fresh air. She soon fell into the habit of going up to the hotel pool for a swim most mornings and could feel all the exercise doing her good after too many years of what she now was beginning to recognise had been overwork.

She was lying in the water on Friday, gazing up at the sky, when she came closer than she had ever been towards making a radical change to her career and her life. What if she were to rent that house in the village and get a simple job – maybe selling vintage clothing at the local markets – which would give her enough to live on while she made up her mind what she wanted out of life? She had a decent amount of money saved up and knew she should be able to survive on a no-frills basis for at least a year, maybe even two. That way she could live here in the country, get herself one of Farmer Luciano's Labradors and enjoy a more easy-going, stress-free life.

She climbed out of the pool and was dabbing herself dry when common sense once again kicked in and she reminded herself that fulfilment and job satisfaction counted for a lot as well. The great outdoors, a cosy little village and a big black dog had undoubted attraction but she knew she needed more. She needed a job that involved her head and her heart as well as her hands; a job that satisfied her and gave her a reason to get up in the morning. This was what her present job provided and somehow she knew that although it came at a cost in terms of its stressful, rootless, nomadic lifestyle which left her with little or no chance of forming a meaningful and lasting relationship, it was eminently satisfying professionally and she knew that life as a market trader would be hard pushed to match it. Besides, after the failure of her previous attempts at relationships, maybe she would do better just to accept that her career came first and concentrate all her efforts on getting as far up the ladder as she could.

That afternoon, as she was mushroom hunting with Leo in Vito's private woodland, she got a phone call from Domenica.

'Ciao, Louise, I wonder if you could spare me a few minutes this afternoon.' She sounded more tense than normal and Louise's antennae immediately started twitching.

'Yes, of course. Is something wrong? Trouble at the hotel?'

'No, nothing like that. It's a personal matter. I was wondering if you felt like coming up to see me in my apartment – say around five for a cup of tea?'

Louise knew of Domenica's apartment over the stables in the same block of red brick buildings behind the hotel as Ernesto's cantina but she had never been inside. 'That's fine. I'll be happy to come up. But, are you sure you're okay? You're not sick, are you?'

'I'm fine, thanks. I just need to talk to you.'

'Well, I'll be there. Is it all right if I bring the dog?'

'Of course, bring Leo. See you at five and thanks.'

Louise slipped her phone back into her pocket and glanced down at the dog.

'That was strange, Leo. I wonder what she wants.'

The only response she got from him was a slobbery lick on her bare knee.

At five o'clock sharp she and Leo turned up at Domenica's apartment. Access to the front door was up an old wooden stairway squeezed between the cantina and the garage where Beppe kept his tractor. The steps creaked as she walked up and Domenica – her ears no doubt attuned to the sound of approaching feet – opened the door at the top before Louise had to knock.

'Ciao Louise, thank you so much for coming. I'm sorry to interrupt your holiday like this.'

'I'm delighted to see you any time, Domenica.' She walked into the flat and looked around. It was a characterful place with a high ceiling spanned by hefty wooden beams. The floor was made up of terracotta tiles and the windows looked out over the rear of the building onto the tree-studded hillside. Standing by the open fireplace was Calogero, and Louise gave him a little wave.

'Ciao, Calogero. What's this, a party?'

'Ciao, Louise, thank you for coming.' He was looking and sounding unusually formal and she could see he was tense. What on earth could have happened?

'Do sit down, please, Louise.' Domenica indicated an old sofa opposite the fireplace. 'Can I get you a drink? I promised you a cup of tea but maybe you'd prefer some wine?'

'A cup of tea would be lovely, thank you.' Louise admired the view out of the window for a few moments before taking a seat and looking around approvingly. It was a charming apartment, redolent with history and atmosphere. In the meantime Leo had wandered over to say hello to Calogero and was stretched out on the floor having his tummy scratched. Louise waited for Domenica to come back with her tea, feeling intrigued and wondering what was going on. She didn't have long to wait.

'We have some news, Louise.' Domenica handed her a cup of tea and as she did so, Louise suddenly realised what had happened. There, on the fourth finger of Domenica's left hand was a ring that hadn't been there the last time they had met. Louise stared at it for a moment and then looked up in wonder.

'Is that what I think it is?'

She saw Domenica's cheeks colour as she nodded. 'That's one of the things I wanted to tell you: Calogero has asked me to marry him and I've said yes.'

Louise jumped to her feet, narrowly avoiding spilling her tea all over herself, and threw her free arm around Domenica's neck. 'Warmest congratulations to you, Domenica.' She kissed her on the cheek before heading across to do the same to Calogero who still had a nervous expression on his face, now tinged with pleasure. After congratulating him she turned back towards Domenica. 'You said "one of the things you wanted to tell me". Is there something else?'

It was Calogero who replied. 'Yes, Louise, you see, we have some news that may come as a bit of a shock to you.' He cleared his throat uneasily. 'The thing is, I'm afraid I have to hand in my notice. My mother's all alone in Sicily and, as the only son, I feel my place is with her. She's not well and ever since my father's passing, she's been looked after by her neighbour but, to be honest, that lady is even older than my mother and no longer up to the task. I had a long talk on the phone with my mother this morning and she was in tears. I can't leave her on her own like this.'

Louise nodded slowly to herself. This didn't come as a total surprise. Ever since his father's death, she had been wondering whether Calogero might have to return to his roots to look after his mum. But, of course, now that he and Domenica were getting married, did this mean…? Her brain was still churning over the implications of this announcement when Domenica confirmed what she was thinking.

'The thing is, Louise, I need to be with Calogero. You do understand that, don't you?'

She was sounding very anxious now and Louise's heart went out to her. Setting down her so far untouched tea, she went over to Domenica and caught hold of both her hands.

'Of course I understand. You have to go where Calogero goes, and I fully understand that he feels it's his duty to look after his mother.' She glanced over at Calogero. 'I imagine you'd like to return to Sicily as soon as possible.'

'Yes, but I wouldn't want to cause any trouble for the hotel. This place has been my life for so many years and the last thing I would want – *we* would want – is to leave you in the lurch.'

'I know that, Calogero, really. Don't worry about it. I would never question your commitment to the hotel. Besides, your mother is far more important.'

'And it's not as if we can get her to move here to Moncalvo. The winters here are too harsh and we're very isolated. I'm so sorry…'

'I understand completely, Calogero. You have no choice.' Louise's brain was churning frantically. When all was said and done, even if Calogero left tomorrow, it wouldn't be too hard to replace him. In fact, one of the new restaurant staff should be able to step up and fill his shoes. Domenica would be harder to replace, but the new assistant manager, Federico, while no older than Louise herself and still fairly inexperienced, should be able to cope for a few weeks as long as he had her at his shoulder to start off with.

She was supposed to be on holiday… but so what? She could always take her holiday another time. She wanted to help these two lovely people to whom she had grown so close over the past few months so she made a quick decision.

'I need to speak to the boss about this but the way I see it it's imperative for you two to get off to Sicily as soon as you can. I totally understand that and I'm going to do everything I can to make it happen. Give me time to talk to Joseph but, one way or another, I'll try my hardest to see that you get away as soon as possible.' She read relief on both their faces and reached for her tea again. 'But, first things first, we need to drink a toast to the two of you. Many, many congratulations. I couldn't be happier for you, really.' She clinked her cup against theirs and could see tears pouring down Domenica's face.

'Thank you so much, Louise. I'm… we're so sorry to break up your holiday. If it helps, Calogero and I have been talking and although it would be lovely if he could be excused quite soon so he could fly down to be with his mother, I can easily stay here a while longer and join him once things have been settled.'

Louise gave her a big smile. She would have expected no less from this lovely lady, but she steadfastly shook her head. 'No, I don't see why you shouldn't be able to go together. Surely that's the least the hotel owes you after over a quarter of a century of service each. Give me until tomorrow to talk to Joseph and I promise I'll sort something out.'

That evening she had arranged to meet Silvana for dinner to hear all about the honeymoon which had involved a whistle-stop tour of China. They met halfway, in a roadside pizzeria not far from the autostrada entrance. It was a nondescript-looking place that Louise had passed and ignored many times without stopping. On the phone Silvana had told her it had an excellent reputation so Louise suspended her disbelief as she walked in through the battered old front door and surveyed the equally scruffy bar within. A large man with an apron around his waist greeted her.

'*Buona sera, signora.*'

'*Buona sera. Il ristorante?*'

She had been looking around in vain but he pointed to an archway at the end of the bar. She set off in the direction of his finger and found herself in a smart, spotlessly clean room filled with tables covered with red and white gingham tablecloths. Half the places were already taken, but she spotted Silvana sitting in one corner and made her way over to hug her.

'Welcome back from your honeymoon, Silvana. I hope it all went to plan.'

'It was great, absolutely great.' Silvana launched into a detailed description of the trip – which did indeed sound fantastic, if exhausting. The flow was only interrupted by the arrival of a waitress to take their order. On Silvana's recommendation Louise also ordered a *Quattro Stagioni* pizza and a glass of beer. Neither of them felt like any antipasti and Louise sat back to wait for the pizzas while Silvana continued with her saga. They only had to wait a matter of minutes before two enormous thin-crust pizzas arrived, laden with olives, mushrooms, ham and artichoke hearts. Louise glanced across the table at Silvana.

'Thank goodness we didn't order anything else.'

Louise was already well over halfway through her excellent pizza by the time Silvana reached the end of her exposé and Louise was able to give her Domenica's news. Silvana listened intently before giving her advice.

'This is your chance, Louise. Why don't you take over as manager? That way you get to give up your itinerant lifestyle, you'd still be doing a job you love and, presumably, they'll pay you well.'

Ever since hearing the news the previous evening, Louise had been thinking along exactly the same lines. 'Don't think I haven't been considering it. It's just that…' Her voice tailed off helplessly and she took solace in a big bite of pizza.

'It's Vito, isn't it? That's why you're hesitating.'

'Mmh, yes, sort of, but it's not just that…'

'The problem is that you're scared he'll never get over his late fiancée and you'll find yourself stuck here just a few hundred metres from the man of your dreams but unable to get any closer to him.'

'I wish it were that simple.' Seeing her puzzled expression, Louise took a deep breath and told her about the scene with the brunette she had witnessed three weeks earlier and read incredulity on her friend's face.

'I just can't believe that of Vito. Davide and I were watching the two of you at the wedding and you looked so good together. He was smiling and laughing and I was fully expecting to come back from my honeymoon to hear that wedding bells were going to be in the air for you two as well. Is it possible this woman was his sister or a cousin or something?'

'You didn't see them kissing. She was all over him, and I mean *all* over.'

'I still find it hard to believe that he could be so two-faced.' Silvana swallowed a big mouthful of beer. 'So, you're afraid that living close to him might become unbearable.'

'It might be weird living so close to him, but there's more to it than that. By giving up my current role in the company I'd be giving up the chance to see so many interesting places, meet so many interesting people, and probably I'd be giving up any chance of working my way any further up the career ladder. Besides, I'm still only in my early thirties. That's unusually young for a hotel manager.'

Silvana scoffed. 'Yes, but think of the experience you have. That's not going to be a problem. Let's face it, I'm the same age as you and I'm allowed to perform surgery on other human beings. It's not how old you are that matters. But haven't you been telling me over and over again that it was your current job that caused – or at least contributed to – the break-up with your boyfriend in England? "I'm travelling all over the place and I can never settle down and form a decent, stable relationship." That's what you've been saying, or maybe you've forgotten.'

'I haven't forgotten. It's just that it's such a big decision.'

'And what does your boss say? Have you spoken to him about it?'

Louise shook her head. 'I phoned him straightaway but he's in a meeting and can't be disturbed.'

As he was incommunicado she had spoken to Annabelle at length and found her immensely supportive, promising to fill him in later that night and get an answer to Louise early next morning. Interestingly, she too had suggested she might like to consider the position of manager and hadn't batted an eyelid at Louise's concerns about her inexperience.

There was no doubt it was tempting. When all was said and done Louise had known for some time now that she needed to consider a change to a less nomadic lifestyle but, as ever, Silvana had put her finger on the real stumbling block – Vito. Having him right there, only a short walk away, but knowing she could never be everything to him she wanted was bound to be immensely frustrating and, in the long term, might drive her away. It was all so terribly complicated.

Chapter 32

Next morning there was a call from Joseph just before nine o'clock.

'Louise, hi. Annabelle's told me all about it. What do you think we should do?'

Louise had been expecting this. He had never been one to impose orders blindly and always believed in dialogue.

'Hi, Joseph. My feeling is that the hotel owes it to Calogero to let him go as soon as possible and, as they're now engaged, the same applies to Domenica. Both of them are contractually obliged to give a month's notice but after all the years they've been here, I'd really like to make exceptions in their case. After all, without them, the hotel would almost certainly have ceased to exist years ago. Do you agree?'

'I'm sure you're right, but what about replacing them?'

'Replacing Calogero won't be a problem. One of the new restaurant staff, Romolo, has been doing particularly well and I'm sure we could move him up to maître d'. As for the manager…'

'How would you feel about taking on the job?'

Louise wondered whether this had spontaneously come from him or whether Annabelle might have been lobbying on her behalf behind the scenes. 'But aren't I a bit young? It's my birthday next weekend and I'll only be thirty-three.'

'So you'd be a bit young, so what? You already have far more experience than most hotel managers. You're bright, you speak several languages. I reckon you'd be perfect. I'd be sorry to lose you from your troubleshooting position, but I'd be delighted if you decided to become manager of our newest hotel.'

Louise was genuinely overcome and was glad this wasn't a video call as she could feel her cheeks burning. 'That's lovely to hear, Joseph. Thanks so much.' She hesitated for a few seconds. 'I'll definitely take over from Domenica on a temporary basis straightaway so she and Calogero can head south and I'll think seriously about making it permanent. Could you give me a day or two to think it over? It's a big step.'

'Of course but, like I say, I know you'd be perfect for the job.'

After the call ended, Louise took Leo and hurried up through the fields to the hotel. Domenica was in reception and she looked up as she saw Louise approach.

'Ciao, Louise. Have you spoken…?'

'Yes, and it's all good.' Louise went on to tell her what she had agreed with Joseph and saw relief and gratitude on her face.

'That's wonderful, Louise. Thank you so much. I've been thinking… today's Saturday. Would it be too soon if we left next weekend? That way we should have time to organise everything – like moving all my stuff out of the flat and taking it to Calogero's house in Moncalvo. Graziella and Rodolfo want to carry on working at the hotel and so they'll still be living there.'

'I'm so happy they're staying on. They're both doing really well and, of course, next weekend will be fine for you to leave. I'll come in next week so you and I can go through everything one last time and you can hand everything over to me.'

'Does that mean you're going to take over as manager? Calogero and I were hoping that would be the case. You could move into my apartment – it's a lovely cosy spot. It would be perfect for you and I know you'd be perfect for the hotel.'

Louise was touched that Domenica had used the exact same word that Joseph had used. 'Thank you, and I'm seriously thinking about it. It's just not an easy decision.'

That afternoon, Louise felt the need for a long walk so, although it was yet another stifling hot day, she and Leo crossed the river at the little bridge and set off up the hill on the other side. This was the first time she had been up here and she had to pick her way along a maze of paths and tracks through the fields and vineyards en route to the top. When she finally emerged from the trees onto the curiously rounded summit of what turned out to be one of the highest hills around, she was hot and sweaty but felt a considerable sense of achievement. She pulled a big bottle of water out of her backpack as well as a plastic bowl she had brought from the old mill and gave the dog a drink before upending the bottle into her own mouth and splashing some of it on her forehead.

Suitably refreshed, she squatted down on the bare hilltop and looked around. Although the heat had made the air hazy, she could just pick out the distant cordon of the Alps, stretching around in a crescent from the Mediterranean to the south towards the distant Dolomites in the east. The urban sprawl of Turin was clearly visible, as was the unmistakable shape of the city's most famous landmark, the *Mole Antonelliana*, like a gigantic hypodermic needle reaching high into the afternoon sky. Closer by was the delightful tapestry of the Monferrato with vineyards, fields and woods interspersed with little towns and villages. Moncalvo, where Calogero had been living, was set on another hill, only a few kilometres away, with a tall, slim tower dominating the jumble of red roofs. The trees below prevented her from catching even a glimpse of the old mill, but there was a stunning view across the valley to the hotel. She pulled out her phone and took several photos, idly wondering if the quality might be high enough to blow up into a big print to go on the wall of the entrance lobby of the Grand Hotel.

She settled back in the grass, the panting Labrador stretched out alongside her, and thought long and hard about the hotel manager job, doing her best to behave like the grown up, intelligent woman her employer believed her to be. The longer she spent here in the Monferrato, the more she loved it. The opportunity of being able to put down roots in such a charming spot among people she had grown to know and like was too good to turn down just because she was feeling scorned. She was bigger than that. This was a job that offered fulfilment and satisfaction and she would be a fool to say no. So Vito had another woman, so what? Nobody; not Vito, Tommy, Paolo or any man should dictate the direction of her life. A good job, a nice house, a new puppy and a job that ticked all the boxes was what counted.

She called Joseph that evening and confirmed her grateful acceptance of the position of manager of the Grand Hotel del Monferrato, starting forthwith. She felt a massive surge of relief to have made the decision that she knew to be the right one. To celebrate, she opened a bottle of sparkling wine produced in nearby Asti – not the sickly sweet Asti Spumante she and her teenage friends used to buy from the local Co-op and renamed 'Asti Spewmante', but a delicate dry sparkling white wine that knocked the spots off most Prosecco she had drunk. She also felt it only right to give the dog one of his biscuits so he could celebrate with her. She took her drink outside to the bench by the millpond and phoned her mum to give her the good news. As ever, her mum was incredibly supportive, just like she had been when Louise had rung her immediately after the shock of seeing Vito and that woman together.

'I'm sure you're doing the right thing, dear. How many girls get the chance to become manager of a top-class hotel at the age of thirty-two? That's marvellous. By the way, what are you doing for your birthday next Sunday? Are you having a party?'

'I don't think so, mum. I'm sure we'll have some sort of celebration on Saturday evening to say goodbye to Domenica and Calogero, so I'll just tack on any birthday celebrations to that. To be honest, I don't think I'll tell the folk here. I wouldn't want them to think I was angling for presents, so best not mentioned.'

The one person she did tell was Silvana, who had big news of her own. Louise drove down to Turin the next day and they met up for ice cream in Piazza San Carlo as usual. Louise's choice today was an indulgent mix of dark chocolate, banana and peach. After listening to Louise telling her about how she had agonised before accepting the manager job, Silvana added her endorsement to that of Louise's mum and then casually dropped into the conversation the fact that she had just found out she was pregnant. Louise almost overturned her ice cream as she jumped up to envelop her friend in a warm hug.

'That's fantastic, Silvana. I'm so happy for you.'

They chatted for over an hour and by the time Louise went back out into the suffocating city heat – the warmth radiating up from the flagstones along Via Roma was almost as intense as the direct sunlight coming from above – she was feeling delighted for her friend but couldn't help a little twinge of regret that everybody's love lives appeared to be forging ahead apart from hers.

Chapter 33

Louise started work again on Monday. Her all too brief break had definitely done her good and she arrived at the hotel in a positive mood. It had taken a long walk with the dog on Sunday evening followed by a mini barbecue of prawns and pecorino cheese to lift the pall of self-pity that had been hanging over her. She was – as everybody was telling her – immensely lucky to have been chosen to manage a prestigious hotel at such a young age and who knew what the months and years to come might bring her? She could now settle down, and this part of the world was ideal as far as she was concerned. She had discussed it at length with the dog – who listened intently in return for a few bits of cheese and a slice of toasted bread to supplement his evening meal – and she came to the conclusion that her happiness was not conditional on Vito or any man and that was that – although she had to admit that a little bit of romance would have been the icing on the cake.

It was a busy week with an ever-increasing influx of new bookings and by Saturday evening the hotel was buzzing, with almost all of the rooms full and the restaurant catering for over a hundred covers. As a result the farewell party for Domenica and Calogero was limited to a couple of bottles of champagne at midnight after all the guests had retired to bed, and was accompanied by a farewell cake especially baked by Graziella. It was all very emotional and Domenica was in tears for most of the time as she said goodbye to everybody and to this place which had been her life for so many years. Louise gave a short speech, thanking both of them for all they had done and wishing them every happiness in the future. Domenica and Calogero promised to come back and visit as often as they could and appeared delighted to receive the hastily printed blown up photograph of the hotel that Louise had taken the previous weekend and had had framed for them.

At the end of the evening, Louise knew there was something she needed to do. Taking Domenica to one side, she finally told her about Vito and the brunette, finishing with the words, 'It's been driving me crazy, but in order to get some sort of closure I really need to know what's going on, and you're the only person I can ask. I don't suppose you have any idea who that woman might be, do you?'

To her amazement, she saw a broad smile of comprehension spread across Domenica's face. 'That's just Bianca. Don't tell me you've been bottling it all up for weeks thinking that Vito's been deceiving you?'

Domenica might know what was going on, but Louise felt completely at sea. 'You know her? And it's not that I feel Vito's been deceiving me – there was nothing much going on between the two of us. It's just that he never once mentioned another woman… So, are you saying that this woman isn't…?'

Domenica stretched out her hand and caught hold of Louise's arm, steering her towards a table and two chairs in a far corner of the lounge. 'Let me tell you all about it. Bianca and Vito have known each other more or less since birth. They're almost exactly the same age and she's the daughter of the people who own the bar in the village.'

'The man with the beard?'

'Exactly, Bruno with the beard is her father. Anyway, Bianca and Vito played together as kids and were inseparable. They went to school together and have always been close. As far as Vito's concerned, she's the nearest thing to a sister he has. But even if he doesn't realise it, it's been clear to me for years that she sees him in a very different light and she mooned after him for years without success. It was only when he went off to university in England that she finally got the message and promptly went out and married Luciano – he's a local farmer.'

'Luciano and his Labradors.'

'That's him. The thing is, she clearly never got over Vito, and now that he's suddenly become rich after selling the hotel, it looks as though she's back on the prowl even though she's still married to Luciano.'

Louise was slowly beginning to make sense of it all. 'Are you telling me that there's nothing going on between the two of them? It's just that she sounded so emotional. She said she was going to kill herself if he left.'

Domenica shook her head. 'Bianca always was a drama queen. She didn't mean it. After all, he's been gone for almost a month now and she's still alive. I only saw her in the village the other day. No, there's nothing going on there – at least not on Vito's part. Try to think back on the scene you witnessed; who was kissing who?'

'She was all over Vito, kissing him like there was no tomorrow.'

'But was he kissing her?'

Louise paused for a few seconds' reflection before replying. 'No, I suppose he wasn't.'

'Exactly!' There was a note of triumph in Domenica's voice. 'She was just putting on a theatrical show for his benefit and he's too nice a guy to be unkind to her. So did you genuinely think Vito could be so two-faced?'

Louise hung her head as the truth sank in. 'I did, I'm afraid, and I feel awful. I just leapt to the wrong conclusion. So this means…'

'So this means that for the past few weeks you've been getting yourself into a right state because you thought he had another woman when any fool can see he only has eyes for you.'

'He has?' Louise had never felt so gormless.

'Louise, you're an intelligent woman and you're going to make a wonderful hotel manager, but this proves the old saying that love is blind… and clueless.'

Louise grabbed hold of her and hugged her tightly before running out into the night and trying to call Vito. She didn't know what time of day or night it was over there or what she was going to say to him, but she knew she had to hear his voice. Alas, all she got was a *number not available* message and she snorted in frustration while, at the same time, desperately trying to dominate the surge of hope and joy rising up inside her. Of course this didn't automatically mean that Domenica was right and that Vito had serious feelings for her, but it did extinguish the black cloud that had been hanging over her. Although it was almost one o'clock in the morning she phoned her mum and gave her the good news, a few tears – but not unhappy ones – trickling down her cheeks as she did so.

First thing next morning she tried Vito's phone again but once more without success. Presumably he was off in the jungle somewhere remote. She went in to work as usual and told nobody it was her birthday. In the afternoon, still unable to talk to Vito, she went for a walk with Leo, stopping off at the hotel to check that Federico, the assistant manager, was going to be all right on his own that evening. Finally she returned to the old mill, poured herself a glass of wine, and settled down on the warm grass by the millpond as the sun began to slip towards the horizon. She lay there, with the dog snoozing alongside her, and felt at peace. She had made her big decision and she felt sure that, whatever happened, it would prove to be the right one. In just under two weeks' time Vito would return from Brazil and she would be able to see if their relationship might progress as she so dearly hoped it would. But, she cautioned herself, if it did, great. If not, it wasn't the end of the world. When he came back she would move into Domenica's former accommodation alongside the cantina and what would be would be. As the Italians would say, *Che sarà, sarà.*

She was humming that old tune to herself when Leo suddenly sat bolt upright and gave a single woof before setting off towards the front of the mill. Louise heard the crunch of gravel as a car approached and she jumped up in her turn and followed him. She saw that it was a taxi and her heart leapt for a moment. The passenger door opened and a familiar figure emerged, but it wasn't the familiar figure she had been hoping for.

'Paolo.' She choked back the surge of disappointment. Maybe deep down she had hoped it might be the man from Brazil. 'What're you doing here?'

He walked over to her and held out his hand. In it was a gift-wrapped package. 'Happy birthday, Louise. I've been in Milan for a conference and I wanted to make a flying visit to see you in person to say thank you.'

'Thank you for what?' She took the present from him and stared down at it in bewilderment. 'What have I done to earn your thanks?'

'Open the package.' He was smiling.

She tore the wrapping paper off to expose a box of her favourite sweets: marrons glacés. Along with it was a card in an envelope.

'Check out what it says on the card.'

She opened the envelope and did as instructed. Inside was a simple message. It just read, *To Louise with thanks. Katharine and Paolo. x*

Two and two suddenly became four and she looked back up again, a smile forming on her own face now. 'You and your wife, you've made up?'

He nodded. 'I took your advice and we went to a therapist back in Denver. We've only had a handful of sessions with her but she's set us straight, and I've moved back home. I owe it to you for making me see sense.'

'Well, I'm really delighted for you both. That's wonderful news.' She held out her hands and the two of them hugged before he stepped back and gave her an apologetic look.

'I'm afraid I can't stop. I have a plane to catch. Ciao, Louise, I wish you all the luck in the world, and thanks again.'

He climbed back into the taxi which set off out of the gates and back along the gravel track. Louise watched the car disappear and the dust gradually settle behind it. She was truly happy for him and she hoped he and his wife would be able to make their marriage work. Finally she glanced down at the dog.

'Do you think I should maybe set up as a relation-ship counsellor? I would appear to be better at it than I thought.' She reached down and ruffled his ears. 'Now, if only I could get *myself* sorted out, things would be perfect. Don't you agree?'

Leo looked up at her and wagged his tail.

She went up to bed at just before eleven and was asleep within minutes. Barely half an hour later, she was woken by the sound of barking downstairs in the kitchen. Leo rarely barked and she wondered what had set him off. She couldn't hear anything going on outside so she went down to comfort him and to check that nothing bad had happened. She found him standing in the darkened room with his nose to the back door and as she stroked him she was surprised to feel the hackles on his neck standing up. Even more unusual was the fact that, although he had stopped barking, he was now growling, something she had never heard him do before.

'What's the matter, Leo? Is somebody out there?'

She was still whispering to him when she heard the unmistakable sound of footsteps outside and he barked again, making her jump. She looked around the room urgently, searching for her phone. Suddenly realising that it was still upstairs by her bed she grabbed a hefty piece of firewood from the old wicker basket by the fireplace and returned to the door. No sooner did she reach it than she heard scraping from outside and the dog produced another loud woof. To her horror, it sounded as though somebody out there was trying to pick the lock. She was trying to make up her mind whether to rush upstairs and barricade herself into her room while she called for help when she heard the hinges creak and saw the handle turn as the door began to open. Flattening herself against the wall, she raised the heavy log and waited, her heart in her mouth.

The door swung open and to her surprise the dog suddenly stopped barking and began to emit a series of yelping whines of delight. Louise was still trying to process what was happening when she heard a man's voice, speaking in a hoarse whisper.

'Leo, for God's sake shut up. You'll wake the whole house.' And then he found the light switch and turned it on.

Louise was still frozen into her aggressive pose, arm raised, makeshift weapon at the ready. He turned towards her and did a double-take.

'Whoa there, Louise, it's me. Please don't beat me to death with the firewood.'

'Vito...?' She could hardly believe her eyes. She lowered her arm and let the log drop from her grip onto the tiles. 'I didn't know...'

'I'm so sorry. The plan was to get here long before dark and surprise you on your birthday, but the flight into Rome was delayed and I had to take a later connecting flight to Turin. All the lights were off so I assumed you were in bed and I didn't want to disturb you, so I got the taxi to drop me off back along the track a bit and walked the rest of the way. I hadn't banked on Leo barking the house down.' He was still standing by the open door, his happy dog standing on his hind legs, giving him a rapturous welcome.

'Carrying your suitcase?' It was a banal thing to say but her befuddled brain was taking a long time to come to terms with the fact that he was here, Vito was here. Then, like a blinding light, realisation dawned and she felt herself beaming with delight. She held her arms towards him. 'It's wonderful to see you again, but weren't you supposed to be in Brazil until the end of the month?'

He took a step towards her and a smile spread over his face – a genuine broad smile of joy that lit up his face and the whole room. 'Happy birthday, Louise.' He glanced at his watch. 'Eleven fifty, I made it just in time. I had to come.'

'You travelled all the way across the Atlantic just to wish me a happy birthday?'

'Not just for that. I came to tell you that being separated from you has made me see things clearly at last.'

She caught hold of his hands and tugged him gently towards her.

'Such as…?'

'Such as the fact that I've been missing you terribly. I've been thinking of you all the time but it's taken me almost a month to work out what's going on in my head… and my heart. It's something you said. You told me I needed to move on with my life and I now know you're right.'

She felt a surge of joy rise up inside her and she was barely able to speak. 'So what does that mean?'

'It means I've wasted four whole months. Do you want to know something? The very first time I saw you, in the lobby up at the hotel, it was as if I'd been punched in the heart. It's taken me until now to realise what that meant.' He caught her in his arms. 'You've changed my life, Louise. You've brought me joy. You've brought me companionship. You've brought me love.'

'Love?' Her voice was little more than a whisper.

'Love.' And he kissed her. Her knees threatened to give way but his arms held her tightly as though his life depended on it. Beside them, she was vaguely aware of the Labrador standing up on his hind legs, pawing at them both. They stayed like that for many minutes until, finally, she took a tentative step back. One look at his face told her he was in the prey of the same wave of emotion that had washed over her. She caught hold of his hands and looked deep into his eyes.

'There's so much I need to tell you, but the only thing that counts for now is that you're here with me and I never want to lose you.'

'And I want to be with you for as long as you'll have me.'

'It's a deal.' She reached up with her lips and sealed it with a kiss.

Acknowledgements

Thanks, as always to my lovely editor, Emily Bedford, and everybody at my publishers, Canelo. Special thanks to my oldest Italian friend, Vittorio, for introducing me to the wonderful world of mushrooms and truffles.